Malice in Memphis: Ghost Stories

Malice in Memphis: Ghost Stories

Edited by
Carolyn McSparren
Malice in Memphis Writers Group

Copyright Acknowledgments

Malice in Memphis: Ghost Stories

Cover design by Allan Gilbreath
Image by Paul McKinnon via Dreamstime.com

Published by
Dark Oak Press
Kerlak Enterprises, Inc.
Memphis, TN
www.darkoakpress.com

Trade Paperback
ISBN 13: 978-1-941754-78-8
Library of Congress Control Number: 2016956953
First Printing: 2016

This book is printed on acid free paper.

Printed in the United States of America

Introduction

Mention ghosts around most southerners, then stand back for at least one story of a ghostly encounter that happened to them, a friend or relation. Is it because we have such a close connection with death and dying that everybody has a tale to tell?

Many lost people in the Civil War. Then came the Yellow Fever epidemics, the flu epidemic after the First World War, the Second World War and the wars since. And along the way, plain old natural disasters like floods and tornadoes, murders, and other hateful occurrences. Plenty of misery for the ghosts to feed upon. Many interesting locations to attach themselves to. And heaven knows, most southerners are raconteurs to the depths of their bones. Just ask them.

Ghosts are often thought to be those who die suddenly, and don't get the word that they are supposed to go to the light. Some are attached to the places they lived or the people they loved and refuse to let go of. Some look for vengeance or to right some wrong. Some are just mean and want to bedevil those they left behind. Some relive their last hours or days again and again trying to get it right.

The ghost stories and the characters in this book are pure fiction, even if the locations in which we set them aren't. The tales were written by members of Malice in Memphis, our local mystery writers' group.

This anthology follows our first, Bluff City Mysteries. This time we've expanded the geographical locations to include the Mississippi River and the area across from Memphis, as well as several of the villages and farms that survived the onslaught of Union soldiers. We've included graveyards and battlefields, some Memphis landmarks that survive and some that don't.

Whether you believe in the supernatural or not, we hope that you'll enjoy these eerie stories of southern supernatural doings.

And check out Bluff City Mysteries, our first anthology of mystery short stories.

Carolyn McSparren

Table of Contents

A Grave Situation
Elaine Meece

April 1962: Collierville, Tennessee

In the attic, boards creaked. It sounded as if someone had walked across the wooden planks. A crash, then something swinging back and forth.

Lying in her bed, Elizabeth Owens shuddered.

It was the house settling or raccoons prowling. In its day, it must've been a magnificent home, but now it was in need of repairs and paint. Plus, it smelled old. Apparently that was why the rent had been so cheap.

It'd take a while to grow accustomed to the sounds.

She and her husband, Raymond, and their two children had moved into the two-story Victorian home over the weekend. Despite being worn out from moving and unpacking, Elizabeth couldn't sleep. Instead, she stared at the high ceiling and wondered where her husband was. Ten O' clock, then eleven, and finally midnight passed without his coming home.

No doubt he was boozing it up.

When he lost his new job and the rent didn't get paid, they'd end up moving again.

The baby kicked, so she placed her hand over her stomach.

Another creak interrupted her thoughts. This time the noise came from the steps leading up to the attic.

A chill ran down her spine.

Could someone be hiding up there?

She slipped from bed and checked on her two sleeping children. She covered Timmy, her five year old, before crossing the room to check on Anna, who'd turned seven over the summer.

Elizabeth left and closed the door behind her. She stopped by the bathroom, grabbed a hammer she'd used earlier to nail curtain rods up, and held it ready to clobber anyone who jumped out at her. At the bottom of the stairs leading to the attic, she turned on the dim light. Something grated over the boards above. Her heartbeat surged. She had a difficult time keeping her hand steady. She stared wide-eyed up the staircase.

Nothing.

Relief flooded through her.

She glanced at the clock. One a.m. and Raymond hadn't come in. If she had any way of making a living, she'd leave him. Without any typing or dictation skills, an office job would be out of the question. The only thing she could do was wait tables, but it wouldn't pay enough to support her and the kids.

She returned to bed and for an hour or two she slept. The front door downstairs opened and closed, waking her. Footfalls came up the stairs and down the hallway.

Raymond had finally come home. Elizabeth feigned sleep. Since he'd been drinking, confronting him tonight wouldn't be wise. The bedroom door squeaked open. He eased into bed and the mattress shifted. He sounded winded. Rather than alcohol, she breathed in a leather scent.

Despite her common sense's telling her to wait until he was sober, she couldn't let him get away with staying out half the night. She couldn't postpone giving him a piece of her mind until morning. She rolled over ready to unleash her anger.

Raymond wasn't there.

The other side of the bed remained empty. The mattress dipped down as if someone lay there.

The heavy breathing beside her continued.

Her heart thumped in her chest, her breath froze in her lungs.

She whimpered as she crawled off the other side of the bed and grabbed the hammer. She ran to the children's room and slammed their door behind her, waking the kids.

"What's wrong, Momma?" Anna asked.

Looking dazed, Timmy dropped his teddy bear and rubbed his eyes.

Elizabeth couldn't breathe, let alone speak. Finally, she found her voice. "There's a rat in my room. I didn't want it to come in here. Everything's fine. Go back to sleep."

She locked them all inside the bedroom, then stretched out beside Timmy and closed her eyes.

A short while later, the door downstairs slammed again.

Would whatever crawled into her bed attempt to enter the children's room?

Dread twisted her stomach.

She recalled the small family cemetery in the right corner behind the house. The headstones were too old to read. Was the intruder from the cemetery?

Footfalls came up the main staircase.

Elizabeth closed her eyes. She wondered how she'd protect them from a ghost. A hammer wouldn't stop it.

"Lizzie," Raymond shouted from their bedroom. He crossed over to the kids' room and tried to open the door. "Lizzie, what's wrong?"

She left the bed, unlocked the door and jerked it open. Immediately, she wrapped her arms around him, sobbing.

The scent of whiskey and cigarettes lingered on his clothes. She didn't care. She was glad he was home.

Unsure of what was happening, the children sat up in bed and cried.

*****

The next morning, Elizabeth stood at the stove and stirred oatmeal. When Raymond came into the room, she glanced up from the steaming pot. "I won't stay in this house another night. Now I know why the rent's so cheap. It's haunted!"

"Hogwash. Is that what all that hysteria was about?"

"Yes. Something was in our bed, but when I looked, there wasn't anything there."

"Your imagination is working overtime."

"I want to move."

"We don't have the money for another deposit. Hell, I had to sell the car in order to get this place. It's close enough that I can walk to work."

Her parents had paid off their 1959 Pontiac. They wouldn't be happy to learn it'd been sold to cover the deposit for this house. But Raymond had been fired from the cotton gin in Bartlett, and they'd lost the nice house on Court Street that her parents had paid the deposit on. She wouldn't call them and ask for more money. Hopefully, Raymond could keep his new job at the Wonder Horse Company long enough to pay her parents back and build a little nest egg.

As Raymond grabbed his lunchbox and headed out the back door, she shouted out, "Come home right after work!"

He didn't reply and slammed the door behind him.

Before meeting Anna at the school that afternoon, she and Timmy strolled to the small library on Walnut Street. Surely, there were books that could teach her enough to get a job. She entered the library housed in a white stucco block building. Inside it smelled more like hamburgers and onions than books.

"Momma, look at all the books," Timmy whispered.

"Maybe they'll have a lot of children's books." She spotted a child's table with picture books on it. "Sit there while I speak with the lady at the desk."

"Yes, Momma." Timmy picked up a book and buried his face in it, pretending to read.

"Can I help you?" the petite middle-aged librarian asked.

"I need books that teach shorthand and typing."

"Do you have a card with us?"

"No, I don't. How do I get one?"

The librarian placed the paperwork in front of her. "Fill this out."

Elizabeth nodded. "We just moved into the old Cameron place."

The lady appeared taken aback. "That old two story house on Natchez that looks like it needs painting and a new roof?"

"That's the one."

"Everything okay there?" The lady's eyes held a curious glint.

Elizabeth glanced back to make sure Timmy wasn't listening. He waved, then walked over to a bookshelf with more children's books. "I heard some peculiar noises last night. My husband claims it's my imagination."

"Well...I shouldn't say anything, but no one stays in that house long."

"After last night, I know why. It's haunted."

"And I know who is doing the haunting."

"I figured it was one of the people buried in that small cemetery out back."

"No. It's Riley Miller of the Union Army's Sixty-sixth Indiana Regiment."

"Why him?"

"In 1863 he was captured in that house and executed by his own division."

This piqued Elizabeth's interest. "Why? What'd he do?"

"During the Battle of Collierville, his younger brother, a confederate in the Seventh Tennessee, was shot in the head. That's when Riley decided to steal the gold and silver coins that had been confiscated from the rebels. General Oglesby planned to hand them over to Sherman when his train arrived on the Memphis to Charleston railroad connecting the Mississippi River to the Atlantic. It was very important to control it during the war."

"So, Riley planned to return the coins to the Confederacy and join them?"

"Exactly. He still had another brother fighting with the Confederacy. But he was tracked down to the house you're living in. Before they caught up with him, he hid the money, and no matter what they did, he refused to tell its whereabouts."

"How'd they execute him?"

"Hanged him from a rafter in the attic. The last renters swore they saw him hanging there," the librarian whispered. "They moved out the next morning."

Elizabeth swallowed hard. "Did the Union Army get the coins back?"

"Couldn't find one single coin. They searched every inch of that house and destroyed the furniture and belongings of the family who owned it in the process."

"It has to be somewhere." Elizabeth paused a moment in thought. "Unless one of the Union soldiers found it and didn't tell the others."

"A lot of people have searched for the coins. It's assumed Riley Miller haunts the place to keep everyone away from the treasure."

"I had no idea the house was so old."

"It's around one hundred and twenty years old, give or take."

Elizabeth handed her the library card. "I don't have a typewriter, so maybe I'll start with a dictation book."

"Wise decision. You plan to get a job?"

She placed her hand on her bulging stomach. "I can't until this one gets old enough at least for nursery school. Hopefully, I won't get pregnant again."

"Is he your only one?" the librarian asked, glancing at Timmy.

"No, I have Anna. She's in second grade."

"I don't know how you feel about this, but there is a birth control clinic here in town, and it's free."

Elizabeth didn't reply, but she would definitely check into it after the baby came. Between Timmy and Anna, she'd had two miscarriages. She didn't want any more children after this one. What she wanted was a divorce, but her parents would rather she put up with Raymond than let family and friends know her marriage had failed.

*****

To her surprise, that evening Raymond came home after work. The man was sober. For some reason, she decided not to share the ghost story the librarian had told her.

It turned out to be one of the best evenings they'd had in a long time. It conjured up memories of how he'd been when they'd first married, before he'd taken up the bottle.

It wasn't until they went to bed that the haunting started.

First the room turned bitter cold, turning their bones to ice. No matter how many blankets they tucked around them, the cold still stung her skin.

"It's sixty degrees outside," Raymond stated. "Why the heck is it so blame cold?"

She suspected Riley Miller was making his ghostly rounds, but she wouldn't say anything for the moment. Maybe, it'd make more of an impression on Raymond to let him figure it out for himself.

After several loud pops and screeches in the overhead rafters, the air warmed.

The attic rafters creaked in a rhythmic pattern as though something swung back and forth. She recalled what the previous renters had claimed. Well, she wasn't about to go into the attic and check it out. When it stopped, other strange noises started up.

Downstairs the kitchen cabinets opened and closed, slamming shut each time with force.

Raymond sat up. "You locked the door, didn't you?"

"Of course. Are you gonna check it? After all, you're the man of the house."

She could tell he didn't want to, but finally he tossed back the covers and walked out of the room.

The house seemed to groan.

Chills ran down Elizabeth's back. She hurried to the children's room to check on them. They slept soundly. Their room had a calm quietness to it. After she returned to bed, someone shouted muffled words. No matter how intently she listened, she couldn't make out what was being said.

Raymond returned, panting. He climbed back in bed. His body trembled.

"Did you find anything?"

He didn't answer.

"Raymond," she said as she turned on the lamp. Not only was he pale, but his eyes held fear. She rubbed his arm, comforting him. "What'd you see?"

"Something placed a hand on my shoulder," he said, his voice shaky. "I couldn't see it, but I knew someone was there."

"Did you hear the noises?"

"Yeah, I did. But it was coming from inside the wall."

"See it wasn't my imagination. So are we going to find another house?"

He didn't answer at first. "No, we don't have the money. As soon as we get a little put back, we will."

Around three a.m., the air cleared and the house settled. A peace fell over the structure. The haunting had ended.

*****

For the next two weeks, Raymond didn't come home. Elizabeth didn't know where he spent his nights, but it wasn't in their bed.

Both Sundays during his absence, she dressed Anna and Timmy and attended the service at the First Baptist Church on the corner of Walnut and College. The church secretary befriended her, and made Elizabeth promise to ask for help if she needed it.

Maybe God heard my prayers.

They had another problem. The man who owned the house died, leaving no heirs. What would happen to it? Would the courts allow them to continue renting? She'd like to move, but she wasn't sure if they could afford to. With the man deceased, could they get their deposit refunded? The county sheriff who'd stopped by couldn't answer her questions.

Payday came and went without Raymond checking on them. Monday after meeting Anna at school, Elizabeth walked to the Wonder Horse Company on Main.

Raymond headed toward a new blue Impala. Behind the wheel was a red-haired woman.

Though it didn't surprise Elizabeth, it still hurt. She swallowed back the pain and fought tears. If not for the children, she'd never ask him for another dime, but they had to eat. She stopped by the fancy car and glared at him.

He rolled down his window. "What are you doing here, Lizzie?"

"We don't have any food. I need grocery money."

"I'm broke."

"But you got paid Friday."

"I spent it. Look, I'm not going back to that house."

"Coward. You won't stay there, but you expect us to."

The woman started up the car and gunned the engine.

Elizabeth wanted to smash something through the windshield. "Go, don't come back. The kids and I won't be there. We're done."

She grabbed Timmy's hand and walked away. She forgot to mention the issue with the owner dying. It didn't matter. She planned to return to her parents' home.

"Momma, why is Daddy with that lady?" Anna asked. "Why doesn't he want to come home?"

"It's complicated, Anna. We'll talk later. Right now we need to get to the church before the office closes."

Timmy didn't say anything, but the sadness in his eyes meant he understood.

The church secretary gave them as many groceries as they could carry. The lady had also allowed Elizabeth to call her mother, who promised to send enough money for her and the kids to ride the Greyhound to Nashville. She had only a few more nights of being haunted.

*****

That night she snuggled her children in bed with her. She waited until they fell asleep before she cried over Raymond and her situation. Penniless and pregnant, but she had to be strong for her children. She hated placing the burden of taking care of them on her retired parents. Sadly, Raymond had been full of big ideas and plans when they'd married, but alcohol had come between him and his dreams. She'd never expected it to be like this.

The creaks...bumps...doors slamming...footfalls in the hall...muffled voices...groans, interrupted her. Riley Miles seemed more agitated and restless tonight. Well, if he kept it up, he'd wake Anna and Timmy.

She wiped her eyes and left the bed. She'd had enough. This ghost was about to see more than the light.

The hallway remained dark, but the scent of leather engulfed her.

The noise came from the stairs leading to the attic.

"Riley Miller, leave this house! In case you don't know, you're dead and have no reason to drive me crazy every night. I'm sure you have family waiting on the other side."

She didn't mention the South hadn't won the war. The last thing she needed was to depress him even more. He'd never leave.

For a moment the house grew still. Had it worked?

Heavy footfalls came down the stairs, toward her. A misty figure glided into view and shaped into the form of a man wearing a tattered Union uniform. She could see through him as easily as one sees through glass.

Her heart leapt in her chest. She tried to run, but couldn't. As the ghost drew nearer, she boldly said, "In the name of Jesus Christ what do you want?"

"Seek the dead."

"I don't understand."

He moaned loudly, and the house creaked and popped louder. For a moment, she thought the ceiling would fall down around her. Her body quaked in fear.

"Our little angel," he said, barely audible.

She forced herself to stay calm and consider what he'd said.

Seek the dead. Our little angel.

"Jennie..." He faded into thin air.

Oddly enough she wasn't afraid of him.

She returned to bed but couldn't sleep. Clearly, he was trying to give her a message about the house, but it didn't make any sense. Why not just say it? Maybe it was difficult for a ghost to speak to the living.

The cemetery.

Would she find Jennie buried there?

But how would she know which grave? The names were no longer visible on the headstones. Elizabeth returned to bed. She'd wait until morning.

*****

With only a small streak of sunlight on the horizon, Elizabeth left her sleeping children and headed for Anna's book satchel. She removed several sheets of tablet paper and some pencils. Outside, she walked through the yard to the small graveyard and pushed on the rusty gate. Vines ripped away as it creaked open. She pushed fallen limbs from her path and waded through weeds to the aged tombstones. One of them had crumbled from age. The dew covered ground sank in over the five graves. She breathed in the pungent scent of earth and grass.

Elizabeth placed the paper over the first one and rubbed the pencil lead over it.

It revealed the words Edward Hoffman. No, he wouldn't be considered a little angel.

Get smart, Elizabeth. Little angel, try the smallest headstone.

She applied the same principles to it and the carbon rub revealed the name Jennie Hoffman. She rubbed below the name.

Our little angel.

Her heart surged with excitement, not fear. Not wanting to leave her children alone, she hurried into the house. She'd continue once Anna was at school. Timmy would be easily distracted by his cars and trucks. He wouldn't ask questions, as her daughter would.

On her way home, she stopped by the library and returned the book on shorthand. None of it had made any sense. She wasn't cut out to be a secretary. *Cross*

13

that one off my list. But she checked out a book on how to sell rare or valuable coins.

The librarian smiled. "Treasure hunting?"

"Not really. Just interested."

*****

In back of the house, Timmy played with his Tonka dump truck in the grass while Elizabeth dug in the cemetery nearby using a handheld garden shovel. It required all her strength to dig into the hard soil.

Guilt edged its way into her mind over digging up some poor child's grave. But she was desperate. Finally, she hit something hard and pushed the mound of soil away.

The wooden domed chest had roots growing around it, holding it captive. Elizabeth chiseled them until it came loose. Earthworms wriggled in the soil around it. She struggled to pull it from the hole, expecting the wood to fall apart due to age. It weighed a ton. Below where the chest had sat rested the remains of Jennie Hoffman.

It wasn't until she had the chest on the ground and brushed away the dirt that she realized it was made of cypress. No wonder it had survived intact. She tried opening it, but from rust and decay the latch wouldn't budge. Using the wooden end of the hammer, she knocked off clumps of dirt from around the lock, then set it aside. Before taking it inside, she packed the soil back over the grave. She didn't want Jennie haunting her tonight.

Forgive my intrusion, Jennie.

In the house, Elizabeth washed the soil from her hands, then fixed Timmy's lunch all the while keeping an eye on the simple chest. Her heartbeat surged from the anticipation. She couldn't wait a second longer. While Timmy ate, she took the hammer and banged on the latch. Finally, it broke off. She pulled the lid open and gasped.

Gold and silver coins sparkled.

Tears filled her eyes.

Thank you, sweet Jesus. And thank you, Riley Miller.

She'd sell the coins. She didn't plan to tell Raymond about it. The only thing he'd get from her would be divorce papers. It didn't concern her that she'd be the first in her family to get a divorce.

She carried the coins upstairs and placed the small chest in her grandmother's large cedar trunk.

With the money, she planned to attend college. It'd be enough to buy a house in Nashville. She could even afford a car and television. She'd be able to pay her parents back as well. She'd make arrangements to sell the coins before leaving for Nashville.

That night the house remained silent. She breathed in deeply, but no longer smelled the leather that she had come to associate with Riley Miller. Had he moved on?

"Riley Miller," she called near the bottom of the attic stairs.

He didn't appear.

Disappointment flooded her. She wanted to thank him.

After meeting Anna at the school, Elizabeth walked to the library to return the book. The librarian took the book and checked it in. "That was fast."

"I didn't find it very interesting." Actually, she'd stayed up half the night reading and taking notes, but she didn't want people getting suspicious. She hated lying, but this had to remain a secret.

Timmy grinned at the lady. "Momma found a treasure."

Elizabeth choked a moment, then forced a laugh. "We played pirates today. The pictures in the book charged up his imagination. We found my sewing buttons and pretended they were gold coins."

The librarian studied her intently. "Any more strange noises in the house?"

"Yes, but I'm getting used to them."

*****

That night after the children were in bed, Elizabeth waited for Riley Miller, but the house remained silent again. She finished washing the dishes, then draped the wet dish towels over a chair to dry.

A key jiggled in the back door.

Raymond walked in. His blood shot eyes and snarly grin indicated he was soused. "Heard you found a fortune."

"What are you talking about?"

"It's all over town."

"If I had, I'd be at a Holiday Inn instead of this spooky place."

He rubbed the stubble over his chin, appearing in thought. "Something's changed. You're not afraid. So, what? You made friends with Casper the Friendly Ghost?"

"Leave now, Raymond. The kids and I don't need you."

"One of my drinking buddies told me a story about a military deserter who hid gold he'd stolen. The guy said it could be in this house. You've suddenly become a little uppity. I think you found it."

"Don't be silly."

"I'm not. Be a good girl and tell me where it is."

"No! It's not yours. You don't deserve anything."

"We're still married. That makes everything you own mine."

"Not for long. I want a divorce."

"You know your parents want us to work out our problems." He glanced around her. "Where'd you put it?"

She didn't answer.

He appeared to be in thought, then grinned. "I know exactly where you hid it. Your grandmother's cedar trunk."

"No! You're not taking it." Elizabeth grabbed him, and he shoved her to the floor. She pulled herself up. "You walked away from us."

She chased after him but stopped suddenly at the bottom of the stairs.

On the top landing, Raymond screamed as his body flew backwards and tumbled down the stairs.

The form of Riley Miller stood above him a few moments before vanishing.

She rushed to Raymond. Thank God he was still alive. Though she'd stopped loving him, she still didn't want anything to happen to him.

Good thing that my children slept through the commotion.

She slipped out and called the Collierville Police from a neighbor's house.

Without mentioning the coins, she told the sheriff that Raymond had knocked her down. The officer eyed her very pregnant belly and hauled Raymond to jail.

*****

Three months later: Nashville, Tennessee

Elizabeth smiled at her new daughter. She'd been released from the hospital that morning. Her mother had come to their new colonial home to help with Timmy and Anna.

Elizabeth's mom dropped a manila envelope on the bed. "This came in the mail."

She handed the newborn to her mother, took the letter and opened it. "It's from my attorney. She read it and sighed with relief. "Raymond signed the papers without contesting. By spring, he won't be a part of our lives. That's when I'll start college."

Elizabeth had decided to become a teacher. It'd allow her to be home with the kids on holiday and summer breaks. Her parents promised to help. She tossed the papers aside and reclaimed her new daughter, cuddling her closer.

Timmy and Anna entered the room. He frowned. "Why does she sleep all the time?"

"That's what babies do," Elizabeth explained.

Anna appeared bored. "When will she be old enough to play with?"

Elizabeth's mother smiled. "That's going to be a while."

"I want to send her back," Timmy insisted.

"Riley is here to stay." Elizabeth peeled the blanket back, giving Timmy a closer peek. "Now could you really send something this precious back to heaven?"

Timmy shook his head. "Guess not. Did you name her after the man who lived in our house?"

Elizabeth thought she'd swallow her tongue. "You knew about him?"

He nodded. "At night, he helped me find my way back to bed from the potty."

"You weren't afraid of him?"

He shook his head. "He's gone now."

"You sure?"

"Yep. His brothers were waiting for him."

Hopefully, Riley Miller had passed on to a better place.

Elizabeth smiled, then kissed Riley, his namesake.

She owed him everything. Without him, Elizabeth and her children would still be in a grave situation.

*****

Sherman's Visit to Collierville:

While the Battle of Collierville and Sherman's visit to the small Tennessee town really took place in 1863, this ghost and his problems were created for this story. My Aunt Gertrude lived in one of the huge Victorian homes in Collierville for a while. I used to wonder if it were haunted.

Many of the haunted incidences that occurred in this story actually happened to me when I lived in Bartlett, Tennessee. The one that scared me the most was when someone I couldn't see stretched out in my bed beside me and breathed heavily. This happened often after my husband left for work in the early morning hours. It served as a good motivator to make me jump from bed and start my day.

After Hours
Richard Warren Powell

With the strap over his shoulder, Joe cradled his guitar across his chest to protect it from the crowd on the sidewalk. It had taken him many years to save up the money for it. One clumsy step in this crowd could easily shatter his baby.

The lighted sign for B.B. King's hung over the sidewalk a block away, but it might take him a half hour to get there. After midnight on Saturday Beale Street foot traffic always moved slowly. An accidental bump between drunks could erupt into pushing and shoving matches that could escalate into full-blown fights.

Street performers raced up and down the pavement. Some were on foot, others rode every type of pedal-powered vehicle imaginable. They performed stunts, danced, or juggled. Spectators clogged progress even more.

The breezeless May heat did not bother Joe, but most people looked sweaty. Their pungent body odor mingled with the aroma of food cooking either in the restaurants or in the vender's trucks parked down the street.

As Joe approached the Hard Rock Cafe, the door swung open. A couple came out of the club holding hands while the sound of Credence Clearwater's *Born on the Bayou* spilled into the street. The music faded to just the loud thump of the bass as the door closed.

Finally, he reached the entrance for B.B.'s. The doorman seemed to look through him but opened the door for a couple ahead. As they halted to pay the cover before getting their hands stamped, Joe passed without stopping. An instrument provided a passport on Beale.

He moved around the edge of the crowd to a dark corner. A young black man crooned lyrics from an old Muddy Waters standard, *Hoochie Coochie Man*. The crowd sang along with the chorus. Someday the boy might be good enough to sit in with them. After hours.

"He is gonna be great if he keeps hisself clean," a voice said behind him.

Turning, Joe found a tall black man with a shaved head standing next to him.

"Joe Weaver, you ain't gettin any prettier with age!" the man said with a smile.

"Sam!" Joe exclaimed as he put his arms around the big man's shoulders. "I jus' thinkin' that boy might be able to sit in one day."

"Glad you think so. He my grandson." Sam handed Joe a small flask and said, "Wet your whistle with this. One of the boys just got in, brought it from Kentucky."

Joe sniffed, then took a long pull on the flask. The sweet taste of bourbon mixed with the warmth in his throat made him slightly dizzy.

"I was worried you wouldn't make it back tonight," Sam said as he watched his grandson.

"Just took some time to check on my people, you know? Like to see 'em once in a while, see how they doin," Joe answered. "You playin tonight?"

"Don'know yet. If a lot of you acoustic guys show up I might get to set in. Them electric guys are hard for a mouth harp guy like me to keep up with. Also, they like to do they own wailin'. Don't like us blow hard boys stealin' they thunder."

"Lots different, now'days.

"Yeah, back in the old days smoke be so thick in here you couldn't see across the room."

"Too bad didn't stop it years ago."

"Yeah never needed to buy any back then. Hell, used to smoke three packs a night without lightin' up."

"Luther never smoked a day in his life."

"Yeah, but lung cancer still killed him."

"That cat was somethin' else on the piano. Here's to Luther," Sam said, raising the flask in a toast.

"Yes, sir, here's to him," Joe replied.

"So you think he'll make it?" Sam asked as the lights on the stage dimmed.

"I hope so," Joe replied as the lights in the rest of the club became brighter. "Closin' time. Let's go back and see who else is here."

As the club's patrons filed out, the servers and bartender hurried through their clean-up. Joe and Sam walked to a vacant room behind the stage. Joe took his guitar out of its sack and polished it. As the last of the employees left, Joe tuned it.

Satisfied, he thumped out a bass rhythm. Sam placed his harmonica to his lips to begin a soft harmonic rhythm matching Joe. When they finished, someone shouted from the main room, "That may be old school, but it still kicks ass!" Sam and Joe made their way back to the main stage. Now lit, leaving the audience in shadows. Joe launched into a rendition of *Its Tight Like That*. After they finished several men in the crowd laughed. A woman cried out, "You built right, they all tight like that." The crowd hooted.

Joe and Sam started in with the *Crossroads Blues*. As they played, others joined the jam. A young white man with a broad-brimmed hat played an electric guitar, but did not drown out Joe. Instead the two traded riffs. Another man added backup on an electric keyboard while a muscular black man played the drums behind them. The sound gradually amped up as the band rocked.

After several numbers, Joe left the stage to sit with the crowd as others came up to join in with the session.

*****

Officer Bill Waterston sat in the Sky Watch Tower overlooking Beale. From twenty feet above the revelers, he watched for problems requiring intervention from the foot patrol officers. So far the throng moved peaceably to the parking areas or Trolley stops, while the die hards headed to many of the after-hours establishments still serving food. Graduated only six months earlier from the Police Academy, Bill had been surprised to be assigned to this important post. Since coming to this shift, he routinely had been assigned to foot patrol.

Starting at nine in the evening, foot patrol officers roamed the street, defusing confrontations, escorting drunks to safe places, finding medical attention for those seriously over the limit. Kevlar vests were standard. Too many guns on the streets.

City government wanted tourists to feel safe. No matter what happened elsewhere in the city, there always seemed enough money in the budget for patrolling this street.

As the foot traffic thinned below him, his Sergeant's voice came over Waterston's radio. "You can come down now. I think we got a handle on the crowd."

Waterston acknowledged. As he stepped to the pavement, Sergeant Johnson moved from the shadows.

"Let's take a look around here to make sure nobody's stranded," Johnson said, as he led Bill down a nearby dark alley. As they rounded a corner, Johnson stumbled. Bill saw a leg extending from behind a dumpster. He aimed his flashlight at it. A white man lay with his upper body against the building. His shirt front looked wet. The smell of beer mixed with the sour odor of vomit overpowered the stench from the trash bin. The man's pants and underwear had been pulled down to his knees. "Sir, are you all right?" Bill asked and shone his flashlight on the man's face.

The man raised his hands to shield his eyes and blinked. He looked up at the officers then glanced from side to side as if puzzled by his surroundings.

"Can y'all help me up?" the man asked as he raised a hand.

Bill grasped the man's to pull him up. As he stood, the man's trousers dropped to his ankles.

"May I see some identification, sir?"

"Sure, right here," the man replied and bent down to grasp his trousers. He pulled them up part way while checking his pants pockets. "Shit, my wallet's gone!"

"What happened, sir?" Sergeant Johnson asked as Bill grasped the man's upper arm to help him maintain his balance.

"See, I met this little doll at the Club around the corner. She suggested we come back here and get better acquainted." The man gave a sheepish grin, "We came back here and were really getting it on when I blacked out. Don't remember a thing from there."

"You've got a nasty lump on the back of your head. You might have been hit," Bill said as he examined the man's head with his flashlight. "Sounds like they lured you back here to steal your wallet."

The man glanced down at his pants now bunched around his ankles. "Looks like they stole my girl too!"

*****

Inside the bar, another man made his way on stage, bowed politely to Joe, who tipped his hat in acknowledgement and stepped down from the stage.

The new man also carried an acoustic guitar, but wore a glass tube on the little finger of his left hand. As he played, he rolled the tube down the neck between the frets and made the guitar whine. While the rest of the group provided a rhythm, the man made the acoustic sing almost like an electric. Someone shouted "Yeah baby! Get on it," as several clapped in rhythm. Another whistled in appreciation while the player smiled smugly at the crowd.

A hand reached across Joe with a tall frosty glass of beer. He accepted the offering, but couldn't see the face of his benefactor. A voice came out of the dark, "You earned it man. I sweatin' just watchin you." The beer tasted smooth and cold as it looked. Joe took a long swallow and nearly drained the glass.

"The place is really getting' hot, man," a man sitting next to him said with a grin as he clapped in time to the beat. Joe took a bandanna from his pocket to wipe the sweat from his brow.

"Music good too!" Joe replied with a grin.

The man chuckled. "Always better after hours!"

*****

26

After the ambulance left with the semi-nude man, Bill and the Sergeant returned to the alley to see if they could find anything related to the robbery.

"The guy got lucky. They must have just taken his cash," Johnson said as he held up a wallet. "Driver's license still here. Bunch of credit cards. I'll turn it over at the change of shift. Let them have all the credit for finding it."

"Anything else happen tonight, Sarge?" Bill asked as they returned to the empty street.

"Pretty quiet for a Saturday night. Had one fight, but that's all. How'd you like your first night in the Tower, Rookie?" Johnson asked.

"I just wonder how this guy got rolled right under me. I never even knew it," Bill said.

"Can't catch it all. If you called in every time you saw a couple sneak off into one of the alleys, we'd be running all over the place. 'Sides you stop a guy like that from experiencing the natural consequences of stupidity, you interfering with Natural Selection."

Bill had to chuckle, but he felt sorry for the guy. Stupidity was not against the law.

As they resumed their walk up the street, they paused to check the shadowed areas to make sure no one else needed assistance.

"Lotta history on this street, you know?" Johnson said. "Yeah, All the clubs, Handy Park ahead, the old Daisy theater," Bill said. "People get to walk on these brass musical notes in the sidewalk, with all the famous singers' names on 'em."

"Up there is that Marker to Ida B. Wells." Johnson swelled with pride. "She was one of my great aunts!"

As they passed the Hardrock Cafe, they could hear the thump of a bass ahead, apparently from B.B. King's. As they approached the music became louder, clearly the club was functioning after hours in violation of its license.

*****

Sam came down from the stage to sit next to Joe. The light faded and he saw people moving in the shadows on stage.

As the stage light brightened, a heavy-set black man with close-cropped gray hair and a guitar strap over his shoulder stepped to the front of the stage. Nearing the microphone, he moved the gleaming black electric guitar from behind his back to the front.

"It's him! He made it!" Joe exclaimed, slapping his knee while he nudged Sam.

The backup musicians began a rhythm as the man at the microphone made the guitar cry out a trademark introduction.

"This here's Lucille. She brought me from the plantation to where I am today," the man spoke as he played. His fingers danced on the neck as his pick stroked the strings. The backup band laid down the rhythm. As he played, the man talked about his life. Lucille always pulled him through. Some in the crowd clapped in time to the music. Others shouted out or whistled their appreciation to his comments or particularly challenging riffs.

*****

Bill reached for the club door's handle, found it locked, and rattled the door, but got no response. He tapped on the glass door with a coin to make a sound loud enough to echo off the nearby buildings. The music continued, but no one came to the door from inside.

"Forget that!" the Sergeant said as he played his light over the Security Company sticker on the door. "You would have to be loud enough to wake the dead to get their attention in all that racket."

"So what do we do, Sarge?" Bill asked.

"I'll call the Security Company to let us in." Johnson punched numbers into his cell phone. "The security system would have been triggered if they broke in. The owner or the manager might be inside with them. See if this place has a back door while I talk to Security."

Bill walked around the corner and found an alleyway that passed behind the club. Dumpsters lined the wall, but a space between two of the bins revealed a door that appeared to be for B.B. King's. Locked. The alley dead-ended, so anyone coming this way would have to pass him.

Blocking these doors violated fire codes, but Bill decided he could safely block those inside for a couple of minutes. He shoved one dumpster across the door, then strode back to the front where Johnson waited facing the street.

"The back door is locked," Bill reported. "I pushed a dumpster in front of it to keep anybody from going out that way."

"That'll be all right for now. If the place catches fire, we can still get them out fast. The Security Company is sending somebody to let us in, but, listen to this, he told me the system is set, and the place has motion detectors. Anybody moving around in there would trigger it."

"Maybe somebody forgot to turn off the jukebox," Bill said. "Wouldn't be the first time one of these security systems failed." Johnson took out his radio,

"Just in case we need to call in backup. That's no jukebox. It's a whole bunch of people. More than you and I can handle if they get rough."

*****

Joe had heard the man play before years ago. His skills had only grown, but his voice sounded rough from age and hard living. He shouted out a few lyrics that brought the crowd to its feet. He made his instrument cry and sing.

"Someone asked me where Lucille got her name. I was playin' in a little club in Twist, Arkansas. Ya'll know where that is, right?"

Several people laughed.

"During the show fight broke out, and a woman knocked over an oil drum stove that heated the place." The man continued. "The fire spread all over the floor around the stage. Set fire to the place and burned it to the ground. If I hadn't been up on the stage playin', I might'a burned up that night. That woman burned that place down was named Lucille. From that day to this all my guitars called Lucille to remind me how lucky I am to be alive."

Up on stage came a tall, desperately thin man with a gold tooth in a central incisor. The man at the keyboard stood and relinquished his spot to let the tall man slide behind the keyboards. He rolled up his sleeves and began to play. The band again picked up behind him.

"Look there, Luther made it too!" Joe turned to Sam in surprise. "He sat in a lot with the man up there."

"Well we had to make sure B.B. know we need him after hours," Sam replied with a knowing grin.

"The Thrill is gone, babe, gone away from me," the guitar player growled into the microphone. As the man played, the room seemed to be lit by a golden light. Joe felt himself rise as if floating. He felt better than he ever had in his experience. The music could not compare with anything on earth.

*****

"Shit, can't be B.B. King in there," the Sergeant said as he walked back to the door to listen "News said he was real sick in Vegas!"

"That's the news for you," Bill answered.

A car the security company's emblem on its door pulled to the curb. A man wearing a baseball cap climbed out.

"You Sergeant Johnson?" the man asked. "Got a call that you may need to get inside to check the place out."

"You hear that? Party goin' on inside after hours violatin' their license," Johnson answered. "We need to wait for backup. May have to haul in a crowd."

The security man smiled as he listened.

"One hell of a party," the man said. "Whether you arrest them or not you're gonna need help to handle this bunch."

"Called it in. They should arrive soon. As soon as they get here you can let us in, we'll take it from there," Johnson replied. "Bill, keep an eye on the back door. If they try to come out that way let me know and we'll back you up."

Bill badly wanted to get off duty at the regular time. He had made plans tomorrow. But now they would have to stay to process this bunch, which might take hours.

31

Eventually, Bill heard several vehicles approach. A squad car, light bar flashing, pulled up to the alley's entrance. Two black officers got out.

"We're goin' in the front now," Bill heard the Sergeant on the portable radio. "Stay there in case they try to slip out the back."

"Roger," Bill responded.

"Hear you guys are making a big bust tonight," the first officer said to Bill.

"Big after hours party. Probably take days just to process them all. Judging by the noise, must be a big crowd."

"Big place," the second officer, added looking at the building, "Came here once, and I think there was a couple hundred just in the bar."

"Probably a bunch of the Memphis-in-May crowd. May end up callin' in a couple of buses to haul 'em to 201."

"Maybe we can call in the Mounties. They can march 'em like one big herd," the second officer said, "Walk might sober 'em up."

"Nah, can't do that. Some of these jokers might pass out or get sick along the way. Can you imagine the papers gettin' ahold of that?" the other officer added, "Probably call it the Death March of Beale. End up makin' 'em all heroes."

Just then the door opened. A smiling, uniformed officer beckoned them inside.

"The big bust all over?" Bill asked.

"You won't believe it."

Their footsteps echoed, as they strode down the hallway's hardwood floor. They entered what appeared to be the main area. Fully lit, the room looked empty except for the police. The Sergeant stood near the front door talking to the security man as several officers moved quickly up the stairs to search the upper floors.

"Did you take them out already?" Bill asked.

"You are not gonna believe this kid," Johnson Sergeant answered. "The place is empty."

"No way! The place was packed with people, Sarge."

"Johnson, you been partying with the crowd?" A short black man wearing a dark blue polo shirt with a gold badge embroidered on the breast said as he walked in the front door. "As a command officer we expect you to set a good example for the younger members of the force."

"Shit, Lieutenant, I know what I heard. The Rookie here heard it first."

"Yes, sir," Bill said. "There was music, and you could hear a crowd."

"Sounded like a real party," the security man added. "Don't know why they didn't trigger the motion detectors. Have to send someone over to check them out tomorrow."

The lieutenant now strolled around the main room followed by Bill and Sergeant Johnson. "This place got a basement? Maybe they heard you and slipped out some secret tunnel."

As Bill now looked for a door that might lead to the basement, Johnson alerted the men searching upstairs to check for doorways that might connect to an adjacent building. He finally came to a door that opened onto a stairway going down.

"I think I found the basement," he called and soon both the Sergeant and the Lieutenant joined him.

The basement was filled to the ceiling with cases of liquor and restaurant supplies. The walls were solid concrete. No trap doors. Dust on the floor had not been disturbed.

Returning to the main floor, they found the remaining officers gathered there. Most stood near the stage talking and laughing. Three stood off to the side studying an old jukebox setting in a corner.

"Looks like a false alarm, guys," the lieutenant shouted. "Go back to serving and protecting."

As the men strolled out, some snickered as they glanced back at Bill and the Sergeant.

"Hey Sarge, take a look at this." one standing near the jukebox called out, "This is a real Wurlitzer Bubbler, must be worth a mint, man!"

The arched wooden cabinet trimmed with chrome and neon plastic stood silently in front of them. The coin slot had been covered in tape, but the machine remained plugged in. Sergeant Johnson shined his light inside the machine. A forty-five disk remained on the turntable. With the light, he could read the label. As they stood in front of the machine, a short black man came in past the officers who were leaving. A younger black man trailed behind him. Both looked surprised by the scene.

"What's happenin' officers?" the older man asked. "Been a break in or somethin'?"

"Who are you, sir?" The lieutenant asked.

"Names Bob Ralston, me and the boy here come to do the early mornin' cleanin'," The old man replied. "Manager called me to come in early today on account'a the news. Thought they might want to have a big thing today. Maybe a wake."

"What news is that?"

"B.B. King died last night in Vegas," the man said. "This bein' his place figured a lot a people be comin' by today to say goodbye. That old thing been actin' up again?" he added as he pointed to the jukebox. "It don't work real good, but it just come on sometime at night. Play a few tunes and then go dead. Spooks the hell outta me," the old man added. "Yeah, look here, Ronnie. Stuck on a old Joe Weaver song. Now it's stuck on B.B.'s *The Thrill is Gone.*"

"You mean it just comes on every so often?" the lieutenant asked. "If it doesn't work, why don't you just unplug it?"

"Can't. It would break the covenant. Man had it put in the deed when he sold it to B.B. that it has to stay plugged in. They can unplug it to move it, but if the electricity is off it for more than a hour the deed is forfeit."

"Maybe that was what caused this ruckus tonight?" one officer near the jukebox said.

"That why you'all here?" the old man asked, "Noise comin' outta here after hours?"

"Yeah, that's about it," the lieutenant replied.

"You'all must be new to Beale then," the old man replied with a chuckle. "Check with the boys that used to work outta the Beale precinct. They clue you in. If you don't mind, me and Ronnie gotta get busy gittin' the place ready."

After the Lieutenant left, Bill and the Sergeant walked to a waiting police cruiser to drive in for change of shift.

"What do you think of all this tonight, Sarge?" Bill asked.

"Damned if I know kid, but the old man was right. You and I have only been down here for six months."

Later that morning Sergeant Johnson stretched as he stood at the conclusion of the church service. Even though he had been up all night, he faithfully attended church on Sundays with his wife and two daughters. Dealing with low-life all week, he felt this routine refreshed him. After he took them out to breakfast, he then could lie down to rest, before he had to return to duty.

As they left the church, he spied a familiar figure ahead.

"Excuse me, honey. Why don't you take the girls to the car? There's someone over there I need to talk to real quick." He kissed his wife on the cheek. "This won't take a minute."

"Tavis!" He shouted as he approached a heavy-set man moving down the sidewalk with an equally plump woman.

The couple turned.

"Kevin, how you been?" the man said.

"You lookin' like retirement suits you, man," Johnson said.

"This here Kevin Johnson, Louise, I had him as a rookie in trainin' years ago," Tavis said to the woman at his side, as she nodded to Johnson. "I hear you in charge of the night shift on Beale now."

"Yes sir, just took it over six months ago. Nice bunch of officers there, but there is something I wanted to ask you about since you used to work out of the Beale Precinct." Johnson told him about the previous night. The older man listened, nodding his head occasionally.

Tavis turned to his wife. "Honey, me and this man need to talk shop for a minute. Why don't you head over to the car and I'll be right along."

"It was nice meeting you, young man. I need to get out of this sun and rest my feet."

"So, nobody clued you in?" Tavis said as he took Johnson by the arm to walk to a nearby shade tree. "Oh that's right, you took over from Robinson. Damn shame him dyin' in that wreck and all."

"What do you mean, clued me in?" Johnson asked.

"That happens all the time at that place. Been goin on for years. Back when I first started out, we got

36

those calls all the time about after hours shenanigans at that place. Same as what happened to you last night. We'd go in there ready to bust a bunch of late night partiers and find nothin'. Brass started sayin' stuff about our shift that wasn't exactly flatterin', you know?"

"So what did you do?" Johnson asked.

"Finally we let it go one night, and the next day nothin' happened. No complaints from the owner—nothin'," Tavis replied. "If other places violated curfew we responded, but we learned to leave that place alone."

"So what do you think is happenin' there?" Johnson asked.

"Don't know. I know there are things that happen in this world that I don't understand, and no one else does either. This thing is one of those. Just be glad it's not something you have to solve."

"How do I explain this to the men on the shift?" Johnson asked.

"You won't have to." Tavis smiled. "By now most of the guys who showed up last night couldn't wait to talk about the crazy thing. Others who know will set them straight."

"This just seems unreal to me, but thanks, Tavis, for filling me in," Johnson replied. "I am still not sure how I can handle it, though."

"Like I said, you probably will not have to do a thing. Just accept the fact it will happen again from time to time. The more you respond by the book, the crazier everybody will think you are," Tavis said with a look of concern on his face. Johnson probably now dreaded his future on Beale. "There is one thing you could do next time it happens though."

"What's that?" Jonson asked.

"Enjoy the music. It is better than you'll ever get to hear anywhere else."

*****

Beale Street

Although Beale Street actually starts down on Riverside Drive by the bank of the Mississippi River, the actual partying portion runs from Second Street to Danny Thomas Blvd. That's where you find the crowds and the noise, the clubs and the restaurants. That's the street where W. C. Handy played the blues and where today his disciples continue the tradition. Good barbecue, good liquor (even during Prohibition), good music, and good times have always hung out there. A few folks never want to leave, even if they died a long time ago.

Noblesse Oblige
Carolyn McSparren

You don't expect to find a grey stone castle with crenellated roofs and towers in the middle of Central Gardens in Memphis. When it was built in 1896, the Hall was considered a country house. It overlooked three thousand or so acres of cotton plantation that reached south across the Tennessee border into Mississippi.

Unfortunately, after the elderly lady whose family built it finally died, it began a long period of decline. None of the rest of the family wanted to move in. It was sold and sold again. It went through various incarnations as restaurants, only one of which did well, several crazy discos, which did not, and new (and peculiar) décor designed by people who must have been on legendary substances when they commissioned the work.

None of that took away from the eccentric bones of the place. The wealthy cotton man whose family built it in the first place was sophisticated, educated, and in love with Sir Walter Scott. I never saw the house in its glory days, but from what I hear, the Great Gatsby had a real rival for king of the party-givers during the Roaring Twenties. And upper-class southerners know how to party. Prohibition? Fogettaboutit.

I'd loved it since I passed by when I walked home from school. Although I had slight acquaintance with the granddaughter of the dowager who lived there in solitary splendor, she was older and never invited me inside, no matter how much I angled for an invitation. Her grandmother was not well and had become a recluse. I also got the feeling she had the temperament of a Cajun gator with an abscessed tooth.

I finally got my chance to see the inside after I became a grandmother myself. The women's circle of which I am a member puts on a house tour of homes in Central Gardens every year or two for charity. This particular year the committee finally convinced the bank and the trust lawyers who were in charge of the hall after its latest foreclosure, that with a little cleaning inside and out, it would be an asset to the tour. Might even help to sell the place.

I always thought it would make a perfect bed and breakfast. Okay, so it would be a bit like spending the night in Hill House (as in Shirley Jackson's *The Haunting of Hill House,* the scariest book I ever read). A lot of people enjoy the frisson of fear. Look at all those haunted castles in England and Scotland that are booked years in advance.

From the enthusiasm generated in my Circle when the announcement that we had permission was made, I was by no means the only person who longed to see the place. It was quite a coup, even if we did have to spend a thousand dollars to have the vines that climbed all over the porticos disposed of and the garden and lawn at least mowed and cleared of copperheads. The bank even agreed to add a thousand, so we'd barely be out of pocket.

The bank's thousand would go to a cleaning team to give the inside a thorough brush up. We'd more than recoup that little bit in additional ticket sales. Their one stipulation was that at least one of the members of the Circle committee had to be on hand at all times to supervise the cleaners and gardeners.

Guess who volunteered? Thank heaven it was October, the only time Memphis houses don't usually need furnaces or air conditioning. In its present incarnation, the hall had neither in working order.

Sissy Houston and I unlocked the giant front door at eight in the morning on a brilliant October morning to allow the five cleaning people—three men and two women—to start vacuuming and dusting and scrubbing. The team of gardeners was already at work tearing down lianas outside and trying to unearth a least a portion of the lawn from the undergrowth. The place was like Sleeping Beauty's castle—festooned with vines so thick the outside portico couldn't be reached from outside nor could the French windows be opened from inside. The windows were perpetually shadowed by ghostly green fingers.

"Oooh!" Sissy said when the door finally creaked open on the foyer. "Tell me again why we're doing this. This place is creepy."

"Won't be once it's cleaned up and the lights are on," I said. I was already staring down at the beautiful mosaic tiles of the coat of arms centered on the front hall. "Once this floor is scrubbed, it'll be lovely, you'll see."

Ahead of us rose the grand staircase. "Oh, for pity's sake," I said. "What idiot did that?"

At some point it had been painted a dazzling white all the way to the second and third floors before ending under a filthy skylight high above our heads. "It's antique mahogany. That's vandalism."

"Well, we don't have the time or the money to strip it, so we'll just have to suck it up." Sissy sounded downright piqued. "And just how do you know it's mahogany? You and Bill ever come here when it was a restaurant?"

"Of course not. Everybody said the food was overpriced, and both badly cooked and served. No wonder they went bankrupt."

"So how do you know about the woodwork?"

"I must have seen a photo sometime." Maybe, but I didn't think so. I just knew. We wandered through the big rooms downstairs with more white woodwork and crumbling red paint on the walls. Good restaurant practice. Red walls make for faster dining, bigger appetites and more conversation. I worked in a fancy restaurant in college, so I know what I'm talking about.

"Tara meets Sir Walter Scott," Sissy whispered. "Talk about your *mésalliance!*" She shivered. "I'm freezing."

So was I. The house was much colder than it should have been in early October after a very hot summer. It was as if the heavy stone with which it was built refused to allow warmth inside.

I could almost hear the house talking to me.

"All right for you," it said. "Abandon me to the mice and the spiders and the dust. I'll sit here and molder and freeze your asses off, you see if I don't."

It was definitely angry. I don't generally sense auras. My friends say I am as sensitive as your average paving stone, but something in that house glommed onto me at once. For whatever reason, I was chosen. Unfortunately.

"I hate this place."

I jumped a foot. Sissy, who is small and light, had slipped up behind me. She stood hugging herself inside her heavy cardigan sweater and stamping her feet in their Sketchers. "It's eighty degrees outside."

"It's the stone walls," I told her. I was cold too, but since I have a much thicker layer of blubber on my bones, I don't feel the cold the way skinny people do.

"Actually, I love it, despite the dumb stuff they've done to it. Want to go exploring?"

"No. I intend to sit myself down on that bench and wait for you. I feel as though the whole house is watching me. One mistake and poof! I'm gone."

"Go sit in your car. That counts as being on site. If anybody questions it, you can say you were overseeing the gardening crew."

"I hate to leave you..."

"I'll come get you if I need you. Go."

"I have a thermos of coffee in the SUV. Come out and join me, okay?" She was gone out the front door, across the wide portico, down the steps and on her way to her car before I had time to turn around.

Somewhere overhead I could hear the cleaners walking on the uncarpeted floors. I started up the stairs, running my hand along the ornate (nasty white) banister. Half way up I looked down at the palm of my hand and found it was filthy. I could hear one of the cleaners on the landing above me. "Don't forget to dust this banister," I called. No answer. Okay, so the house cleaning service didn't waste words.

"I'm getting to it." I turned to look over my shoulder, nearly tripping on the stairs in the process. One of the cleaning ladies stood behind me. She was the size of a yearling rhinoceros. I should have heard her footsteps.

"I thought I heard you all upstairs," I said. I had met all five of the cleaners on their arrival. "Augusta, isn't it?"

"Yes, ma'am. We haven't gotten upstairs yet. We're still working on the main floor and the kitchen. Just hitting the high spots is going to take all day."

"You're *all* downstairs?" Then who had I heard walking overhead? Did we have a squatter? The place had excellent security and even better locks, but in this day of expert hackers, any security can be circumvented. "I'm going to do a quick tour of the second floor," I said. "We don't have to touch the third floor and the attic. Nobody will be allowed up there."

"Not in the basement either," Augusta said. "I took a peek down there. It's a mess, but there are still tables and chairs stacked against the walls. I guess from the restaurant, maybe the disco. There's French doors leading out onto the portico. Looks like there used to be a swimming pool out there."

"There was. It was filled in at the start of World War II. All the private pools were filled in for the war effort. I have absolutely no idea why. It's not as though Memphis has a water shortage. It simply was considered unpatriotic to keep one's swimming pool."

"If was a real big one for a private pool," Augusta said. "You can see the stones around what used to be the edge. Real pity to fill in something like that. You know, this place gives me the creeps, but whoever lived here must have been real rich."

"Rich-rich. Farmed half of north Mississippi." I turned away to go up the steps, while she went back to her dusting and scrubbing. I was one step from the second floor hall when I heard it again—a footstep, and not a light one. "Hello?" I called. "Whoever's up here, y'all come on out." The steps ceased for an instant, then started again. The same measured tread. If it was a cleaner, they were making slow going of it. I had an instant of fear. What if I ran into some kind of crazed derelict who'd been living here and didn't want to leave? My husband Bill says I blunder in where angels fear to tiptoe, much less tread.

"Look, you won't get into trouble, but you're going to have to leave. The house will be open to the public this Saturday and Sunday for the house tour." I felt like an idiot speaking to footsteps. That had already quit.

Great. Whoever it was had gone up to hide on the third floor or in the attic. Well, one of the muscular gardeners could dislodge whoever it was. I refused to come face to face with your friendly neighborhood axe murderer. If I had to, I'd call the police, although the Circle would have a hissy fit at the bad publicity if the papers picked up the call. And they would.

I'd reached the second floor landing by this time. The six bedrooms on this floor had not been restored for the restaurant, so they were pretty ratty. At least the woodwork up here—beautiful old golden oak— had not been painted, although it had darkened almost to black the way varnished oak will do if left unloved. I longed to get my hands on some varnish stripper just to see what it had looked like in its glory days.

Thud, thud, thud!

I jumped a foot and spun around. There was somebody up here, and it sounded as though it was coming from the front bedroom. I felt the floor bounce. "Who's there?" I tried to sound big and important. That's how you're supposed to frighten grizzly bears. I wasn't sure how it would work with squatters.

I actually sounded like a frightened mouse.

Thud!

I would have fled back down the stairs, but I was too scared to move.

"All right now, that's enough," I said when I could breathe again. I was an English teacher for thirty years. I know how to handle rowdies. I took a deep breath and stomped into that front bedroom. Or at least to the door. I figured if somebody chased me, I could beat them down the stairs easy.

No one there. Uh-huh, so they slipped through the connecting door into the adjoining bedroom. Except there wasn't any door, and like most houses of its era, there was not a closet in sight. Just scrofulous walls dripping cabbage rose wallpaper.

Okay. The gardeners had done something with the furnace that made the radiator thump. Except there wasn't one. There was a fireplace designed to burn coal, which meant the opening was small and the flue smaller. Santa wouldn't be able to get down that chimney after a year on Weight Watchers.

So what had I heard?

Thud, thud, thud!

Again I spun. This time the sound seemed to come from the back bedroom on the other side. "Now cut that out!" I shouted as I sprinted for the room.

To find precisely the same nothing I'd found in the front.

This room was over the entrance portico and had a bank of windows across one wall looking out over what must at one time been the front garden and the Porte-cochère. I stalked across, yanked the tail of my ratty t-shirt out of my jeans, and used the end of it to clean one of the small panes of glass so that I could see out. I expected to find a ladder outside and a gardener cutting honeysuckle away from the windows. I saw the gardeners, all right. Every single one of them down by the swimming pool.

I knelt on the filthy window seat under the window, largely because my legs wouldn't hold me. I was well and truly scared. "There is some rational explanation," I said aloud. "There always is."

Thud! Thud!

I came to my feet. That noise was coming from directly in front of me. If it had been tangible, I would have been able to touch it. But there was nothing to see.

I have absolutely no idea where my words came from or how I was able to speak them, my mouth was so dry. I said, "Who are you and what do you want?"

Nothing.

I dropped onto the window seat and the aged silk upholstery sent up a cloud of dust so thick my eyes watered. I thought I was going to choke to death. Whatever it was waited politely while I coughed my guts out and wiped my streaming eyes on what was now a filthy Kleenex.

"Look, I don't believe in ghosts and I'd prefer not to be convinced otherwise. If, however, you are one, all this banging isn't helpful. Who are you and what do you want? And enough with the thudding, please." Sounded nearly normal. I hoped only I could hear the quaver. I kept my hands clasped in my lap to cover up the shaking.

The room was quiet so long I'd decided it must have been the radiators after all. Then right beside my head, words began to appear in the dirt of a second windowpane. I couldn't see the finger, but I could see the words take shape. "Home Leave."

"You want to leave home? Can ghosts do that?"

Big thud! Obviously wrong question.

"All right, we'll leave that one. Who are you?"

Nothing. I slid over to give it room to write. After a minute, the word *Belle* appeared in the dirt.

"Are you family? From the family that lived here, I mean?"

Thud!

"I take it that's a no. But you did live here at some point, didn't you?"

Double thud.

"Now we're getting somewhere." I am a puzzle solver. I can never finish the *Sunday Times* puzzle because I refuse to look the answers up on the Internet, but I'm pretty good otherwise. Sudoku? No way, I deal with words. And thinking about words lowered my fear level.

"So who *were* you?" When I took my Yankee husband to our first big Memphis party, and somebody came up to me and asked that same question, "Who were you, dear?" He had no idea what they meant.

I did. They wanted family history, where I went to school, whether I had ever been in Cotton Carnival, and on and on. So that I could be neatly filed in the proper slot. I assumed my southern ghost would understand as well. And she did. I knew it was a woman, though Lord knows how. "Were you a friend?"

Thud.

"Servant?"

Big thud.

Who else would have lived here? Not family, not servant, not friend.

Thud, thud, thud, thud, thud. Annoyed. Obviously I was being woefully dumb.

"Nurse. You were her nurse, weren't you?"

Thud, thud. I could hear the satisfaction.

"All those years when the old lady was an invalid, you were with her." Once I got out of here, I could go look up who she was, but at the moment all I knew was Belle. I assumed it was her first name.

So why was she still here? She was probably much younger than her patient. After the old lady's death, she would have found a new job or been reassigned to another patient. Unless..."Did you die here too?"

Softly this time—thud, thud.

"Oh, Belle, I am sorry. Was it the big flu epidemic?"

Thud.

"Later?"

Double thud.

"But why did you stay?"

Silence. And then voices from the hall and the rattle of mops and pails and the thump of vacuum cleaners being dragged upstairs. I looked at the windowpanes. That was evidence that Belle had been here.

I've always thought the worst moment in *The Lady Vanishes* comes when the message disappears in the steam from the train engine. As I looked, something or someone wiped the words away and left only streaks. "No!" I shouted.

"Hey, ma'am. You okay?" Augusta stood at the bedroom door with the whole crew behind her. I started to tell her, but stopped myself.

Instead I took a deep breath and pasted a smile on my face. "Just going over a list in my head. Y'all ready to move up here already? I'll go downstairs then."

I slipped by them and fairly catapulted down the broad staircase and right out the front door, down the steps, and into Sissy's front seat.

"What on earth?" she said.

"Coffee, please. Lots of sugar if you have it." In my headlong flight down the stairs and out, I figured out what I had to do. If we were going to be safe from intrusions during the house tours, I had to find some way to get Belle out of that house.

At this point I might be the only one she'd revealed herself to, and I intended to keep it that way. Otherwise, we'd have first, bad publicity, and second, probably insurance problems from falls down the

49

stairs and coronary thromboses. "I have got to get out of here, Sissy," I said. "Mary Alice is due to take over in an hour. Can you hold the fort until then?"

"You sick? It's not like you to renege on a job."

I knew she'd think I was crazy, but I absolutely had to tell someone, and I couldn't tell Bill. He'd have me committed. So I told her from the first footsteps through the last thud, and the cleaning team's appearing at the bedroom door. I didn't dare look at her after I finished.

"My Lord," she whispered. "You, of all people."

"I am not crazy, Sissy."

"I know you're not, honey. Bless your heart." She patted my arm. Now those three words can conceal everything from fury to pity and everything in between. As in, *"That witch stole my husband, but bless her heart."* I suspected I'd wound up on the pity end of the spectrum.

"So you're running away?" Now she sounded as though she was coaxing a cat down from a tree. "I do not blame you one little bit. You go on home and rest. Mary Alice and I will handle everything."

"I am not going home. I'm going to the library. I have to find out who this Belle was and why she won't leave that house. Then I've got to figure out a way to get her gone before the house tour. If she starts banging and thudding on Saturday, we could be in a pickle. She wants to stay there, and she wants to stay there alone. I got that much. I have to convince her someplace else is better."

"Go to the liiiggghht." Sissy snickered.

I opened the car door. "I knew I shouldn't have told you."

She grabbed my sleeve. "Yes, you should. As a matter of fact, I do believe you. It's just weird that she went for you and not for me. You are not the most sensitive person in the world. We had three ghosts in the house I grew up in down in Marshall County. Never bothered the family, but scared the daylights out of houseguests." She took a deep breath. "All right. I'll take care of the crews. You go hit the library. Bound to be scads on this house. But I warn you, I am not going in that house alone."

"I'll call your cell if I find anything. I'll pick us up a couple of barbecues for lunch and come back as soon as I can. Will you still be here?"

"Unless Belle whisks me away I will."

Our public library has an extensive collection of historical data about Memphis and the neighborhood. In my teaching days I'd often used it to assign essays to my advanced placement students, so I know the librarian of the collection well. I think he dresses to type. He has a fluffy halo of white hair and a small goatee. Despite the October day he was still wearing his seersucker suit. Surprising. I wouldn't have thought he'd be caught dead in seersucker after Labor Day. We hugged and squealed and spent ten minutes bringing one another up to speed. Then I told him I wanted the records from the Hall for the last years the old lady lived there.

"Pictures too?"

"If you have them."

"Oh, we have them. The family gave us all the records and the albums from the time the house was built until the old lady died, and it was sold the first time."

I expected microfiche. I was instead given folders of clippings, elderly leather bound ledgers, and photo albums, also leather bound.

"I'm actually looking for the name of one of the nurses who looked after the old lady. Possibly the last one she had."

He picked up a ledger and opened it on the scarred library table. "If she was paid, her wages should be noted in here. The old lady died in 1958, so we'll start there."

Trust Henry to know the date she died. The ledgers were in a beautiful Pittman cursive. Not many people write well anymore and half my students didn't even know cursive. Pity. Not, however, easy to read and the letters and numbers were teensy.

We started when the old lady died. "I would expect a final check—severance pay, maybe a small bequest," Henry said.

Nothing. After some searching we did find payment to a home health care group, but not the name of the nurses.

"Wouldn't have only been one, you know," Henry said. "You'll have to call the health care people, but they probably won't give you names, even if they are still in business and still have the records."

I ran a hand over my face. My eyes were smarting from the dust and the exertion. I cleaned my glasses, which were as usual filthy. I was sliding them up my nose when Henry asked, "Why are you looking?"

"I wish I could tell you, but you'd think I was nuts."

He sank back against the tall leather chair that dwarfed him, a gift from a generous donor. Probably belonged to some confederate general. He crossed his legs at the knee and templed his fingers before his face. "You've met Belle."

I sat up so fast I bashed myself in the nose with my glasses so hard my eyes watered all over again. "What the Sam Hill do you know about Belle? Who was she?"

"I don't know precisely who she was, but I do know you have been privileged. She usually only makes a to-do when she's annoyed. I used to go over there for dinner when I could afford it while it was a restaurant." He tittered. "She drove Jeff Richards, who owned the place, barking mad. He'd planned to turn the second floor into private dining rooms and conference rooms. He gave it up after Belle tried to toss him downstairs. She knocked a painter off his ladder while he was painting the banister..."

"Good for her."

"I agree, but Jeff wanted the place to look trendy."

"Bad taste is never trendy."

"Again, I agree, so did Belle." Jeff persevered. "He did, however, give up his idea of using the second floor. She never makes her presence known downstairs."

"So she probably died on the second floor. And if all my ghost story reading bears any semblance to reality, she died suddenly and probably violently. Does she speak?"

"Jeff said she simply made noise and knocked things around."

I picked up another ledger. "She's got to be here someplace. If you'll help me look, I'll take you out to lunch." I'd have to pick up barbecue for Sissy on my way back, but this was more important.

"It is, my dear, what I'm here for."

If this is what real detectives do, it is mind-numbing, eye straining, and about the most boring job I have ever undertaken since I gave up crocheting. We even gave up chatting to one another and worked on in silence and, in my case, despair.

My stomach rumbled so loud Henry looked up.

"Lordy, it's almost two-thirty. You must be starved!" I said. Sissy would kill me when I got back.

"I seldom eat lunch," he said. I could just bet. He was whip thin. "I feel we are close. One more ledger each and we call it quits for today, all right?"

What could I say? I am not whip thin and never skip lunch. I grabbed the next ledger in the stack and began to scan the salary columns. In the end I nearly missed it. Near the bottom of a page with coffee stains on it, I found an entry called "termination of contract. No severance pay for lack of notice."

And a name. Belfontaine Bishop. "Gotcha!" I shouted and received a nasty look from Henry.

"Hush!"

So I whispered. "Belfontaine Bishop." I showed him the entry. "She left without giving notice."

"Or did not leave."

The hair rose on the back of my neck. "No home health care firm listed, so she was privately hired. What happened to her?"

Now that we knew who to look for, we found her salary listed the previous year, the year before that, and on back for eight years. Then her name disappeared.

"She stayed for eight years. That's hardly a lifetime. Maybe she was reaching retirement age and just died," I said. I flipped the ledger closed and looked at the date. 1942. The war had started in December of 1941. Maybe Belle left to join one of the war nursing groups, but surely she would have given notice to people who had paid her for eight years. "She must have been fond of the old lady..."

"What makes you think that? She was a real martinet, and until she became bedridden, she ran her poor family ragged."

"How do you know?"

"I am older than you are, my dear. I used to go to what I suppose are now called 'play dates' with Vicky, who disliked her grandmother thoroughly, by the way. The old woman hated having strangers in the house, especially little boys. She loathed noise and change, so I only came a few times."

"More than I did," I said. "Vicki never invited me. I was younger, but not that much younger. You wouldn't have known Belle then, would you?"

"If so, I don't remember her. We avoided the second floor. We used the back stairs to get up to Vicki's room on the third floor."

"Okay, so why did Belle disappear and where has she gone? Or not gone?"

"Maybe the old lady hit her with her cane in one of her fits," Henry said. "She drank an amazing quantity of bourbon, to hear Vicky tell it."

"Someone would have had to cover it up."

"Anyone in the household would have done that, family or old retainers."

"They wouldn't want the old lady sent to prison..."

Henry snorted. "Prison? They would have died if her name had ever appeared in the *Commercial Appeal* except on the society page."

"Wouldn't they have called it an accident anyway? Maybe the old lady pushed her down the stairs. They're pretty treacherous now. They must have been deadly when they were kept polished."

"They were covered in an oriental runner," Henry said. "It's in some of the photos."

"If she had family of her own, wouldn't they have come hunting for Belle?" I asked.

"Big if. Maybe she was estranged from them or had none in the first place. Plenty of young women went off on their own as private nurses or companions."

"Can we find out if she was a registered nurse?" I asked.

"Undoubtedly, but it will take a little time."

"I don't have a little time, and it doesn't matter anyway. What matters is why she died in that house and what they did with her afterwards, whoever they are."

"Well, you can't ask any of the family. Nobody is left. Vicky moved to Paris and died about five years ago. She was the last."

I hate hearing that people I knew as a child are dead, even if they were a few years older than I. "Let's look through the rest of that ledger. Maybe we'll find a clue to what happened."

"Certainly. No doubt we'll find an entry for 'new cane, finest Malacca, braining nurses, for the use of.'"

I rolled my eyes. This time we shared the ledger. Even in 1942 the bills for groceries and alcohol were staggering. A portion of the tile roof over the Porte-cochère had to be replaced because it leaked. The chauffeur left to join the navy. One of the housemaids joined the WACS. Nothing on Belle.

I am no genius, and I doubt if Belle's aura could reach five miles across town to land in the library, but the minute I saw the payment, I knew we'd found it. "Henry, look here."

He looked. "So? Everyone was doing it."

"One week after Belle disappeared?"

"Surely they'd had it planned for months beforehand."

"Maybe. Maybe it was serendipity. Maybe it was the cause. Maybe hearing the equipment out her window is what set the old lady off. Didn't you say she hated change and noise? That would definitely have done it."

"You think the old lady killed her?"

"Makes sense. It was summer, so Vicki was probably off at camp with the rest of us. By that time the rest of the family was living elsewhere..."

"War effort gearing up. New regs about farming. Problems getting people to chop the cotton. The family would have used anything as an excuse not to visit."

"So she's alone with a smaller staff than she's used to. Nobody to dance attendance on her except Belle. Maybe she didn't dance fast enough."

"Or tried to pry the bourbon bottle from her hand." Henry was starting to get into this. "I have no idea what size this Belfontaine was, but the old lady was taller than I am and as big-boned as a full sized heifer. Armed with a cane, she'd have been a formidable opponent, if she went off the rails."

"Say the earth moving equipment could have set her off," I said.

"Destroying her view, desecrating her land. And all without a by your leave."

"Was she in a wheelchair?" I asked.

"I don't think she was stuck in one until after the war," Henry said. "Stumped around with the cane. With a heavy silver fox head, as I recall. She fox-hunted when she was a girl."

"Perfect weapon. She whacks at Belle, then either keeps whacking or discovers one whack was enough to land her with a dead body. She wouldn't call her son, would she?"

"She'd call her man-servant. He was not called a butler, although he served as one. As I recall, he received an extremely comfortable retirement package a couple of years later."

"Dead now?"

"Good grief, yes. But he could have done it. He was the size of a small buffalo. The two of them actually loved one another, I think."

I raised my eyebrows. Henry shook his head. "Not that kind of love. It was, after all, the forties, and he was ten years younger than she and African American. But love nonetheless. He'd have said something like, "Don't you worry your pretty little head, ma'am. I'll take care of it."

"And he would. Ready-made grave down below all ready to be filled in."

"Big grave. It's a big swimming pool. We'd never find the skeleton, even if we dug the entire thing up. Nobody'll do that on this little piece of conjecture."

"Maybe we don't have to," I said, and picked up my bag from under the table.

As I surmised, Sissy was furious at me, but a giant brown barbecue and a big diet coke mollified her. When I got there Mary Alice was out working with the gardeners. I walked over to report to her I was back and release her from duty.

"Good," she said. "I have a million things to do if we're going to open this tour on time." The subtext was that she was behind because I had been irresponsible. I kept my mouth shut.

The garden crew had done a miraculous job in a short time. They had scythed the tall grass and underbrush from over the pool, cut down the lianas, raked and pruned and piled up an entire trash hauler with debris.

I sat on the portico steps that were now clean and swept, and stared at what had been the swimming pool. Maybe someone would buy the old place and restore that too. I'd be interested to know if they found any trace of a skeleton. Maybe Henry and I were dead wrong.

But it felt right, and for one of the few times in my life, I was willing to trust my feelings.

So I trudged up the main staircase expecting thuds. But I heard nothing. I went back into the master bedroom and stared out the old lady's bay window. She would have had the perfect view of the pool and garden. How she must have hated losing it.

I heard no thuds, but when I turned I knew something was there. Until that moment it never occurred to me that the ghost might be the old lady herself, who would definitely not want Belle's story to come out.

"Belle?" I asked tentatively. "Belfontaine?"

Nothing, although I knew she, or something, was there. "Look, I can guess what happened to you. She probably already had dementia or Alzheimer's. I don't think she would have hurt you on purpose. What she did in covering it up was dreadful, but times were different then."

This time instead of a thud I heard a skitter as though a mouse ran across the floor. I don't mind mice, so I didn't react. "I don't know whether you're staying because your body is buried in the swimming pool and not in a cemetery, but frankly, it's not a bad resting place, all things considered. If I can convince the police to dig it up, we may or may not find you, and if we did, I don't know what we could do about it. Everybody who had anything to do with it is dead.

"I'd like to see this place preserved, maybe turned into a bed and breakfast. Certainly better than letting it go to wrack and ruin. I would think that's what you'd want too.

"I'm not asking you to leave. That's your choice. But you were a nurse, remember? A care giver? A nurturer? Stomping around scaring people is not what care givers do. If you don't want to leave this place that you called home for eight years, I can understand that. If you want to go to the light, or whatever happens after we die, I can understand that too. All I'm asking is that you stop scaring people and quietly enjoy having them around." Then I explained about the house tour and everything that had happened since the old lady died. I doubted anyone had told her.

"Scaring people won't protect this place from developers. So could you do your haunting when it's empty and be quiet when there are people around? I truly think it's in everybody's best interest."

I prayed the cleaners hadn't heard me talking to an empty room.

Which suddenly wasn't quite empty. She hadn't been particularly pretty, although there was a country girl freshness about her. Her hair had been mousy brown, as had her eyes. The uniform she wore was too big and kind of droopy, and she wore white stockings and nurse shoes. Nobody does that any longer.

When she turned her head slightly, I caught my breath. A dark stain ran from above her ear down into her collar, and her skull on that side wasn't the same shape as the other. "So she did hit you," I whispered. "I'm so sorry."

She ducked as though the crushed skull embarrassed her. Then she raised her eyes, and smiled at me.

That was it. She vanished. But I knew we had a bargain. Maybe when she felt comfortable, she'd move on. The house tour would go off without a ghostly hitch or a single thud.

I looked over my shoulder as I left the room. "Belfontaine is a beautiful name," I said.

Two months later the house sold yet again and is in the process of being restored again, this time for a small hotel. I hope Belle is happy wherever she is.

And I hope I never, ever, have an encounter like that again. My heart won't take it.

Noblesse Oblige

*****

Ashlar Hall

Ashlar Hall, named for the Ashlar stone of which it is constructed, was built by Robert Brinkley Snowden in 1896. After the Snowden family sold it many years later, the massive Gothic revival house went through several incarnations as restaurants and is presently being revived once more. It has been on the National Register of Historic Places since 1983.

Cadence
Seth Wood

My cousin Angus, unfortunately, neither lives up to the masculinity of his name nor the adventuresome spirit it implies. He is a fair skinned, redheaded lad. His parents named him Angus because of the red hair and because they are 'Irish.' Their last name is really Schmidt, which sounds nothing like an Irish name. I should know. My last name is Kelly, which means 'frequenting churches' or 'warrior' depending on who you ask and when you ask. Everyone just calls me Kel.

Imagine my surprise when the normally timid Angus starts whispering at me in the middle of the night.

"Kel."

I ignore him. He most likely needs to pee or wants a glass of water.

"Kel!" Angus whispers. "You awake?"

"I'm not walking you to the toilets," I reply. "It's too far from the tent. And it's dark. Like, real dark."

"What? No. I don't have to pee," Angus says.

"Then what?" I ask.

I try to turn my sleeping bag over so that I can see Angus. Against the distant glow of one of the campground's few floodlights, I make out Angus's slump-shouldered form leaning on one arm.

"Shh!" Angus says. "Don't make so much noise."

"Why not?" I ask.

"You'll wake up Grandma and Grandpa."

"They aren't waking up anytime soon," I say, "Grandpa is deaf from his own snoring, and Grandma pops sleeping pills every night to deal with Grandpa's snoring."

"What?" Angus asks. "Never mind with the jokes."

I was not joking.

"What?" I laugh. "They are in their RV. We are stuck out here in the tent."

"I just don't want to wake them up, Kel," Angus says.

"Fine. I'll be quiet." Angus is smart–incredible smart. But, he lacks a sense of humor. I have this feeling that he does not find my jokes amusing. In fact, I'd bet the sleeping bag that I am curled up in that joking in general irritates him no end.

I slide out of my sleeping bag without unzipping it. Through the tent's thin canvas, I can see the moon shining brightly overhead.

"Shhh," Angus whisper yells.

"Angus," I say. "You are making more noise shushing me than I am getting out of this sleeping bag."

Under the soft canvas glow of the moonlight, I see him glaring at me. What a prick. It was either the sound of the metal-on-metal zipper or the sound of a shuffling sleeping bag.

I keep my mouth shut. After all, he is my cousin, and his immediate family sucks right now.

So, I slip my shoes on without undoing the previously tied laces.

"Ready?" I ask.

"Yeah," Angus says. "Be quiet with the tent zipper."

The tent zipper is no metal-on-metal affair. It is a plastic-on-plastic style that harkens back to the warehouse-style quality of its roots: it's cheap. As I pull the zipper slowly around the tent's canvas, flexible zipper doorframe, I can't help but wonder if Moses camped in this very tent. If he had, he probably would have told Angus, "Thou shalt have a sense of humor."

But, I digress.

A cool rush of air flows in through the flapping canvas tent door.

"Might want to grab a hoodie," I say. "It's pretty chilly."

"Thanks."

I climb out of the tent into the darkened campgrounds. Grandma and Grandpa's RV putters ten feet or so from the tent. I stretch and yawn.

The campgrounds look so different during the night. The solitary light source in the entire area is an appropriated streetlight hanging off of a pole above the squat building that houses the campground showers and bathrooms. The building is a good distance away from our campsite, and I am nearly positive that fourteen-year-old Angus is still afraid of the dark.

Angus climbs out of the tent, rear-end first as he usually does.

"We need flashlights," I say.

"No. I've got something better," Angus replies.

I see a familiar strap hanging around his neck.

"Why are you bringing that?" I ask, and point to Angus's prized DSLR camera.

"You'll see," Angus says, as he arranges the camera's shoulder strap into a comfortable position. He tosses me the camera's foldout tripod. "Carry this, will you?"

"I guess," I say. "What have you got that is better than a flashlight?"

"A new lens," Angus says. "Well, it is more of an attachment really. Night vision. My Dad got it for me for this trip."

"Night vision?" I ask.

Angus pulls something that is shaped like a lens from his pocket and tries to show it to me in the dark.

"Yeah. But only if we need it."

"What are you talking about?" I ask. "It's dark. We need a flashlight."

"Let your eyes adjust to the dark, Kel," Angus says. "It'll make it easier later."

"What are we doing here?" I ask.

"You'll see."

Angus typically is not one for suspense or mystery. That's my area of expertise. So, whatever he is planning, I know it will be fairly good for him at least. I will probably get bored as I usually do with the things he finds 'fun.'

"Lead the way," I say.

Angus walks towards the campground's exit, the main road.

The main road is a two-lane affair that looks to be freshly laid asphalt. The moonlight shining off the road provides just enough light to see which direction we are going.

"Why are we going towards the battlefield?" I ask.

"Less light," Angus says. "We need as little ambient light as possible."

I focus on the misty breath that comes out every time I exhale. I try my very best to make rings and spaceships out of the exhalation, but I am not as skilled as the smoking guys in the old movies that Angus likes to watch. Or, maybe you have to actually breathe out smoke for it to work. I don't know, but I try anyway.

"Why did they call this place Fort Pillow?" I ask.

"You went on the tour."

"Yeah, but I was looking at all the canons and stuff," I say.

"It was named after some general," Angus says.

"Oh, right," I say.

Angus remembers stuff like that. It is his gift. Mine is my sharp wit and sharper tongue: wordsmithing. I shiver in my hoodie. What are we doing out here this late at night anyway?

"Why'd they bring us out here?" Angus asks. "Grandma and Grandpa?"

"I don't know," I say. "Probably because of your mom and dad."

"Yeah," Angus says.

I can tell by his voice that his head had fallen forward. Angus's mom and dad are divorcing, and from what I know from my own mom and dad, it is an ugly one

"How are you doing with all that anyway?" I ask.

"I'm fine. Things at my house are..." Angus trailed off. "Tense. I don't know how else to describe it."

I stop and turn to Angus, and say, "I know I give you a hard time and joke and stuff, but you can always come stay with me on the weekends. You know my mom and dad will come pick you up."

"I know," says Angus. "I think me being at home is the only thing keeping my mom and dad from killing each other."

"Tense," I say.

"Yeah. Tense," Angus says. "See that field over there? I want to follow the road to that spot."

"What are we doing out here?" I ask.

Angus is being coy, not normally like him. He must have something special to show off. I follow him a few more steps along the road. Angus leads us to a spot

67

in the road with a wide-open field on either side of the two lane street. In the moonlight, the field looks white and dreamlike. I can see the wind shifting the grass in waves that crash silently upon each other.

"Ok. This is a good spot," Angus says. "Close your eyes."

"Angus—"

"Just do it," Angus says.

"Fine," I reply.

"You've got your eyes closed?" Angus asks.

"Yes."

"Are you sure?"

"Yes, Angus," I say truthfully.

"Ok. Good," Angus says. "Ok. Your eyes are fully adjusting to the dark."

"You do know we are standing in a road in the middle of nowhere at night with our eyes closed, right?" I ask.

"Come on, Kel," Angus says.

"All right," I say. "I'm just messing around. What am I supposed to be doing?"

"Nothing. Your eyes are doing all of the work," Angus says. "Like I said, they are adjusting to the dark."

"Gotcha," I say.

"Ok, open your eyes," Angus says.

I open my eyes and Angus is right. I can see much more clearly than I could before. The fields are no longer solid waves, but individual crests and peaks and valleys as the wind whispers among the grasses.

"Now," Angus says. "Look up."

I look up.

"Oh," I say because I can't think of any other word.

"Cool isn't it?" says Angus.

But, I am barely listening.

Above our heads the sky sings with so much light. My wit and metaphors fail me. Ten thousand pinpricks of light vibrate against the blackness above. Ten thousand more flank the ones above. A tangible trail of twinkles litters the dark sky in a fantastic array.

I am so rarely at a loss for words.

"I never knew there were so many," I stammer.

"Stars?" Angus asks. "There are hundreds of billions of them. And that is just in our galaxy."

"I know that," I say. "I just didn't realize you could see them with the naked eye."

"You can't in the city. Too much light."

The stars form structures and broken lines and semblances of tangibility just beyond my comprehension.

"So, this is why I brought the camera," Angus says. "I want to take some pictures, but with it being so dark, the shutter has to stay open awhile to let in enough light. So, I have to hit the shutter and wait. Hit the shutter and wait."

"Yeah," I say. "Yeah. That's fine. Can I get a copy of those pictures?"

"Sure thing," Angus says.

He takes the tripod that I have been carrying. The legs are multi-jointed, and Angus attaches the camera to the base of the short tripod.

"When was the last time you got out of the city?" Angus asks. He slides the telescoping legs out from beneath the tripod.

"A while ago," I say. "But I don't remember this."

"Yeah, if you take the highway, there are so many cars that their headlights keep your eyes from adjusting to the dark."

He sets the camera and tripod on the road and manipulates it so that the top-heavy tripod does not fall over when he aims it upward.

"This is really something, Angus," I say.

As we sit, I imagine Angus Schmidt, famous astronomer. Me? I am the budding, wisecracking sidekick. Wait. Why am I the sidekick in my own imagination? I shake my head. I see no signs of any sort of life on the dark, empty road, car or otherwise. No RVs. With all of the senior citizens here at the campgrounds, recreational vehicles are a must.

"All right, I am hitting the button," Angus says.

I wait for a 'click.'

"Did you do it?" I ask.

"Yeah," Angus says.

"I didn't hear a click," I say.

"It doesn't click yet," Angus says.

"Hmm," I say.

Click.

"There," Angus says. "It clicks after it takes the picture."

"All right," I say. "You going to look at the picture on the screen?"

"No. I don't want the light blinding us," Angus says.

He steps away from the camera to look up for what I can only guess is a better angle of the sky.

"Fair enough," I say.

"Ok, I am going to take the second picture," Angus says.

Tat.

"I thought you said it wouldn't click?" I say.

"I haven't even pressed the button yet," Angus replies.

Sure enough, Angus is not at the tripod yet.

Rat-a-tat.

"Did you hear that?" I ask.

"Yeah. I heard that," Angus says. "I didn't touch the camera."

Rat-a-tat.

"That sounds like drums," Angus says.

"Drums?" I ask.

Rat-a-tat.

"OK. That does sound like drums," I say. "There must be some re-enactment going on."

"I would think that the tour guide would have said something about that," Angus says.

Rat-a-tat. Rat-a-tat.

"Ok. The sound's coming from that direction," I say, pointing to a field.

"Should we check it out?" Angus asks.

"What?" I exclaim. "No way. I am not going into some field in the dark. Even if my eyes are adjusted."

"We can use my night vision lens," Angus says.

Rat-a-tat.

"Do it," I say.

The drum sound is unnerving. It is almost keeping time, but the beat is slightly off. Just slightly. I turn to face the field and squint trying to make out any abnormal shape or shapes in the billowing grasses.

Nothing.

Angus snaps the night vision attachment onto his camera. "Ok. The night vision only works when I snap the shutter."

"What?" I ask. "It only works when you actually take a picture? I thought it was going to be like in the Army or a video game or something. You know, video?"

"No," Angus says. "All right. Are you ready?"

"Yeah."

Rat-a-tat.

Angus raises the camera and aims it towards the drumming sound.

Click.

"Ok, the view screen is going to be bright," Angus says. "Shield your eyes."

I cover my eyes and see by the light streaming through my fingers that Angus has the view screen on.

"Uh. Kel—"

"What is it?"

"There is something out there," Angus stammers.

"What? Like a cow?" I ask.

"Not a cow at all."

I pull my hands away and look towards the blindingly bright view screen. It takes my eyes several seconds to adjust but when they do I see what he is talking about.

I nearly drop the camera. Angus catches the camera strap.

"Freakin—" I stutter. "What is that thing?"

The view screen is night vision green. The field is an eerie glowing green thing. I can make out individual waves of tall grass. In the middle of the field stands a brightly glowing green figure holding some contraption in front of it.

"Is that—" Angus trails off.

"The drummer? I think so," I say.

"But, where are rest of the marchers? And why is the drummer looking at us?" Angus heaves.

Rat-a-tat. Rat-a-tat.

Angus is frightened. I am terrified. The breath in front of my face thickens. I am breathing too heavily. Calm down.

Deep breaths.

"Snap another picture," I say.

Click.

"Oh my—" Angus trails off.

"What? What is it?" I snatch the camera from his hands.

The figure has moved closer. I can clearly see the drum strapped to the chest of what looks to be a young boy in old garb. In each hand are two roughly hewn drumsticks.

Rat-a-tat.

"I saw him," I exclaim. "I saw him do it."

Rat-a-tat. Rat-a-tat.

Click.

"He's closer," Angus whines.

"I can't see anything out there," I say, squinting into the dark.

Rat-a-tat.

Click.

"Kel. He. Is. Right. There," Angus breathes. "On your left."

Rat-a-tat. Rat-a-tat. Rat-a-tat.

I freeze. I cannot move. I try to work my legs, but the stupid things just will not do what I tell them. The boy is not here. I cannot see him. What is happening? Why can I not move?

"Run. Angus. Go," I whisper. Click.

Angus screams.

My legs start moving on their own. I snatch Angus by the collar and yank.

Rat-a-tat. Rat-a-tat. Rat-a-tat. Rat-a-tat.

Click.

I do not look back. I do not look at the camera screen.

I run. I run as fast as I can while dragging Angus behind me. He is clicking away.

"Wait," Angus says. "Kel. Stop. Let go."

I do not listen. I keep dragging him back towards the campgrounds.

"Kelly," Angus says. "Stop. He isn't following us."

I let go of Angus and nearly collapse from hauling two human beings uphill.

"Look," Angus says.

I do. And what I see frightens me.

A single torch floats between the trees obscured by the undergrowth. Sounds and groans of marching men fill the air. Heavy footsteps slap the ground in rhythm.

Rat-a-tat. Rat-a-tat. Rat-a-tat.

The drummer boy has the beat now.

A second torch winks into existence in the woods several paces behind the first. Then by a third. Then, a fourth.

"This has to be a re-enactment," I say.

"I don't think so," Angus says.

He hands me the camera.

"Look at the pictures," he says.

I fumble around on the camera until I find the right button. The blindingly bright screen turns on. A green, empty road flanked by green empty pastures on the screen.

"But..." I trail off.

I flip through all of the pictures that Angus took.

Rat-a-tat. Rat-a-tat. Rat-a-tat.

"But, I saw the first one. With the boy," I say.

The picture shows an empty field. No drummer. No boy.

"Take a picture of the torches," Angus says.

The torches now number more than ten. I snap a picture of the forest and the torches. The camera screen lights up to reveal a glowing column of men and horses tramping between the trees. The men wear uniforms like the ones we saw back on the battlefield tour—too far away to tell if they are blue or gray. The camera screen fades to black. I quickly turn it back on to focus on the same spot.

The forest is empty.

No men. No soldiers.

Only trees.

And the sounds of invisible men marching with their torches.

"What is this?" I ask.

"Something amazing," Angus says.

"Where did the boy go? The drummer?" The winding column of torches and invisible men nears the edge of the trees where the forest meets the field we just fled.

"He wasn't following us," Angus says. He stares off into the distance and towards the marching columns.

"Then what was it?" I ask.

Angus seems amazed, but my palms are sweating in the cold night air.

"I think he was leading the way," Angus says.

"The way to what?"

"To the battle. They are going towards the fort," Angus says, "We were just in the way. I saw it when I was taking pictures while you were dragging me down the road."

"I think we should go. I don't think we are supposed to see this," I say.

The first torch reaches the edge of trees. It winks out as it hits the tree line where it should enter the field. The second torch in the column hits the edge of the field, and it too winks out.

"I want to stay," Angus says. "I am going to stay. Go if you want. Go if you are scared of these ghosts. I'm not."

"I don't believe in ghosts, Angus," I say shakily. "And I don't know what I am seeing."

"You wouldn't have seen the stars in the sky if you hadn't really opened your eyes and looked, Kel," Angus says.

I know he is right. Angus may not have a way with words like I do, but sometimes, he gets lucky. So, I stand there next to my cousin whose life is falling apart, while we watch an army of ghosts vanish on their way to some ridiculously named fort.

"Want me to try to take some more pictures?" I ask.

The torches keep disappearing as they reach the edge of the forest.

"No. I just want to watch," Angus says.

I put my arm around Angus to keep us both warm. I feel him shudder, and I pull him closer. I know he is crying, but I will not say anything. The last torch in the line winks out and the sounds of marching men and their equipment dies out.

"You know," Angus says. "What I wouldn't give to be able to march off like that. Just leave everything. Have everything provided and just do a job without having to worry about picking sides. The side would be picked for me."

I do not know what to say. That is twice tonight.

"Those guys at least have a place to go to, and they wear a uniform that tells them which side they are on," Angus says. "If you are from the North, you wear blue. If you are from the South, you wear gray. Simple. But what am I supposed to do when both sides wear beige?"

"Beige?" I ask.

I feel Angus chuckle under my arm.

"You get what I am saying," Angus says.

"Nobody wins," I say. "There may have been more blue uniforms on the ground after this battle than gray ones, but the next one has more gray ones on the ground than blue ones. Everyone loses in war. Even people who wear beige."

Angus chuckles again. He pulls away and wipes at his eyes.

"Are they really asking you to pick sides?" I ask.

"Not verbally," Angus says. "But, I can feel it. You know?"

"Tense?" I ask.

"Tense," Angus says. "Can we stay out here for a little while longer?"

"Sure, we should just be back before sunrise. So, which side is it going to be?" I ask. "And desertion isn't an option."

"I don't know yet," Angus says. "Mom and Dad are still forming their troops into position."

"Ah," I say like I understand.

But I do not understand. Maybe I have not given Angus enough credit. Perhaps there is more to him than I think.

"What do you think happened to that drummer boy ghost, Kel?" Angus asks—ruining his previously gained ground in my opinion of him.

"He's a ghost. What do you think?"

*****

Fort Pillow

Fort Pillow was a series of fortifications built at a strategic point in west Tennessee along the Mississippi River north of Memphis. Union soldiers captured the fort to protect the United States' control of the river and were subsequently attacked by a

Confederate army under the command of Major General Nathan Bedford Forrest. During the battle, Confederate troops massacred the defending black Union soldiers. Fort Pillow is now a National Historic Landmark and state park.

A Dance with the Devil
Juanita Houston

Jenna knew she could not let her daughters go to their grandmother's funeral alone. They were too upset, and their father and his trophy wife would be there. She needed to protect them from the added stress of family discord. Jenna had been fond of her former Mother-in-law. Delores had always treated her well, even after the divorce. She wanted to pay her respects. Even though her marriage didn't last, she had no ill feelings toward the rest of her ex-husband's family. This was going to be a long and difficult day for everybody, but not even Jenna could have been prepared for what was about to happen.

She was glad that her best friend had agreed to tag along for support, which was saying something, especially since Elena despised Max and his family.

So far they had not seen Max or his trophy wife, Susan or Suze, as she insisted her stepdaughters call her. She had told them that she didn't want to be called mom because it made her sound like an old woman.

A noise in the back of the chapel brought Jenna out of her thoughts. She turned to watch as Max and Susan made their way to the front of the room. Something seemed off but she couldn't put her finger on what it was. They appeared to be arguing about something, and she was practically dragging him up the aisle.

"What's up with what's-his-face?" Elena slid into the pew beside her. "He looks like he is going to keel over just any second."

"I don't know, but he doesn't look good," Jenna agreed.

"He looks like a zombie," Elena quipped, "and he probably needs brains. After all he never had any."

"You're terrible." Jenna hid a smile behind her hand. This wasn't the time or place for ex-husband jokes, but it did help lighten her mood, if only for a moment.

"Keep an eye on the girls, I'm going run to the restroom," Jenna told Elena, who nodded as she slid out of the pew, and headed out of the chapel.

A few minutes later she was washing her hands, glanced into the mirror to see an odd reflection of her ex-husband reaching for her. She yelped, flung herself out of his grasp.

"What the hell?" she said with her hand on her chest. "You damn near gave me a heart attack. What are you doing in the women's restroom anyway?"

"I need your help." He dropped his hand to his side. The movement seemed almost wooden. Sure, it was her imagination.

"Yeah, that's not going to happen. We're not married anymore." Jenna grabbed a couple of paper towels to dry her hands. "Why don't you ask Susan for help?" Jenna glared at Max a little closer. "What is wrong with you? You look horrible."

"I think I am dead!" Max told her. "And I can't ask Susan. I think she is the reason I am dead. That is why I need your help."

"If you are dead, how do you think I can help?" Jenna stared at him skeptically. She couldn't believe she was having this conversation in the ladies room with her ex-husband.

"You need to find out what happened to me. I think I was poisoned," Max pleaded.

A scream interrupted their conversation. Jenna glanced back. Max was gone. Now, she knew she imagined the whole conversation with him. She had not heard the door open or close indicating that he had left. He was just...gone. She knew it had to be the atmosphere of a funeral home. Otherwise, she must be losing her mind. Jenna ran back out into the hall and towards the lobby only to see people pouring out of the chapel where her former mother-in-law's body lay.

Jenna searched the crowd looking for her daughters but didn't spot them right away. So, she approached their aunt. "Hey Angie, what is going on? Where are the girls?"

"Max just passed out. The director is trying to revive him and an ambulance has been called but it doesn't look good." Angie appeared as if she might faint any second. So, Jenna led her over to a seat. "Angie, I need to you tell me where the girls are."

"They are still in the chapel. Tommy stayed with them when they refused to leave. I tried to get them to come out but they wouldn't, and I had to get out of there. First mom and now Max." Angie sobbed as if she just realized the gravity of the situation.

"You stay here, I am going to go check on them," Jenna stated as she headed into the chapel. She made her way to the front where several people worked on her ex-husband.

It couldn't be true. She had just been talking to him in the ladies room. Hadn't she? Yet there he lay, on the carpet next to the casket of his mother, and it didn't look like the CPR was helping.

Jenna moved over to where Elena sat with her daughters who cried as they watched the attempt to revive him. She sat between them and held them close as the paramedics moved in to take over.

The paramedics worked for at least 30 minutes without any luck. He was gone. The medics put away their equipment, called the police, and called the Medical Examiner's office.

Jenna and Elena led the girls into the lobby where more people had gathered for the funeral, and wondered why they hadn't taken him to the hospital.

One of the paramedics tapped her on the shoulder, and asked if he could talk to her in private.

"I am not family, maybe you should talk to one of them," Jenna told him as she moved out of earshot of her daughters.

"I need to talk to someone who will keep a level head, so please just five minutes is all I am asking for," he told her.

Reluctantly Jenna nodded and followed him across the lobby to the far hallway, and sat down on a bench.

"I am not sure how to tell you this, Ma'am but..."

"Jenna," she interrupted him. "I am the victim's ex-wife so you don't have to be so formal."

"Jenna...I think that your ex was murdered, and we have contacted the police and the Medical Examiner."

Jenna stared at him in disbelief. "Are you sure? How?"

Before he could answer the funeral director interrupted advising that the police had arrived. "I'll be right back," the paramedic Brian told her, and followed the funeral director, leaving Jenna alone.

When the paramedic didn't return after ten minutes, Jenna decided she needed a drink. Since she didn't have alcohol, she would have to settle for water. She went down the hall to the little reception room, and had just filled her cup with cold water from the cooler when her ex popped in behind her, and touched her shoulder. "Jen," Max called.

"What the hell?" she screeched, and dropped her cup of water. "What are you doing?" she asked keeping her voice low. "Wait...how in the hell are you here? You're dead."

"I know and I need you to find out why," Max's spirit told her.

"Max, or whatever you are, I don't have to do anything, and for the record I don't really care why. Thanks to you I have to worry about how this is going to affect Katie and Brianna, and personally, I don't have time for your theatrics," she told him as she grabbed some paper towels to clean up the water.

"That is why you have to find out, for the girls sake," he pleaded. "Find out what happened, please?" And then he popped out just as a man dressed in khakis and a polo shirt came through the door.

"Who were you just talking to?" He stared as she stood.

"Excuse me?" Jenna grabbed some more paper towels to continue the cleanup.

"You were talking to someone in here," he accused. "Who was it?"

Jenna narrowed her eyes at the stranger. "I was talking to myself. Did you hear anybody else in here?"

"Well, no but you were clearly talking to someone," he challenged.

"Who are you?" She grabbed more paper towels to finish her task.

"I'm sorry. I'm Detective Durham, and you are...?" he asked.

"Jenna Daniels." She stood, tossed the damp towels into the trash.

"Any relation to the deceased?" Durham inquired.

"Which deceased are you referring to?" Jenna asked with mocked innocence. "After all, this is a funeral home and we were here for Delores Daniels's funeral."

"The gentleman who just passed away rather suddenly at his mother's funeral. Any relation to him?" he asked again.

"Max Daniels was my ex-husband and the father to my daughters, Katie and Brianna," Jenna told him as she sat down at one of the small round table with a new cup of water. "Was he really murdered?"

"What makes you think he was murdered?" Detective Durham asked suspiciously.

"Well for one, you are here, and I don't think they would waste tax payer's money sending a Detective to investigate a heart attack, do you?" Jenna narrowed her eyes.

"That is true," he agreed. "Why would you say heart attack?" Detective Durham took the seat across from her, and pulled out a notebook and pen.

"You ask a lot of obvious questions. How did you make detective? Did you look at the victim?" She huffed. "I might not be a doctor or even a nurse but heart attack would have been my guess with the color of his skin."

"Yes I have seen him, but I wouldn't have guessed a heart attack," he told her. "Where were you when the victim died?"

"I was in the ladies room when he collapsed," Jenna told him rather flatly. *Talking to my ex-husband's ghost, apparently.*

"How did you know he had died?" Durham asked.

"Well the blood curdling scream was kind of a dead giveaway that something was wrong," she retorted, "but I don't think he was dead at the time, since they were still working on him when I got back to the chapel."

"There is no need to be sarcastic," Durham told her quietly, "unless you have something to hide."

"I don't have anything to hide but I do have two teenage daughters in the lobby who are upset that their father has just died in addition to their grandmother, whose funeral they are here for in the first place. So if that is all the questions you have for me, I am going to go check on my daughters." Jenna stood, tossed her cup into the trash.

"You never answered my question earlier, who were you talking to?" He turned in his chair to face her as she as walked to the door.

"I told you, I was obviously talking to myself unless of course you heard someone else in the room with me?" She cast him a challenging glance as she strode from the room.

Jenna walked to the lobby where her daughters sat with their aunt and uncle. Elena stood nearby keeping an eye on the girls, and nodded when Jenna returned.

The Detective that Jenna had just been talking to in the reception room followed her into the lobby. "Can I have everybody's attention please, the funeral will have to be rescheduled and you will be notified as to that time later. However, you will need to remain here in the building until you have talked to me or a uniformed officer, and given your statement. There has been a possible murder here, and we need your cooperation to find out what happened. The funeral director has set up chairs in one of the viewing rooms for everybody. So, if you would please make your way over there until you are called, it would be appreciated. Thank you."

"Who is that?" Elena whispered in Jen's ear as she watched the detective and a couple of officers direct everybody to the hallway where Jenna had just come from.

"He is a detective with the Memphis Police Department, and he thinks that Max was murdered. Well, actually he is investigating why a man dropped dead at his mother's funeral," Jenna whispered back while she scanned the crowd. "Can you distract him so I can slip back into the chapel for a minute?"

"Sure," Elena said smiling, "he's kind of cute."

"I guess if you like that type," Jenna told her, "but remember you're kind of married."

"And you are no fun," Elena tossed over her shoulder to Jenna, as she headed towards the detective who tried to keep a couple of elderly ladies from leaving.

Jenna watched Elena as she moved in to assist the detective, temporarily distracting him. Now preoccupied, Jenna slipped into the chapel. She had her keys in her hand so she could say she was looking for them if she did get caught. Thankfully, there was no one in the chapel at that moment. While Max's body was still on the floor, they had at least covered him with a sheet. She couldn't think of it being anything other than Max. There was no love lost between them. In fact they had finally gotten to the point where they could be civil to each other.

"Did you find out anything?" Max asked when he popped in beside her.

"Oh good grief, quit doing that," Jenna hissed at him. She tried to keep her voice low so as to not being overheard, and she was sure that the detective thought her nuts since he claimed to have overheard her conversation in the reception room earlier.

"Sorry," Max said, as he realized she stared at his vacant body.

Great, Jenna thought, *just want I need, a ghost who just realizes he's dead.*

Jenna knelt by Max's body, and pulled back the blue sheet that the EMT's had used to cover the body. She looked at him, and just couldn't get over that he was really gone. She had to mentally shake herself, and made an attempt to look at it from a different perspective. Without touching the body, she stared at Max's face, then his fingernails. They indicated that he had been sick for a long time. But that couldn't be possible since Jenna had seen him just a couple of weeks ago, and he didn't seem sick then. She knew whatever had happened was very recent. His skin had a yellow, sickly pallor, and his nails had white streaks in them.

She had just dropped the cloth back over the body, when she heard voices outside the doors at the far end of the chapel. She stood, and quietly made a beeline for the side door. She cracked it open, saw no one, and quickly crossed the hall to the ladies room. At least there she would have a few minutes to compose herself before she crossed paths with the detective.

*****

Her respite was short lived, though, as she heard someone just outside the door. She ducked into the first stall, and quietly slid the lock into place.

The door opened and shut. Then Jenna heard Susan Daniel's voice talking to someone.

She must be on her cell phone, Jenna thought to herself, trying to stay still and quiet so that she didn't get caught.

"I'm pretty sure it worked just fine," Susan grumbled into her phone. "Well they covered the body with a sheet or something, and he looks dead, if that is any indication."

Susan listened for a moment then replied, "Yes, I rinsed out his coffee cup before we left the house. You worry too much. No one will ever suspect me as I will be a very convincing grieving widow who just lost my mother-in-law, *and* husband within days of each other." Susan faked a sniffle or two as if to indicate her acting abilities.

Jenna couldn't believe what she heard. Susan just admitted to someone that she had poisoned her husband, and possibly her mother in law.

"That woman was horrible to me," Susan complained to her confidant as she left the restroom

It was all that Jenna could do not to come out of the stall and beat the crap out of her. *What a hateful vindictive person*, Jenna thought to herself.

A few minutes later, after making sure that Susan had a few minutes to get out of the hall, Jenna stepped out of the ladies room, and took a long drink from the water fountain just outside the door.

"Hiding in the ladies room again?" Detective Durham asked, causing Jenna to visibly jump.

"Stalking me again, Detective?" She turned around as she wiped her chin with her hand.

"No, but you seem to be spending a lot of time in the ladies room." He leaned against the wall across from her. He apparently had just come out of the same door of the chapel that she had escaped through moments ago.

"Well," she drawled, "I did just drink all that water earlier so yes I had to go again. Next time I will try to hold it since we are obviously not allowed to go to the restroom."

"You are free to go anywhere you want as long as you stay in the building," he informed her, "but right now I would like to speak to you in the conference room. That is if you can spare the time."

A few moments later Detective Durham settled in the chair at the head of the table, and motioned her to sit to his left.

Jenna reclined, and tried to appear more confident than she felt but inside, her stomach tightened in anticipation of his questions.

Detective Durham stared at Jenna for a long moment. "So did you learn anything from sneaking into the chapel earlier?" he questioned.

"Excuse me?" She tried not to let her reaction confirm his accusations.

"You thought your friend could distract me that easily? That I wouldn't notice you went back into the chapel." It was a statement rather than a question but it hung in the air for several long moments.

When Jenna didn't answer him, he continued leaning back in his chair. "So, did you learn anything from your snooping?"

"Why are you asking me? I thought you were a detective?" she asked with a little relief.

"I am a detective, but since you think I am unqualified, I thought you might have solved this crime already with your little investigation," he retorted.

"Where is his wife?" Jenna asked the detective.

"What?" Durham asked, taken off guard by the unexpected question.

"Has the Medical Examiner been here to pronounce Max dead and determine cause of death?" She fired off the second question without waiting for an answer to the first.

"The Medical Examiner is in there now with the body. Mrs. Daniels hasn't been here," he responded, "not that any of that is any concern of yours."

"She is supposed to be here, she came in with Max earlier. However, I haven't seen her since they walked into the chapel together. But I am pretty sure I heard her on the phone a few minutes ago in the ladies room, and I am pretty sure she is responsible for Max's death, and maybe even her mother-in-law's death as well. She mentioned to whoever she was talking to that she had rinsed out his coffee cup before they left the house." Jenna finished in a rush, leaned back to watch the detective's reaction to her news.

"Mrs. Daniels..." Durham began exasperated.

"Ms. Daniels," Jenna corrected him. "I am not married, and I only carry the last name because of my kids."

"Ms. Daniels," he began again. "I know what I am doing. I haven't seen or talked to the other Mrs. Daniels. What motive does she have to kill her husband or mother in law?"

"Money and hate for starters," Jenna began but the detective waved a hand dismissing that notion.

"If she hated her husband, why would she marry him?" Durham asked.

"Money...he owns a chain of paint stores, and is worth quite a bit of money that he inherited from his dad. Delores didn't like Susan, and the feeling was apparently mutual, at least according to my girls," Jenna told him.

One of the uniformed officers knocked on the doorframe. "Sir, the medical examiner would like to speak to you in the chapel," he told the detective.

Detective Durham stood and headed to the door, pausing long enough to tell Jenna to stay put, that he would be right back.

After the detective left, Jenna stood and wandered to the window. This was not how she expected to spend her day. Jenna saw the reflection of movement out of the corner of her eye, and by now had come to expect Max to pop in unannounced.

"What are you doing?" she hissed when she turned to gaze at his spirit. His essence began to fade. "What is going on with you?"

Before he could answer, there was a scuffle and a woman screeching a barrage of profanity on the other side of the door.

Jenna ran across the room and jerked open the door. A uniformed officer dragged a very angry Susan Daniels out of a side office in handcuffs. She fought to get away from the officer, and screamed at the top of her lungs, her face almost purple with anger.

"What is going on?" Jenna asked the officer.

"Mrs. Daniels was attempting to leave the premises by way of the back door." He held the other woman tight as she fought for freedom.

Some of the funeral attendees now spilled into the hall to see what happened. Detective Durham moved through the crowd followed by another man who carried a case labeled with the large letters M.E. He moved past and out the front door. Two men dressed in black pants and white shirts, guided a stretcher with the body on it through the crowd. They followed the M.E. out to the black van labeled with CORONER in white letters and loaded up Max's body, and drove off toward the medical district.

"Take her to 201 Poplar for processing. I'll be right behind you." Durham turned to Jenna and the crowd of mourners that had nearly doubled since he had come out of the chapel.

"Everybody is free to leave, but please come downtown to 201 Poplar to sign your statements within the next day or two," he told the crowd. Most started filing out of the building, relieved to finally be able to go home.

Durham turned to Jenna and spoke in a lower tone so that only she could hear. "You were right. Mrs. Daniels had poisoned her husband with what appears to be arsenic, but we won't know for sure until the autopsy is complete and the tests come back in a few weeks. His mother's body will also have to be taken downtown to the Medical Examiner's office and rechecked to see if she had been poisoned as well."

"How do you know for sure that it was Susan that did it?" Jenna asked, surprised how quickly things had happened.

"She was caught sneaking out of the funeral home through a back entrance where the deliveries come in. I had officers stationed around the building because someone always tries to leave. Most people don't leave the scene of a crime unless they are guilty of something. We will have to get a court order to search their home for evidence. We will confiscate the coffee pot and cups, and have them tested. There will probably be some traces of poison in it."

The detective and remaining uniformed officers made their way out of the funeral home's front doors and left.

Jenna found Elena in the lobby. "Take the girls back to your house. I have to take care of a few things here. I will pick them up in about an hour." Jenna hugged the girls.

A little later she sat at the back of the chapel where her former mother-in-law had recently lain in state, expecting her ex-husband to make a final appearance. She wasn't disappointed.

"You did it!" Max told her. "Thanks so much, I really appreciate it."

"Max, I really didn't do anything, I just merely told the detective what I saw and heard, and then they caught her trying to leave. Jenna paused a moment, "I am sorry, but she may have killed your mom as well." She watched him fade, probably since his body had been removed from the premises.

"But you did find out what happened to me. Take care of the girls for me and thank you again." He smiled as he faded out for the last time.

"Good-bye, Max," she whispered.

*****

The Funeral Homes of Memphis
There are a number of excellent funeral homes in Memphis. We couldn't narrow our location down to a single one, but we suspect that there are a number of ghosts wandering around them with private agendas that would certainly startle those attending their obsequies.

Drive-In Miss Daisy
Phyllis Appleby

"You are not driving Miss Daisy," I said.

Uncle Jake confronted me with a determined glint in his rheumy eyes.

I was working out logistics for the upcoming week's viewings and burials with the office manager, Yolanda. I had no time for Uncle Jake's antics.

"I *have* to. It's the only way we can make contact," he said.

"The last time you drove, you made contact with three parked cars and a city bus, and lost your license. You've also lost your mind if you think you're driving daddy's antique Cadillac hearse on my watch. I am the acting mortician, and the buck stops here."

"I'd just love to have a ride in that lovely hearse," Yolanda said as she flashed a brilliant smile at Uncle Jake, "not feet first, of course."

She had a huge crush on Uncle Jake and considered him, in her words, "a major stud muffin." Yolanda has managed the office for decades. She'd been angling for Uncle Jake ever since her third husband died a dozen or so years ago. So far he hadn't taken the bait.

"Jeez, Angie, it's my birthday. You promised me and the boys could go to the Summer Drive-In for the 'Dusk to Dawn Daisy Flowers Creature Feature.'"

"As your attorney, Lennox agreed with the judge that you suffer from potentially terminal O.P.C.D.

Syndrome, otherwise known as Old People Can't Drive."

"You and your brother are both prejudiced against the elderly. It's our chance to establish our cred as legitimate ghost hunters by making contact with the ghost of Daisy Flowers. She haints the Drive-In on the anniversary of her death. This is a perfect opportunity for the Ghost Geezers. I ain't getting any younger. This might be the last time I get the chance. I might not make it to next year."

He had a point, Uncle Jake was turning ninety on October thirty-first, but he didn't look a day over a hundred and ten. He'd be more likely to meet Daisy on the other side before he met up with her ghost. "Don't try to con me," I said. "You will probably outlive us all, and I did not promise you could go in Miss Daisy."

"We have to go in Miss Daisy," PeeWee said. "It's a Daisy Flowers' film festival in honor of the anniversary of her death on Halloween night fifty years ago. All the surviving cast and crew will be there. We got to go in her hearse if we're gonna make contact with her spirit."

PeeWee is an alcoholic dive bar owner and one of Uncle Jake's quartet of antiquated running buddies. They were holding ground in the narrow hallway behind their comrade in arms. H.H. is an elderly African American with a faulty pace-maker. He faints in times of trouble, which are more numerous than you'd think for this crew. Also Billy Running Deer, a mute Native American the size of the Incredible Hulk, and as placid as a lamb.

"You've already had contact with some spirits if you think I'm turning over that hearse to a bunch of geriatric scam artists."

Miss Daisy is my daddy's pride and joy. She is a 1966 Cadillac hearse decked out with a ridiculous array of chrome on her lemon yellow dome with a luxurious white leather interior. The hearse was commissioned by my father to take infamous B-movie horror queen Daisy Flowers to her final resting place in Elmwood Cemetery. It was the claim to fame for the family business, the *Elm in Woods Funeral Parlor.* Uncle Jake wasn't about to wreck it with a wild night of Drive-In hijinks. Daddy and Mom were in Boca for the winter with their Gulfstream cohorts, so I was acting head of the family funeral parlor. Uncle Jake and his buddies would not get their gnarled hands on Miss Daisy. Not on my watch.

Uncle Jake grinned. "Okey, dokey. There's a simple solution to this problematical predicament."

I didn't like the sound of this. Uncle Jake only used big vocabulary when he was about to pull a fast one.

"Angie can drive us in Miss Daisy."

The three other Ghost Geezers bobbed heads in agreement, and Yolanda applauded.

"No way! That hearse is leaving the grounds over my dead body!" I could only hope. Bad pun and even worse prediction.

Unfortunately I lived to drive the crew to the Summer Drive-In in Miss Daisy. Uncle Jake plays dirty, and he dished the dirt to my mother, who then laid down the law to yours truly. Therefore as the sun sank toward the horizon I sat behind the wheel of Miss Daisy, and chauffeured Uncle Jake and his cronies to the Summer Drive-In. Having offered her organizational services as Ghost Geezer stenographer, Yolanda rode shotgun. After sitting in line for what seemed like eternity behind a rust bucket with a faulty muffler and no discernible functioning exhaust system, we finally pulled up to the box office.

The dark-haired woman in the box office window winked at Uncle Jake. "Wow, is that a banana yellow hearse or are you just glad to see me? You're really getting into the spirit, Jake. Long time, no see, how many tickets this time?"

Uncle Jake winked back. "*Lemon* yellow, sweetie, it *is* Daisy's hearse you know. It's my birthday. You do look mighty fine tonight, Mildred. There'll be six of us."

"Fine is my middle name, you old dog, anyone under ten?"

I did a mental eye roll. "Not even if you're counting in dog years."

PeeWee snorted from the back seat. "She's prejudiced against the elderly."

Mildred nodded at the hearse. "You know I'm gonna have to check the back, Jake. Last time you tried to sneak your girlfriend in by putting her in the trunk."

"Arlene and I broke up."

Yolanda winked at me conspiratorially and patted her big blonde wig. Apparently it was apropos to make an appearance as a Daisy Flowers look alike and Yolanda had embraced the opportunity to strut whatever stuff she had left.

"We don't have a trunk," I said. "This is a hearse."

"Duh, missy, but I have a hunch I better check that coffin. Pop the lid. My line is piling up."

I glanced over my shoulder. "Uncle Jake, why is there a coffin in the back?"

"This *is* a hearse," he said innocently.

Mildred's instincts were for once in error. She didn't find a body in the casket, but she did find an assortment of miscellaneous junk that Uncle Jake identified as their ghost hunting paraphernalia. I ponied up for tickets to the birthday party from hell, and Mildred waved us through the gate. I slowly navigated a driveway pitted with fifty years of ruts and bumps, gripped the steering wheel with white knuckles and followed the signs to Screen Two, home of the "Halloween Dusk to Dawn Daisy Flowers Creature Feature."

Uncle Jake squirmed in his seat in anticipation. "Park up near the screen."

PeeWee added, "This place hasn't changed a bit since I came with my daddy."

I glanced around the lumpy lot studded with decapitated speaker poles. "You say that as if it's a good thing."

Pee Wee's seatbelt thunked. "I'm goin' to the concession stand. I want me some popcorn and a cherry Icee before we get down to business. Y'all comin' with me?"

"Let's get this straight, anyone who spills buttered popcorn in this hearse is a dead man. Not a pun, a promise," I said. "Oh, what the heck, get me a corndog."

Three doors popped open in unison and they piled out. Yolanda latched onto Uncle Jake's arm, teetering on her glitter encrusted wedges. They all headed for the lights of the concession stand. Their matching neon yellow t-shirts emblazoned with Ghost Geezers in glow-in-the-dark lettering was hard to miss even in the twilight. If Daisy was interested in making contact there was no way she'd miss them. If she had a lick of sense she'd make a run for it and dive head-first into the light before they caught up with her.

I tuned the radio to the proper frequency and waited for dark, and the return of the fearsome four, otherwise known as the Ghost Geezers, and their predatory Daisyette. As it turns out, I had a long wait for the Geezers but soon found out that Daisy wasn't the patient kind. She had no intention of being a shy wallflower at this supernatural shindig held in her honor.

Screen Two backed up to the Wolf River. As the sun slowly sank, the lot's dips and valleys filled with a miscellaneous assortment of Daisy Flowers fans, or perhaps I should say fanatics. Parking as close as possible to the Miss Daisy seemed to be a creepy badge of honor. I was beginning to feel claustrophobic. The VW beetle two cars over boasted four women of various sizes and vintages wearing platinum blond Daisy wigs and yellow jumpsuits studded with rhinestones. They had settled in lawn chairs munching buckets of popcorn and slurping ginormous soft drinks in anticipation of the start of the first feature. Another Daisy in a gauzy gold evening gown glided past the hearse a half dozen times diligently refusing to make eye contact. I felt the heat of embarrassment in my grey sweats and honorary Ghost Geezers t-shirt. I was decidedly underdressed, and all these pseudo Daisys were giving me the willies.

"Yo, Angie? I didn't know you were a Daisy Flowers fan."

I searched the automotive graveyard for the familiar but disembodied voice of my old flame, Tom Leister. I finally spotted him three rows back sitting on the tailgate of his battered Toyota Tacoma. I didn't dare leave Miss Daisy unprotected, so I waved him over.

"Not guilty. I'm here to ride herd on Uncle Jake and his BFF's. This is his ninetieth birthday bash. What are *you* doing here, looking for crime in all the wrong places as usual?"

"My sister and brother-in-law are having a date night, so I offered to bring my niece Ainsley. She's a huge fan of Daisy Flowers. My sister figured that a homicide detective could handle one precocious fourteen-year-old. She will go nuts when she sees Miss Daisy."

"She's in good company in this crowd. Uncle Jake is a tough old nut, but he's finally cracked. He is positive that Daisy's ghost will pay a visit to her hearse. His gang of Ghost Geezers will make contact and find out why she's haunted the Drive-In for the last fifty years."

Tom's eyes tracked the golden Daisy in appreciation as she sashayed past the hearse again. She turned and winked at him with a wistful smile. He fanned himself. "Whew, *she* is one hot Daisy. Jake's got his work cut out for him. You can't throw a rock without hitting a Daisy wannabe. I don't know how he'd recognize the unreal thing if she does decide to make an unearthly appearance."

I nodded at the casket. "He's got a supply of ghost busting tools."

Tom grinned. "Awesome, maybe I'll lend a hand."

"Et Tu, Brute? Don't tell me a pragmatic, rational detective believes in ghosts?"

"Hey, stuff happens. Sometimes you can't find a rational explanation."

"Well, irrational I got. Every day is the day of the dead for me and no one has communicated with me yet."

"Maybe they know you're a skeptic."

"Uh, huh. Maybe they're just chicken. Why is Daisy supposed to haunt the Drive-In anyway?"

Tom nodded at the screen. "Her last film debuted at the Summer Drive-In, on this very screen. It was Screen One back then. The drive-in had just opened about two months before the debut. Daisy was a Memphis gal, and she thought it would be perfect for the opening on Halloween night. The whole crew came along with Daisy's co-star and fiancé Fred Fabiano and her stunt double, Margie Dawson. They planned to stage a spectacular stunt event featuring Daisy's car. Daisy held court in her yellow Cadillac convertible at the front of the screen and signed autographs. Daisy went to Humes High with Elvis, and rumor has it that even the Memphis Mafia showed up."

"I've heard of Mad Margie, she was a legendary stunt woman. She doubled for every major star back in the day; she was supposed to be fearless. It sounds like a real party, but Daisy died that night didn't she? What happened? Did the stunt go wrong?"

Tom shrugged. "No one knows for sure. They didn't even get to the stunt. Daisy was having a great time holding court waiting for dusk with her cast and crew, and then something set her off. She had one of her legendary temper tantrums and attempted to trash the concession stand. She was whisked off to the private viewing room off the rear of the concession stand that served as the VIP green room by her manager and her leading man. Next thing you knew she slugged her manager and threw her drink at Margie. She roared off in her yellow caddy screaming like a banshee."

"How did she die?"

"She gunned it down the drive, made a left across Summer Avenue burning rubber. She ran a couple of cars off the road and caused a three-car pile-up. She lost control and went off the edge of the Wolf River Bridge trying to avoid a VW van filled with a bunch of flower children heading to the opening. It's kind of weirdly ironic. The car hit low water and ignited into a fireball. Daisy was killed instantly."

"Ya'll, look see who we found!" Uncle Jake shuffled up to Miss Daisy followed by the Ghost Geezers and a tall, slim man with silver hair. He was dressed in khakis and a plaid shirt, and had an easy manner.

"Angie, this here is Jimmy Winters. He's been the projectionist at the drive-in for thirty years! He's actually *seen* Daisy!"

H.H. promptly fainted. His body sagged across the hood. PeeWee pulled a small brown bottle out of his pocket and waved it under H.H.'s nose. The old man snorted and his eyes popped open. "I ain't scared of no haints," he added in a raspy voice.

Billy propped him up against the hearse, wrapped a protective arm around his friend and patted his shoulder, nodding reassurance.

I extended a hand. "Pleased to meet you," I said, "this is my friend Tom. He believes in your ghost."

Jimmy shook hands and grinned. "If you don't believe now, you will soon. Daisy's about due to make an appearance."

PeeWee pumped a fist in the air. "I knew it!"

"How do you know?" I asked feeling a little shiver crawl up my spine.

"She's been real active lately. See back there behind Screen Three at the Wolf River bottoms?"

Yolanda stood on tippy toes and peeked over Uncle Jake's shoulder. "You mean all that smoke?"

"Yep, lots of fires down in the mulch piles lately. Had a humdinger of a bonfire couple of nights ago. Had to call the fire department."

"And that means Daisy's hanging around?" Tom asked.

"Dang straight," Uncle Jake said. "She starts fires to remind folks how she died. She burned down this very screen back in '07."

Jimmy grinned and shoved his hands in his pockets. "Don't know that for sure, some folks think it was a homeless man back there in the shed tryin' to keep warm."

Yolanda's eyes widened. She hugged herself as if she felt a sudden chill. "I remember the night Daisy died. I had just been through my first divorce and was moonlighting by working the concession stand. We were all in awe of Daisy. She was larger than life. She wore a slinky gold dress and smoked like a chimney. The manager even caught her spiking her Icee with vodka. We bought her a huge bouquet of daisies with a fancy yellow bow. We didn't have a clue that before the night was over she'd be pushing up daisies." She looked at Jimmy. "You think Daisy burned down the screen, don't you?"

Jimmy narrowed his eyes and scanned the parking lot. "Yes, ma'am, I do. She died before her time, and I think she's trying to tell us something."

Uncle Jake hiked up his sagging cargo pants and popped the back hatch. "I say it's time to break out the equipment and get up close and personal with Daisy Flowers."

Jimmy leaned against the hood of the hearse and crossed his arms over his chest. "I was here the night Daisy died, too. My brother and I came for the opening night of Daisy's last film, *Dead and Married.* It hasn't played it again since that night until tonight. I guess there was some kinda dust-up over the film rights after Daisy died. What's left of the cast and crew are here tonight and they intend to recreate the spectacular stunt they planned for the opening. I'd like to stay and help you folks, but someone's got run the movies. It's about time to hit the button and start things rolling." Jimmy turned toward the concession stand and waved a hand over his head. "Good luck, you'll need it, Daisy's a real spit fire."

"Did he say that haint spits fire?" H.H. asked eyes wide. "That must be the way she starts them fires. Y'all smell smoke?"

PeeWee fished in his pocket for the brown bottle just in case. "She don't spit fire, she's just high-spirited."

I glanced around at the boisterous crowd and poked Tom. "Judging from the audience, she isn't the only one high on spirits of some kind."

"I'm off duty. I see nothing, I hear nothing. I better take a hike to concession and look for Ainsley. The celebrities are signing autographs, and she plans to get them all."

"And leave me here with to ward off hostile spirits?"

Uncle Jake rummaged through his stash of dubious equipment and handed out miscellaneous items to his team. Uncle Jake slung a camera around his neck and perched night vision goggles on his head. PeeWee had earphones and something that looked as if it had been a Geiger counter in a previous life. Billy had a metallic dousing rod, and H.H. had a small black box with a variety of blinking colored lights. Yolanda grabbed a small recording device and stuck a low tech pencil in her artificial Daisy hair.

They were standouts in a crowd of weirdos. The Daisy aficionados stopped watching the previews to ogle the Ghost Geezers and their ghost hunting arsenal. They would definitely not take Daisy by surprise. I'd lay odds that she was hiding in plain sight amongst the pseudo Daisys, and was having a good chuckle at Uncle Jake's expense.

There was a commotion in the drive that passed in front of the screen and a massive yellow Cadillac convertible passed under the screen heading the wrong direction toward the box office, music blaring from its speakers. The car was driven by an over-the-hill Daisy look-alike waving and blowing kisses to the crowd. The twin exhausts blew a fog of smoke and fire lending a gauzy haze to the twilight. The fans erupted in cheers of appreciation. They began to sway to the beat of Daisy's theme song with lights from cell phones and lighters waving in the gathering dusk like twinkling fireflies.

Uncle Jake and his cronies headed toward the drive to follow the car. They moved pretty fast for a bunch of geezers, as they tracked the progress of the Cadillac with their ghost gizmos. Yolanda fell behind, tottering on her wedges. She nearly fell into a crater worn by time and tires. The woman in the gold dress came to her aid, then promptly disappeared into the crowd.

Just the opening credits scrolled across the gigantic screen, I noticed the whisper of a shadow cross the screen. The smoky silhouette of a curvaceous woman trailed through the title credits and we heard a crackling sound. The screen became hazy and the light from the projection window took on a smoky film.

All of a sudden the air around us took on an eerie ozone odor, and it was so cold, I felt goosebumps. The raucous crowd grew strangely silent, their eyes glues to the drive in front of the screen. The Cadillac screeched to a stop as the grill made contact with the screen enclosure. A woman in a gold lame dress jumped out and rolled across the grass verge toward the gawking Ghost Geezers. I could hear a collective gasp from the crowd. Uncle Jake and the Ghost Geezers parted the crowd half carrying, half dragging an elderly woman in a gold lame dress.

Suddenly the Cadillac burst into flame. In fact, the screen was really smoking and flames rimmed the naked metal framing struts where the Cadillac made contact. I sincerely hoped this was the special effects stunt.

I fought my way through the crowd to the Ghost Geezers. The woman's platinum blonde wig was askew and tears left streaks on her ash dusted cheeks.

"Don't let her get me," she pleaded as she clutched Uncle Jake for dear life with hands like claws. "I swear it was an accident!" The woman collapsed against Uncle Jake, her body racked with heart-rending sobs.

A tall man with thick dark hair peppered with silver breast-stroked through the crowd. He wore a dark suit with a yellow tie and sported a daisy in his lapel. He grabbed the woman by the shoulders and shook her. "Margie, what happened?"

"She did it, Fred! I saw Daisy and she wants to kill me, just like we killed her!"

I now understood the expression, because my jaw literally dropped. "Say what?"

I felt a warm hand on my shoulder. "Did you just confess to killing Daisy Flowers?" Tom asked.

Margie looked as if she'd seen a ghost because, I guess, she had.

"We didn't mean to kill her. It was supposed to be a stunt. Her car was rigged. I was supposed to drive it, not Daisy. We had it choreographed perfectly."

"Margie, you're distraught, shut up!" Fred said, gripping her tighter.

She shrugged out of Fred's hands. "No! I can't live with a lie anymore." She turned to look at the screen that was now rimmed with the flicker of flame. "She found out I was having an affair with Fred. She was livid! She hit Max and threw a drink in my face like a proper drama queen. It isn't as if she loved Fred, she didn't want her fans to find out their engagement was a sham. She was about to sign a contract with a big studio and leave "B" movies behind."

"You mean leave *me* behind," Fred said through clenched teeth. "She got what she deserved. She went out in a blaze of glory just like she always wanted."

Yolanda teetered over to Fred and stabbed a finger in his face. "Shame on you! You shouldn't speak ill of the dead."

"Especially if you killed her," PeeWee added.

"We didn't mean to. It was an *accident*," Maggie wailed. "She tried to kill me to get even."

"You're as self-involved as Daisy," Fred snapped. "I'm glad that selfish harpy was out of my life for good. Who do you think told her about the affair? I knew she'd have one of her infamous tantrums and play to the audience. I made sure the keys were in the car so she could make a grand exit. It was just serendipity that she offed herself and saved me the trouble."

"You let me believe it was my fault all these years!" Margie landed a left hook to Fred's jaw and laid him out cold.

I heard the opening strains to Daisy's theme cut through the wail of sirens from the fire trucks descending on the Drive-In.

Suddenly the opening scene of *Dead and Married* lit up the screen. A giant 50 foot Daisy filled the screen in all her platinum blond glory. She wore a flowing gold lame gown and held a long gold cigarette holder. She took a drag and blew smoke toward the audience. A wisp of pungent smoke seemed to billow out from the screen. Daisy had a wistful smile on her face, looked directly at her captive audience and winked.

I couldn't take my eyes off the screen. "Tom, doesn't that look exactly like the golden Daisy who winked at you in front of the hearse?"

Tom grinned and nudged my arm with his elbow. "Hot dang, Angie, I think you've finally seen a ghost."

*****

Summer Drive-In

The Summer Drive-In is located appropriately at 5310 Summer Avenue. Built by Malco Theaters and opened on Thursday September 1, 1966, it was originally the Summer Twin Drive-In with two screens. In 1985 two more screens were added. Screen Two (originally screen one) burned in 2007 and was replaced in 2009. The Drive-In was upgraded to digital in 2012 and will be in continuous operation for fifty years in 2016. It is one of only 22 Drive-Ins in Tennessee and only 383 remaining in the United States.

Fallen Soldier
Susan Wooten

Eleven-year-old Billye Trueblood loved Halloween. She loved all things spooky, creepy, ghoulish or ghostly. She especially loved costumes that afforded her the aforementioned characteristics. Her costumes required more than the customary design, materials acquisition and construction. Her costumes required negotiation. While Billye was fervent in her belief that Halloween costumes should be terrifying, her mother, Anna Trueblood, was equally fervent in her own conviction that a young lady's attire should be at all times seemly. Today was the big day. Immediately after dinner, this year's costume negotiations would begin.

"Billye, food is to be eaten, not formed into topographical features," Anna Trueblood said.

"Sorry, Mother." Billye filled her fork, thereby destroying the English pea mountain she had constructed in the center of her plate. Too nervous to eat, she slipped her chicken leg to her Staffordshire terrier.

"Henry, please tell your daughter that the chicken is not for the dog," Anna said in a sharp voice.

Dr. Henry Trueblood gave Billye what he hoped was a stern look. "Your mother did not prepare this delicious dinner for Petey."

Billye resisted the urge to point out that her mother had not prepared the *delicious dinner* at all, because Pearl, the Trueblood's housekeeper, had cooked the meal. "I'm sorry, Mother. Really, I am. I'll never do it again. I promise."

Henry pursed his lips to hide his amusement at Billye's panic. Because he knew the importance of this evening, Dr. Trueblood took pity on his eldest daughter and changed the subject. "Mother, what's for dessert?"

Anna huffed and started to push back her chair. Billye saw her opportunity. "Stay seated, Mother. I'll serve dessert."

"It's the lemon pound cake on the kitchen counter by the stove. And bring dessert plates and the correct forks," Anna said.

Oh, great. Now, I have to figure out which forks go with cake. Fortunately, Pearl had put out what Billye prayed were the correct forks next to what she hoped were dessert plates.

Billye returned to the dining room, set the plates, forks and cake on the table, and sighed with relief when her mother gave her an approving look. After cutting four generous slices of the yummy-looking cake, Billye placed each slice on a plate and served each diner from his or her left. Henry stifled another smile and hoped his daughter's excessive apple polishing was less obvious to his wife than it was to him.

As her family savored their first bites of Pearl's delectable pound cake, Billye took a deep breath. "Mother, may Papa and I speak to you about my Halloween costume?"

Anna sighed audibly. "I suppose there's nothing to be served by delaying the inevitable. What do you want to be this year?"

Billye glanced at her father for support and took another deep breath. "I want to be a zombie. You know, like in Haiti? Don't worry, Mother, I don't want to be a Haitian zombie. I want to be a soldier zombie. You know, because of the war."

Looking as if she might faint, Anna gasped and brought her hands to her cheeks. "Henry, are you hearing this?"

While Henry supported his daughter's Halloween costume vision, he was unwilling to overrule his wife. He was, however, willing to assist his daughter in the negotiation process. A repeat of the disastrous negotiations breakdown of Halloween '45 must be avoided.

"Young ladies do not dress as, behave as, or pretend to be, zombies," Anna said with all the calm she could muster.

Billye gave her father a pleading look. Henry reached for his wife's hand, and made an attempt to put negotiations back on track. "Anna, Darling, what would you like Billye to be this Halloween?"

Anna thought for a moment. "Billye Dear, why don't you dress as a bride? Pearl and I can make you a beautiful wedding dress."

Billye looked at her mother as if the woman had just turned green and sprouted antennae. Even Henry looked askance at his wife when she suggested their tomboyish daughter don a wedding gown on Halloween. Henry searched his brain for a suggestion that might promote a compromise between his wife and daughter. "Perhaps Billye could be a ghost bride. She could be the spirit of a bride who died on her wedding day."

While Anna was giving her husband a grateful look, an idea was forming in Billye's mind. "I guess I could be a ghost bride," she said as she bestowed a sweet smile on her mother.

Henry knew his daughter was up to something, but he was so relieved by the possibility of a compromise that he kept the knowledge to himself. His silence was rewarded when his wife spoke. "All right, Dear. Pearl and I will begin work on the dress tomorrow. Halloween is only three days away."

*****

"Hurry up, Pokey!" Billye tugged her younger sister's arm, causing the little girl to drop her book bag. Hoping to save time, Billye gathered Bitty's spilled books. Bitty's given name was Bettye, but the nanny had so consistently addressed the underweight newborn as *My Itty Bitty* that the *Bitty* had stuck.

"I'll carry your books, but you need to walk faster," Billye said in a tone that lacked the smallest vestige of patience.

Bitty increased her pace, and tugged at her sister's sleeve. "Billye, I don't want you to be a ghost on Halloween. I'm scared of ghosts."

"I won't be a real ghost, Silly. I'll be a pretend ghost. And, since when are you afraid of ghosts?"

"Since I found out one lives in our house." Bitty's voice cracked as if she were about to cry.

"What are you talking about?"

"Minnie Simms told me all about the ghost during recess. A soldier lived in our house. He fell down the stairs and died, and now he moves things at night."

"Bitty, that's ridiculous. The Manns lived in our house until Father bought it last spring. Judge Mann died before the war started. He couldn't have been a soldier."

"Not that war. Minnie said the Mann House ghost was in the first war, the one they fought a long, long time ago."

Billye planned to have a talk with Minnie Simms. But first, she needed to calm her sister. Or, maybe not. Perhaps, she could use the ghost to her own benefit. "Bitty, Honey, don't worry about the ghost in our house. If you pay me a dime a week, I will see that he doesn't harm you in any way."

"But, my allowance for a whole week is only twenty-five cents," Bitty whined.

Billye stood her ground. "That's the deal. Take it or leave it. For the price of a dime, I will walk you upstairs every night and stay with you until you fall asleep. Just be sure to keep your hands and feet on the bed and under the cover. The ghost can grab only those body parts that are dangling off the bed. That's in the ghost book of rules."

Bitty was dubious, but her fear was greater than her skepticism or her parsimony. "Okay, it's a deal."

The sisters walked up Forrest Street to Mann House. Their father had bought the magnificent colonial revival home to entice his wife and daughters to leave Memphis, cross the Mississippi River into Arkansas, and move forty-seven miles east to the quiet farming community of Forrest City. The girls' new home town was named after the same civil war lieutenant general as the street on which they now lived.

Billye and Bitty entered their haunted house and sat at the kitchen table to have milk and Pearl's rolled biscuits. When they finished eating, Bitty removed her writing book, pencil and tablet from her book bag, and began painstakingly copying letters of the alphabet. Leaving her own homework untouched, Billye embarked upon a frantic search for her mother. She found Anna and Pearl upstairs in the sewing room where the two women were putting finishing touches on a wedding dress for a ghost.

"Mother, I need to go the library. No one need drive me. I can walk there," Billye said as she fidgeted and shifted her weight from one foot to the other.

"What about your homework?"

"I need to use *The Arkansas Collection* to do research. It is a very special collection that they keep under lock and key. But, Mrs. Proctor told me I can use it whenever I want." Billye was careful to avoid the telling of an outright lie. She did need to use *The Arkansas Collection* to do research. If her mother assumed the research was for a school assignment, well, that wasn't her fault.

"Be home by suppertime. And, take Petey with you." Billye's mother did not altogether approve of her daughter's wandering all over town, but Anna worried less when Billye was in the company of the dog. The faithful Staffie followed the girls everywhere. Anna was confident that no harm would come to her children with Petey on guard.

"Thank you, Mother," Billye said as she rushed down the stairs and out the front door with Petey at her heels. She ran all the way to the library and, leaving Petey sprawled on the bottom step, took the remaining steps two at a time. She burst through the library's front door and nearly collided with a surprised librarian.

"Whoa there, Young Lady. What's your emergency?" Mrs. Proctor tried to look and sound serious as she administered the half-hearted scolding.

"Would *The Arkansas Collection* have information about my house?" Billye asked her question in a halting stammer while she struggled to catch her breath.

"Well, hello to you too, Miss Billye," Mrs. Proctor said.

Billye suddenly remembered her manners. "I'm sorry, Ma'am. Hello, Mrs. P."

Mrs. Proctor studied Billye's earnest face. "What would you like to know about your house?"

"I want to know about the ghost."

Mrs. Proctor briefly considered an attempt to dissuade Billye of the notion that Mann House was home to a ghost. But, the older woman knew that this child who had visited the library almost every day of her summer break would not be easily dismissed. Mrs. Proctor calculated the risks and concluded she should tell young Miss Billye the truth. The child should have an accurate version of the tragedy that occurred at Mann House so she could decide for herself whether or not the ghost existed. "There is no need to consult *The Arkansas Collection*. I can tell you the story of the Mann House ghost."

Mrs. Proctor led Billye to a table at the back of the library where the two friends could talk in relative privacy. "Your house was built in 1913 by a wise judge named Sam Mann. He lived there until he died in 1938. Judge Mann was from Brownsville, Tennessee. In 1919, almost a year after the First World War ended, Judge Mann received a telegraph message from an old friend named Zebediah Falcon. Sam and Zebediah had been childhood friends back in Tennessee. Zebediah Falcon's telegraph message was a plea for help. His son, John, had returned from World War I in sad shape, both physically and mentally. Zebediah's wife had died after a long and expensive illness that left the family penniless and unable to provide proper care for young John. In desperation, Zebediah begged Judge Mann to help his son."

"Did Judge Mann help John?" Billye asked. "He should have helped a soldier. We should always help the soldiers."

"Judge Mann and his kind wife brought John Falcon to live with them soon after the telegram arrived. The Manns did the best they could for the troubled young man. They provided John the best medical care available and made every effort to make him feel safe and loved."

"Did he get well?"

"Billye Dear, I'll never get the story told if you continue to interrupt."

"I'm sorry, Mrs. P. It's just that I really want the soldier to be okay," Billye said in a quiet voice.

"I understand. And, I wish I could tell you that young John did get well. But, sadly, in spite of the medicine poured into him, and the love showered on him, John continued to suffer terrible nightmares that caused him to relive the horrors of war night after night. He began to drink, I suppose to help him forget, or perhaps, to help him sleep. Out of respect for Mrs. Mann, John did his drinking away from the house and always in the evenings. No one is sure where John went at night, but it's said he would always come home quite drunk and always at midnight."

Mrs. Proctor paused to study Billye's face for signs of discomfort. Seeing none, she continued her tale. "About a year after John came to live with the Manns, tragedy struck. John awakened during the night, probably from one of his nightmares. He left his room and started down the stairs. John tripped and fell down the steps to the landing where he struck his head on a cast iron gas heater. He suffered a concussion and lost consciousness as he attempted to negotiate the remaining steps. A pool of blood on the landing was followed by a bloody trail marking John's roll down the last part of the staircase. The Mann's cook found poor John's lifeless body at the bottom of the stairs the next morning when she went to the front of the house to call the family to breakfast."

Billye leaned forward with impatience. "So, where does the ghost come into the story?"

"I'm getting to that," Mrs. Proctor said. "When John was alive, the Mann's housekeeper moved his bed away from the wall each morning so that she could straighten the bed covers. Each night, around midnight, John would arrive home, go to his room and shove his bed against the wall before he retired. Perhaps sleeping against the wall made him feel more secure. It is said that John's ghost continues to climb the stairs at night, and around midnight, attempts to move his bed against the wall."

Mrs. Proctor studied Billye's face. "Are you all right, dear? I hope I didn't frighten you."

Billye gave the older woman a puzzled look. "Why would I be frightened? I love ghost stories, but I don't believe ghosts really exist. Papa says there is a scientific explanation for everything. Well, I'd better get home. It's almost time for dinner. I appreciate your telling me the story of the Mann house soldier ghost, even if I don't believe in ghosts." She hugged Mrs. Proctor and rushed out the door. When she reached the bottom step, Petey sprang from his napping spot, and bounded after her toward home and dinner.

*****

Anna studied her husband's face across the table. He rarely brooded and never in the presence of the children. "Henry, are you unwell? You aren't eating your fish. Pearl's husband caught it fresh this morning and Pearl prepared it just the way you like it, with lemon and pepper."

"A little girl died in my office this afternoon."

Anna gasped. "Oh, my, I'm so sorry. What was wrong with her?"

"Tetanus," the weary physician said. "She stepped on a snake bone, and the puncture went untreated. Her parents brought her to me too late. They are convinced she died because the snake was poisonous. I let them think it because the truth would only serve to add guilt to their grief. A child will not grow up and live her life for lack of a tetanus shot. It's such a tragic, needless, stupid waste."

The Truebloods sat in stunned, saddened silence. Bitty broke the quiet. "What was her name, Papa?"

Henry sighed and answered his daughter. "Susie Clayton. Her name was Susie Clayton."

"I know her!" said Billye. "She's a grade behind me in school, but she's the same age as me." All the children in Billye's age group were a grade behind her. Back in Memphis, she had been so bored and fidgety in first grade that the headmistress had moved her to second grade. Anna worried that her daughter would be socially stunted by being placed with the older children, but Billye was not bothered. With the exception of her new friend, Joyce McConnell, she cared little for socializing with children of any age.

"Susie's parents are very poor, I think," Billye said in a solemn tone.

"Yes, Sweetheart, they are poor," her father agreed. "They have no money for a funeral."

"Henry, we must bring her here," Anna said. "Where is she now? Is she still at your office?"

"Yes. I told the Claytons they could sit with her there until they decided what to do. I could go now and bring them here. Anna, are you sure you're okay with having the girl here? People will be in and out to sit with her and to attend the service."

"We must do what we can for these people. Think how awful it would be to lose one of ours and be unable to do right by her."

Henry put his hands on the table, pushed back his chair, and said, "So, that's what we will do. You girls finish your dinner and then go to your room. Anna, let Pearl know that the embalmers will do their work tonight in the kitchen."

Anna paled. "Not in my kitchen. For heaven's sake, Henry, our food is prepared in there."

Henry refrained from explaining to his wife that many a corpse was embalmed in a family kitchen. "All right, Dear, I'll tell them they can use the empty room at the top of the stairs."

"Oh no, Henry, not that room," Anna said.

Henry spoke with quiet firmness in his voice. "It's either that room or the kitchen."

Anna gave a resigned sigh. "If you feel the room at the top of the stairs is a suitable place for the embalmers to do their work, then so be it. I'll have Pearl put a couple of chairs in the room for the sitters. We can move young Susie to the parlor in the morning for viewing."

"That will be good." Henry kissed his wife on the cheek, donned his coat and hat, and went out the door.

Mother and daughters ate the remainder of their meal in relative silence, and Anna said a prayer of thanks when Billye took her younger sister's hand and led her up the stairs. Anna's thankful mood dissipated moments later when she heard footsteps on the stairs. The footsteps would be those of her eldest daughter returning with some excuse to avoid spending the evening in her room as instructed. Anna quickly compiled a reprimand to deliver before the child had a chance to wheedle. The prepared reprimand flew from Anna's mind when Billye appeared with her best Sunday dress in hand. She held up the frock. "May I give this dress to Mrs. Clayton for Susie to wear? She may not have a nice dress for the funeral."

"That's very kind of you, Sweetheart. Are you sure you want to part with the dress?"

"Yes Ma'am, I'm sure. It's just a dress. Susie needs it more than I do. She should be buried in a nice dress."

Anna took the dress from her daughter and gave the child a hug. "I'm sure Susie's parents will be very grateful to have a pretty dress in which to bury their daughter. Now, go to your room. The men will be here soon with Susie. Mrs. Clayton's friend will come and sit with her until morning. Papa will come in to tuck you in as always. Goodnight, Dear."

Billye told her mother goodnight, and trudged back up the stairs to her room with Petey in tow. Less than an hour later, she heard footsteps on the staircase. She tiptoed to her sister's bed and whispered, "Bitty, are you awake?" When the younger girl made no sound or movement, Billye opened her bedroom door a narrow crack, and peered into the hallway. Two somber looking men in black suits had just reached the top of the stairs with a strange looking wooden table bearing legs that were folded underneath. The men were using the table as a stretcher to carry a small form covered with a white sheet. A third man carried a large, rectangular case and pulled a metal tank on wheels behind him as he ascended the stairs.

The third man wore a white coat that was identical to the one that Papa wore at work. The first two men stopped at the top of the stairs where the third man set down his case, and straightened the legs from underneath the table. The legs were on wheels that allowed the men to roll the table into the room at the top of the stairs. The three men disappeared into the room behind the table taking with them the large case and the portable metal tank.

Billye closed her bedroom door, gathered her schoolbooks, pencil and tablet from her desk, and flopped onto her bed, barely missing Petey as he scrambled to avoid being squashed. After nearly two hours of what she considered superfluous busywork, she heard a door close. The sound of footsteps in the hall prompted her to leap from the bed, causing books, papers and dog to fly in various directions. She ran across the room and opened her door just in time to see the backs of the embalmers as they descended the stairs.

Leaning against the door jamb, Billye steadied her breathing, and gathered her courage. After ordering Petey to stay, she crept out of her room and down the hall to the room where her schoolmate lay dead. Light seeped under the door. Perhaps the men were kind people who did not wish to leave a young girl alone in the dark. Whatever the reason, she was happy that the light had been left burning. She took a deep breath, opened the door and slipped inside.

Billye took cautious steps toward the form lying on the mobile embalming table. She recognized Susie Clayton immediately, as the girl looked very much as she had the last time Billye had seen her at school. Only, now, Susie appeared to be sleeping. She looked nice in the gifted dress, and Billye liked knowing that one of her dresses would soon be worn in heaven.

And, even better, if Susie becomes a ghost, she'll haunt people wearing my dress. But, there are no such things as ghosts.

Billye was interrupted from her reverie by the sound of footsteps and voices on the lower landing. Panicked, she made a flying trip back to her room, and couldn't believe her good fortune when she found herself safely inside, undetected by the approaching adults. When her heart slowed and her breathing returned to normal, she once again cracked her bedroom door to hear what she could hear. The adults were in the room with Susie, but the door had been left open. Billye caught bits of their conversation and could hear sobbing that she assumed came from Mrs. Clayton. A brave peek around her bedroom door told her that the adults were Papa, Susie's parents, and a lady Billye had never seen before. She figured the lady must be Mrs. Clayton's friend who was going to sit with Susie.

After several minutes passed, Billye heard her father instruct the sitter. "Mrs. Snokum, make yourself comfortable. Pearl will bring you something to eat and drink. The toilet is down the hall to the right. Please don't hesitate to wake us if you need something. I'll see the Claytons out and return to ensure that you have all you need for the night."

Billye closed her bedroom door and held the knob so that it wouldn't click until her father and the Claytons were out of earshot. It suddenly occurred to her that, after seeing the Claytons out, her father would come to tuck her in. She tore off her clothes, stuffed them into the wardrobe, pulled on her dressing gown, jumped into bed and feigned sleep when she heard her doorknob turn.

"Are my angels asleep?" Because it was not his first day as a father, Henry was fairly sure that Billye was faking, but he played along. He kissed her on the forehead and then did the same for Bitty. The weary physician paused on his way out of his daughters' room, and turned back for one last look at his sleeping children, his *healthy* sleeping children. He stepped into the hallway, quietly shut the door and looked down the hall at the door behind which laid a third sleeping child, one who would never awaken. The irony, insult and sheer injustice of it all exhausted him.

When Billye was sure that her father was out of her room, she sat up in bed and mumbled to herself. "Must stay awake. How to stay awake?" Because her greatest fear in life was that she might miss something, she had made the firm decision that tonight would not be spent sleeping.

"I'll read. I won't fall asleep if I read." Billye had never understood the concept of reading oneself to sleep. The more engrossed she was in a story, the wider awake she became. Her favorite girl detective never put her to sleep. She dug her flashlight from under her pillow and joined Nancy in her quest to solve *The Mystery of the Ivory Charm.*

Billye read until the mantel clock chimed midnight. When the chiming stopped, she put down her book, crawled out of bed, and stretched. Petey roused himself from his spot at the foot of the bed and blinked at her with a questioning expression. *Do you know what time it is? What are you doing?*

She scratched a spot behind Petey's left ear. "Go back to sleep, Buddy. It's nothing to do with you." Flashlight in hand, she crept out of the room and down the hall toward the room where Mrs. Snokum sat with Susie.

Petey yawned, jumped down from the bed and padded after her. He had no idea where his human was going in the middle of the night, but it was his job to go with her.

As Billye inched toward Susie's room, she rehearsed what she would say if Mrs. Snokum questioned her presence there. *I wanted to see that you were comfortable. Do you need anything?* It was Billye's firm belief that the best way to respond to an awkward question was to ask another question.

When she noticed the absence of light under the door of Susie's room, Billye wondered why Mrs. Snokum would wish to sit in a dark room with a dead body. When no answer came to mind, she shrugged, grasped the doorknob, and turned it slowly and quietly. She opened the door a crack and peered inside. Because the drapes were closed, she couldn't see a thing. Widening the crack in the door just enough to slip inside, she nearly jumped out of her skin when Petey's soft fur brushed her leg. While she didn't want the dog in the room, she didn't dare give him an audible *out* command. She stood still a moment, and debated the pros and cons of switching on her flashlight. When she finally decided to try putting her hand over the lens, her fingers proved to be an excellent filter. After her eyes adjusted to the dim light, she saw that Mrs. Snokum was sound asleep. The woman's lack of diligence gave Billye an instant dislike for her. Staying just inside the door in case the need arose for a quick getaway, she leaned against the wall and wondered what the soldier ghost, if he really existed, would think of Mrs. Snokum's lack of respect for the dead. What happened next made Billye rethink all things ghostly.

A grinding noise brought to mind the theory that the soldier ghost might move things in the night. Billye dismissed the thought, and turned her attention to Susie. She shone her light toward the dead girl, and to her horror, discovered the source of the grinding sound. She stifled a cry when she saw that the foot of the portable embalming table had rolled against the wall, dislodging her dead friend's upper torso which now hung partially off the table. Before she could cross the room, and return Susie to her proper position, screams pierced her ears. Mrs. Snokum had awakened, and the stupid woman was in full-blown hysteria. Billye glanced toward the embalming table, but her strong sense of self-preservation outweighed her desire to right the upper half of Susie's body.

"C'mon Petey," she whispered. With her dog at her heels, she beat her personal best time back to her room. She jumped into bed and prayed that Mrs. Snokum had been too distracted by the dislodged corpse, or just too busy screaming, to notice a young girl and a dog.

"There's no such thing as ghosts. There's no such thing as ghosts." Repeating the mantra, she fell asleep with the covers over her head.

*****

Sugar rationing had limited trick or treating for the past several years. This Halloween, Billye and her younger sister knocked on the doors of a handful of their father's wealthiest patients, and visited a few members of their mother's Musical Coterie. After the girls returned home from trick or treating, Billye walked the two blocks to the home of Joyce McConnell. Although the two girls had met only months before, on Billye's first day in her new school, they had quickly bonded over a shared loved of dogs and Nancy Drew.

"Is the coast clear?" Billye whispered the question as soon as Joyce opened her front door.

"You bet. Mama and Papa are long gone, and your stuff is under my bed." The girls ran to Joyce's room and retrieved a cigar box from under the bed. Joyce lifted the lid of the box, and removed a small tin of talc, a powder puff and a lump of charcoal.

Joyce wore a confused expression as she studied the items. "What exactly are you going to do with those?"

"Just watch," Billye said as she dabbed the puff in the talc. She patted her face with the loaded puff until she was as pale as death. Next, she used the charcoal to hollow her eyes and cheeks, and turned to face her friend. "Well, what do you think? Do I look like a zombie bride?"

"You look exactly like a zombie bride."

Billye asked Joyce one final question. "Did you get the dirt?"

"I can't imagine why you need dirt, but here it is." Joyce opened a dresser drawer, and removed a small paper bag filled halfway with soil from her mother's flower garden.

Billye smeared handfuls of the dark, moist soil down the front of the dress. What she did next made her friend gasp. She ripped the once beautiful dress in several places and practiced walking with her arms outstretched zombie style. "I'm ready for a killer-diller Halloween party."

"Now it's time for you to see *my* costume," Joyce said as she pulled her zombie friend into Mrs. McConnell's sewing room. After instructing Billye to close her eyes, Joyce quickly removed her dress and donned her Halloween outfit. "Okay, you can look now. What do you think?"

Billye was seized by an attack of jealousy the moment she opened her eyes, but she pushed the feeling aside. "It's a swell costume, Joyce. It's the cat's meow. I wish my mother would allow me to wear something like that."

"Can you tell what I am?"

"Are you kidding? You look exactly like a train conductor. The hat is keen."

Joyce pointed to her cap with pride. "That's because it's a real conductor cap. Papa borrowed it from the conductor of the Choctaw Rocket. Papa often rides the Rocket to Memphis for business, and he is friends with the conductor. I love trains. Did you know that the largest freight train in the world comes through Forrest City every night around midnight? It zips by Union Station at more than 70 miles per hour. Billye, are you listening to me? Billye?"

"Shhhh. I'm thinking." Billye perched on Mrs. McConnell's sewing bench, and drummed her fingers on her knees as she contemplated the information Joyce had imparted.

"Did you hear what I said about the train?"

"That's what I'm thinking about," Billye said. "Does your father have a level?" One look at Joyce's face told Billye that her friend had no idea what a level was. "Your father does woodworking as a hobby. Where does he keep his tools?"

Joyce led Billye through the house and out the back door. They walked a stone path to a small, wooden shop painted to match the house. Inside, floor to ceiling shelves were filled with woodworking and carpentry tools of every description. Two levels rested side by side on one of the shelves. Billye chose the wooden one because she figured, if she were caught with one of Mr. McConnell's levels in her possession, it shouldn't be the newfangled metal one. Because she often found herself weighing consequences, she had become astute at choosing the one that would be least dire.

"We'd better get back," said Joyce. "The party guests will arrive soon."

As the girls headed through the McConnell's back door into the kitchen, Billye said, "We need to go to my house."

Before Joyce could protest, the McConnell's doorbell chimed. "We can't go anywhere," Joyce said. "Our friends are arriving for the party."

Billye no longer cared about parties or zombie brides, but she couldn't desert her friend. Glumly, she followed Joyce to the door, and spent the next two hours greeting, and helping to entertain her boring schoolmates in their stupid costumes. As soon as the last guest was out the door, she called out to Joyce. "Get your coat. We have to go to my house right this minute."

Joyce called back. "Tell me again why we have to go to your house *right this minute.*"

Billye pulled on her coat. "C'mon. I'll explain on the way."

As the girls hurried the two blocks to Mann House, Billye told Joyce the story of the soldier ghost and concluded with a description of the unfortunate movement of the embalming table. When the story was finished, she added, "Because there are no ghosts, there must be a scientific explanation for the movement of the table. Your talk of trains gave me an idea of what that explanation might be. Now, we must investigate."

Joyce paused at Billye's front door. "Exactly how sure are you that ghosts don't exist?"

"Very sure. Now, come help me prove it." Level in hand, she opened her front door, and pulled Joyce inside. Billye held her forefinger to her lips for silence, and gestured to her friend to follow her up the stairs.

When Billye put her hand on the knob of the door leading to the room where Susie had been embalmed, Joyce grabbed her friend's arm, and spoke in a whisper. "Wait, isn't the dead girl in this room?"

Billye dug deep for patience. "No, they had her service in the parlor this afternoon, and took her to the cemetery. Now come on before we get caught out here in the hall. I'm supposed to be spending the night at your house, remember?"

"Yes, I remember. And, my house is where we should be right now."

Billye opened the door to the now empty room, pulled Joyce inside and shut the door with care. Billye paused inside the door. "Darn. I forgot to bring a flashlight. I can't see the bubble."

After thinking for a moment, Billye removed her coat, and stuffed it against the crack under the door. Light would still show above the door, but that crack was smaller, and she only needed light for a moment to read the bubble. Deciding that getting an answer would be worth the risk, she placed the level on the floor perpendicular to the back wall where the embalming table had been. Then, she whispered to Joyce who stood frozen just inside the door. "Switch on the light."

Joyce fumbled for the switch. Light flooded the room, allowing Billye to read the bubble in the level. As soon as she got her answer, she gave Joyce frantic instructions. "Switch off the light. Be quick!"

As soon as the girls were safely away from Mann House, Joyce questioned Billye. "Are you going to tell me what we did back there and why we did it?"

Billye skipped and waved the level in the air. "This brilliant invention solved the mystery of the Mann House ghost."

"How? How did that whatchamacallit solve a mystery about a ghost?"

"Level. The whatchamacallit is a level. It confirmed my suspicion that the floor in that room is not level."

"So?"

"Your story about the freight train got me to thinking about vibrations. Freight trains are big and fast. Big, fast things cause vibrations. And vibrations cause things to move on slanted floors."

Joyce finally understood. "And, Susie's bed, uh, table, moved at about the same time the freight train came through."

"Exactly," Billye said. "I'll bet things have been shifting in that room for decades, but no one noticed it until John Falcon died horribly and people came to believe the house was haunted."

Joyce looked at her friend with admiration. "Billye Trueblood, you are brilliant."

*****

"Billye Trueblood, what is your answer?"

The shrill voice startled Billye from her daydream. "I'm sorry, Mrs. Davis. Could you repeat the question?" Absorbed in thought, she had not heard her geography teacher call on her. She was rehearsing the very special question she planned to ask her father if and when the closing bell ever rang. It was Friday, her favorite day of the week. On Fridays, Papa closed his office early and picked up the girls from school in his shiny Buick Roadmaster. After dropping Bitty off at home, he took Billye with him to visit patients who found it difficult to travel into town because of advanced age, chronic illness, or as was too often the case, abject poverty.

"Yes, Miss Trueblood, I can repeat the question, but I have no intention of doing so. You will lose a point for failing to provide the answer, and I trust this will teach you to attend to what is taking place in the classroom as opposed to whatever nonsense is going on in your head."

Just as Billye opened her mouth to apologize, the bell rang. Saying a quick prayer of thanks, she stuffed her books and tablet into her book bag and covered the distance from classroom to car in far less time than was proper. Flinging open the car door, she tossed her book bag inside, and jumped into the front seat. She kissed her father on the cheek and peppered him with questions. "Where is Bitty? Why does she have to be so slow?"

"Probably because she is small and young. By the way, good afternoon to you, too," Henry said with amusement. He wondered what Billye was up to but decided to wait for the scheme to reveal itself.

"Oh, sorry, Papa. Good afternoon. Where is that sister of mine?" Billye looked out her window and caught a glimpse of her younger sister among a group of children making their way along the sidewalk. She lowered the window, and shouted to her sibling. "Hurry up, Bitty!"

As soon as Bitty climbed out of the car and headed for the front door of Mann House, Billye said, "My birthday is next week, you know."

Ah, there it is. "Yes, Sweetheart, I know. Have you given thought to what you might like to have for your birthday this year?"

"Papa, I want something that won't cost you a cent."

While the prospect of making a child happy on her birthday without having to spend money would please most parents, Henry knew his eldest daughter well enough to exercise skepticism. "That sounds interesting. What might this special present be?"

"I want my own room. The room at the top of the stairs isn't being used for anything. I could move in there and have my very own space. I'm going to be twelve, and in another year, I'll be a teenager. A teenager can't share her room with a child. Will you talk to Mother? Will you, please, Papa?"

Henry drove in stunned silence. He didn't know where to begin. While he could overlook his daughter's disdain for her younger sister, the problem of the room at the top of the stairs had to be addressed.

"Don't worry about the ghost, Papa. I don't believe in ghosts. There is a scientific explanation for all phe...phe...nom..."

"Phenomena," Henry said. "How did you learn of the ghost?"

"A girl at school told us about him. But, Papa, I figured out the scientific reason things move in that room. The floor is not level, and vibrations from a freight train that comes through Forrest City at midnight cause movement on the slanted floor."

Henry was, as the British say, gob smacked. When he recovered his power of speech, he asked Billye how she knew the floor was not level. She described the experiment that she and Joyce had performed, and related the statistics pertaining to the size and speed of the midnight train.

"I am impressed with your initiative and your application of scientific methodology," Henry said.

"But, what if your bed moved during the night? Wouldn't that be frightening in spite of any scientific explanation of the phenomenon?"

"My bed is heavy and has regular legs. It's not on wheels like the embalming table." Billye's hand flew to her mouth. She couldn't believe she had been so stupid.

Henry ignored the slip. Given everything his daughter had said and done in the last few days, it came as no surprise to him that she knew about embalming table features. Henry sighed. "Yes, Billye. I'll speak to your mother."

*****

Billye waved goodbye to the last guest, thanked her mother and Pearl for the swell birthday party, and ran up the stairs to her beautiful new room. She stretched out on her bed, and hugged Petey. "What do you think, Buddy? I know, I know. The floral chintz curtains are a little much, but you know Mother."

Just as Billye picked up the latest Hardy Boys mystery, the lights flickered and died. "Darn," she said to Petey. "Arkansas Power and Light is at it again." After fishing her flashlight from under her pillow, she made her way across the room to the chest of drawers, and retrieved a candle and a box of matches. She lit the candle, and turned toward the bed, unaware that Petey had followed her. Tripping over the dog, she sent the candle flying toward the curtains. Startled by the kick, Petey ran under the bed. Before Billye could scramble to her feet, the curtains were ablaze.

Billye jumped up, ran out the door, and shut it behind her just as her father had taught her to do.

An open door allowed oxygen to feed a fire. She ran down the stairs to the parlor where her parents were having their evening brandy. "Papa, Papa, my room is on fire!"

Henry leapt from his chair and flew to the kitchen where he grabbed the fire extinguisher. Just as her father reached the top of the stairs, Billye had a horrible thought. She screamed, "Petey! I shut Petey in the room with the fire!" As she stood paralyzed by the realization that she had killed her best friend, she felt something touch her leg. "Petey! Oh Petey, you're alive! But, how did you...? The door was..."

Billye dropped to her knees and hugged her dog with all her might. With tears running down her cheeks, she whispered into Petey's ear. "Maybe ghosts *do* exist. And, aren't we lucky that our ghost is an animal lover?"

*****

The Mann House

Designed by Charles L. Thompson and built in 1913, Mann House, a historic house in Forrest City, Arkansas, is one of that firm's finest examples of Colonial Revival architecture. The front façade features an imposing Greek temple portico with two story Ionic columns supporting a fully pedimented gable with dentil molding. The main entrance, sheltered by this portico, is flanked by sidelight windows and topped by a fanlight transom with diamond-pattern lights.

The house was listed on the National Register of Historic Places in 1982. The residence is occupied by descendants of its original owner, Judge Sam Mann, and is not open to the public.

Going Back Home
Barbara Christopher

"Just wanted to remind you to be at St. Columba by six tonight."

Shannon breathed a sigh of relief. When she'd seen the name on the phone she figured the weekend planning session had been cancelled because of the threat of snow.

She buttoned her coat, grabbed her coffee and headed to the screened-in porch of Sanders Lodge. She had an hour to relax before the rest of the group arrived. Until then she would do nothing but close her eyes and meditate.

She liked the peace and quiet of the wooded area. Loved the deer, the squirrels, and the birds. Their musical creation was soothing. Right now she needed what it gave her.

Even the threat of light snow wouldn't dampen her mood. Just a dusting, here tonight and gone before they were scheduled to leave. She glanced at the gathering clouds. They were rolling in faster than the weatherman "guessed".

The chilly November wind rustled the remaining leaves clinging to the large oaks. Shannon took a sip of her coffee, tucked the warm cup to her chest and closed her eyes to let the bustle of the day's events float into oblivion.

"Ma'am?"

The child's voice echoed through her mind. Shannon squeezed her closed eyes a little tighter. Not now, I'm not ready to give up my peace.

"Ma'am?"

Shannon opened her eyes and turned her head to where a small girl stood at the door to the screened porch. "What is it, Hon?"

"Can you help me find my Daddy? He's lost and I can't go home without him."

The young girl had a small home-made doll tucked in her arms. Her sweater had several small holes, not large, but big enough to let you know she'd battled with a thorn bush, and the thorn bush won.

Blood gathered on the back of the girl's hand outlining a couple of tiny pricks.

"You're daddy is lost?"

"Yes, Ma'am."

"What's your name?"

"Rachel."

"Well, Rachel, come inside and let me clean up those scratches, then we'll go look for him."

Shannon pulled the screen door open and waited for Rachel to come inside. "I'll get the first-aid kit."

Shannon cleaned the wound as she'd done so many times with her nieces and nephews and put small bandages on them. No cartoons on these, but they would do for now.

"Okay, where was the last place you saw your daddy?"

"He went into the woods to find my brother." She cocked her head to one side and frowned. "Caleb's lost too."

"Well, come on, let's go find them."

Shannon took Rachel's hand in hers and helped her down the back steps. A rack of wood was stacked to the left. On the right stood was a tiny fenced-in cemetery with three old markers.

One of the ladies at last year's planning session joked about having to sleep in the lodge next to a graveyard. It didn't bother Shannon. At least it hadn't until one of the ladies looked up the information about the graves. All it said was that the children died tragically. Three graves, two children.

Beyond the graves was a road leading to the only area they'd been warned not to venture near. The old hermit's cottage.

"This way," Rachel said. She tugged Shannon toward the forbidden road.

"No, hon. We're not supposed to go down there. Why don't we call the office and let them know you're with me."

"My Daddy is down there." Rachel pulled free and ran down toward the road.

"Wait, Rachel," Shannon called. "I'm coming, but I don't want to go too far from the lodge."

Just a few yards, then they would return to the Sanders Lodge.

Rachel caught Shannon's hand and dragged her toward the woods. The further from the cottage they went the colder it got. A light dusting of snow swirled around them.

Shannon frowned and looked toward the sky. When they'd left the cottage the sky had been mostly clear, now it was dense with the kinds of clouds that everyone says, "They just look like snow."

The flurries that dusted the roofs and grass soon turned into thick wind-driven flakes that made seeing difficult.

"Rachel, where do you live? I'm sure your daddy is back home by now with your brother and worried about you."

Tears flooded Rachel's eyes.

"Daddy's not lost, I am. He went to the barn to get Caleb. He told me to stay in the house, but I was scared and followed him, but the barn is all white and I couldn't find it."

Rachel shivered. The thin sweater barely covered her small frame. The girl's tiny feet were jammed into unlaced boots. Shannon doubted the child was even wearing socks.

"Come here." Shannon motioned Rachel closer, then opened her coat, and tugged her close to her. They had to find shelter and fast or they would both freeze to death.

"Daddy told us to find the big Oak, then look up and get under the biggest limb." Rachel said. "He said to put our back against the tree and if we walked straight ahead we'd find home." Rachel touched Shannon's cheek. "Do you know where the tree is?"

"No, but we'll find it. Better yet, why don't we go back to the lodge, we can get warm and call around to let the people at the office know where you are?"

Without waiting for an answer Shannon turned around.

Nothing. No light, no outline of a building, no rack of wood, nothing but white and a smattering of trees that weren't completely coated with snow yet.

They couldn't have traveled fifty yards down the road, but they were lost in a whiteout.

The weather report said flurries. If this was light snow what was a blizzard?

If there'd been storm warnings out the group would have cancelled the meeting and rescheduled to an alternate date.

The other ladies would see her car. Know that she was there somewhere, and come looking for her, or at least alert the authorities that she was missing.

Shannon picked Rachel up and made sure her coat covered as much of the girl as possible.

"We're lost, too, aren't we?" Rachel asked.

The girl rested her chin on Shannon's collarbone. Pain shot through her, but she didn't dare say a word.

They walked in the direction of the lodge.

Shannon felt Rachel move her head from side to side.

"You okay?"

"Yes, Ma'am. Daddy told me to keep looking from side to side. Pick a point and make sure I stayed headed in one direction. That way I'd get somewhere and not go in circles."

"Good information."

Rachel ground her chin into Shannon's shoulder and again turned her head.

"Look," Rachel yelled trying to scramble out of Shannon's arms. "There's my Daddy."

Shannon turned around. The outline of something moved away from them. Was it her father, or the hermit? Or did they have bears here? The barely visible image crept further away.

"Hello," Shannon called as loud as she could.

The figure turned, hesitated then headed toward them. Relief coursed through her as the form took shape.

"You found her," the frantic man said. "I thought we'd lost her too."

"We?"

A small boy clutching tightly to the man's hand came out from behind him.

Shannon smiled. "You must be Caleb."

"Yes, Ma'am."

"Rachel told me you and your daddy were lost and asked if I could help find you."

The man grinned, then sobered immediately. "We need to head back to the cabin before we <u>do</u> get lost. Follow me." He picked up the boy, then held out his hand to her.

"This might be a little awkward, but if you can hold my hand and try to walk behind me in my footprints it will be easier."

Shannon cupped her fingers in his.

He turned, rested their coupled hands against the small of his back, and headed the way she'd been going.

She moved in closer. Fear sent a ripple of laughter through her. They were moving together in tandem like a train, only the tracks were footprints and not rails.

"That's the tree." Rachel pointed toward the huge Oak tree, then giggled. "We're going home."

Shannon heard the man chuckle.

"That we are, Rachel. We are going home."

The man set the boy down, and nodded toward the door. "This is home. It is not much, but the children and I do not need a lot. Please come in."

"Thank you."

Caleb rushed ahead of them, shoved open the door, and stepped aside. "After you, Ma'am."

"It will take a few minutes to get the fire stoked, but you'll be warm before too long."

"I'm fine," Shannon said, "but Rachel is almost to the point of freezing. Do you have a blanket to put around her, and socks? She needs socks on her feet."

The man pulled a blanket off one of the two beds and wrapped it around Rachel. "That should stave off the cold until the cabin gets warm."

"Thank you, Mr...?"

"Just call me Daniel."

He worked in silence until the fire was blazing. Then he turned toward the old wood cook stove and started a fire in it. "I have a stew going. It should be ready in a few minutes. You are welcome to sup with us."

"I can't. I'm supposed to be at the lodge for a meeting. The rest of my team is bound to be looking for me."

"Lodge?" Daniel frowned. "I do not know of any Lodge near here. Besides letting me share what we have is the only way I can repay you for saving my daughter."

Daniel glanced at Rachel and grinned, then gathered the sleeping child and the blanket into his arms, and took her to the bed. "Rough day for a six year old."

"Six? I thought she was eight."

He chuckled again. It was a sound that penetrated all the way to the heart. "She takes after me in size, but she is going to be a fine woman. Just like her mother was."

"What happened to their mother?" Shannon asked as she slipped off her coat.

Daniel took her coat and hung it on a nail beside the door. "Went to Memphis to take care of her parents, got the fever and died. That was three years ago this week. That's what Caleb was doing. He went to the barn to cry. I told Rachel to stay here, but she's a stubborn girl."

He looked toward the door and took a deep breath. When he turned back she could tell he was having trouble holding back his emotions.

"Supper," he said, and dipped out three bowls of stew. "Rachel can eat when she wakes up. Thank you again for what you did." He glanced at Caleb. "Bless the food Caleb."

Got the fever. The words swirled though Shannon's mind. What fever?

Caleb said a quick blessing.

Shannon took a bite. "Oh, my. This is heavenly."

They ate in silence, then Daniel nodded to Caleb

The boy gathered the bowls and put them on the wooden shelf beside a large basin. Then took a kettle off the stove, poured hot water into the basin and added a ladle of cold water from the bucket sitting next to the stove.

Shannon looked around at the furnishings of the cabin. Nothing electric or gas. Where was she? She glanced at the ceiling, no lights, then at the door, no light switch.

Was this even real?

Panic made her breath catch.

Shannon turned toward the sleeping girl. The bandage was gone.

Daniel reached over and touched her hand.

Shannon tensed, and he pulled his hand away immediately.

"I am sorry. I did not mean to be so forward. Please forgive me."

"It's not you. It's just that we were told not to come near the cabin, that you would not welcome strangers."

"Ah, so you are the visitor old man Hayes was talking about the other day. His niece from New Orleans."

"No. I...I live in Bartlett."

"New to the area then?"

"No."

He smiled at her and her breath caught.

"I cannot believe we have not met before. I know most of the families in Bartlett." Daniel glanced at Caleb, then at Rachel. "You..." He cleared his throat and started again. "You mentioned a meeting. Is it with a gentleman friend?"

"Heavens no, I'm meeting with the program committee from church. We're working on our programs for the next year."

"Then you are not being courted by anyone?"

Shannon shook her head and tried to stifle her laugh, but failed. Courting was a word her granny had used when Shannon had brought one of her boyfriends home.

"May I come courting?"

"No." She drew in a deep breath, then said, "Listen, I enjoyed the stew, but I really do need to get back to the cabin."

"I understand. I had hoped you might be open to my courting, but I can tell if you are looking to court someone it will not be me. You are young and I should not have hoped that you would take on a family like mine."

"Wait. Just wait. All I did was help your daughter find you. I am not interested in..." she raised her hands, and did the quotation marks as she said. "Courting" you or anyone else."

"Ma'am. Please, I meant no harm."

"I'm sorry." She didn't want to be rude. For heaven's sake this was a dream, and she didn't need to snap at him for words that were of her own making. "Please take me back to Sanders Lodge."

"As you wish. Your time with us is almost over, Shannon, but you never know when someone will come into your life and touch your heart. Like I said, I had hoped it would be me."

"Daniel," Shannon rested her hand against his chest, "maybe another time. I'm just not ready. If I was interested in courting, you would certainly be in the running."

He moved her hand from his chest to his lips, then whispered, "Be ready, Shannon. You will find someone."

How had he known that's what she'd been thinking from the moment he'd found them wandering in the snow. She'd been so lonely. She wasn't about to admit it to him, but she wanted a family, even a ready-made one.

He reached for her coat and slipped it over her shoulders.

She felt the gentle tug and thought he was going to kiss her, but he closed his eyes and backed up a step.

"Caleb, keep the fire going and watch your sister while I take Shannon to the 'tree'."

Caleb nodded. "Yes, sir." He turned toward her and grinned. "Hope to see you again soon, Ms. Shannon."

Daniel grabbed his coat, glanced at each of the children, then opened the door for her.

They walked together as they'd come with his hand cupped in hers and resting against the small of his back while she walked in the impression made by his boots.

He released her hand as she glimpsed the Lodge in front of her. "I'm sorry I intruded on your privacy."

"I was glad to have the company," Daniel said.

Shannon raced up the steps into the screened-in porch. She turned back toward Daniel, and gasped. He stood inside the small fenced cemetery, holding Rachel in his arms and with Caleb by his side.

Tears trickled down Shannon's cheeks.

"Hey, Shannon, can you come help us bring in some of this food," Trina called from the doorway.

Shannon wiped her cheeks. "Coming, Trina."

She watched the snow-lined footprints that lead from the screen door to the rocker slowly disappear in the snow, then took a quick peek at the three graves.

Daniel smiled at her.

Rachel and Caleb waved. Rachel slipped to the ground in front of her daddy, and stood there. Caleb and Daniel faded into the stones nestled under the giant oak tree.

"We've got work to do, girl." Trina fussed when Shannon finally made it into the tiny kitchen. "Deborah is bringing her brother and his two kids with her."

"Whatever for?"

"He's not staying, but he wanted the kids to see this place. He used to come here as a boy to some camp they had. I told her he could stay for supper and meet the gang, but he can't."

One by one the program committee arrived for the annual planning session. They would get the schedule set, then decide who was going to have the Christmas party to launch the year.

Shannon glanced toward the back porch. Was Daniel real? Were the graves his and the children's?

He'd touched her deeply in the brief time they'd been together. The love he'd shown for his children made her hunger even more for someone who was the type of husband and father he had undoubtedly been.

Deborah made her grand entrance. Behind her, clinging to the hem of her coat was a small girl with a sheepish grin. "This is Rachel, my niece," Deborah said. "And this is Daniel and Caleb, my brother and nephew."

Shannon took a step back, and drew in a quick breath. Their eyes locked. Tears blurred her vision. She felt her coat pocket. Papers crackled. She slipped her hand into the pocket, and pulled out the wrappings of the bandage she'd put on "Rachel's" hand.

She glanced out back. Barely visible in the fading light she saw Rachel give one last wave before she vanished into the darkness.

"Ma'am?"

It took Shannon a moment to realize that the girl was talking to her. "What, Hun?"

"Can you tell me where the potty is?" she whispered.

She heard Daniel cough then laugh.

"Sorry, Miss...?"

"It's Shannon," she said. "And not a problem. I love kids."

Deborah followed Shannon and Rachel to the back of the cabin.

"I'll wait out here for you, Hun," Shannon said as she flipped on the light switch.

"Thank you," Rachel said. "Don't shut the door. It might lock and I don't want to be stuck."

Shannon laughed and left the door open. "How's that?"

"Good," Rachel said.

"Listen," Deborah said. "I hope you don't mind. I thought you might be...I'm trying to help Daniel...Damn it. His wife's death hit him hard. But it's been a year now and he needs to get out some. I don't know if you two will click or not, but you're my friend, and you both need somebody. He told me to bug off, that this was his life, and he would find someone when he was ready."

"Don't try to set us up, Deborah. I...I don't think I'm ready either."

"I saw that look on your face when he walked in. And I know you love kids. Please, if he asks you out, go for his sake. It's been awhile. You know how hard it is to ask someone out. I'm just saying give him a chance. If he knew I was asking you to go out with him he would kick me all the way home and back."

"Okay, okay. If he asks me, I'll go, but I'm just saying maybe you ought to let Daniel handle his own life."

"That's what I keep telling her," the child's voice broke into their conversation. "I gotta go now. Daddy said we needed to finish looking at this place before it gets dark."

Rachel ran between the two women and straight into her dad's arms.

"She's right. We do have to go. I promised Caleb we would drive through the grounds, then we're off to a movie that Rachel wants to see."

"Daddy, maybe Ms. Shannon can go with us."

"Ah, well, yes, but not this time she has a busy weekend ahead of her."

Deborah chuckled.

Daniel stood with Rachel in his arms and faced the two women. "Well, Shannon?"

"Pardon?"

"I think Rachel is impressed. She doesn't usually want anyone to intrude our family time. Since I know you can't join us tonight, how about Sunday night? I'm making stew for Deborah and her family. I'm sure she wouldn't care if you joined us. I'll tell you now, I make a mean stew.

*****

Barbara Christopher

St. Columba

St. Columba Conference and Retreat Center is a 145-acre wooded campus where groups can meet in a natural and peaceful area. Although it is close to Memphis, it feels like the wilderness, but with first class accommodations.

An Indisputable Event
Steve Bradshaw

"If Walter said he talked to a ghost, I believe him."
Jake wiped his hands on the oil rag hanging out his
back pocket and released the airlift. The silver '57
Chevy descended like a treasure from heaven.

"Nice car..." Teddy pocketed his cell and took in the
classic beauty as the wheels pushed into the wells,
and it settled on the stained concrete floor. He
pressed his cheek to the fender then slid his finger
out and back from his nose. "I don't see any damage."

"It was there. Up all night soft hammering that
fender. Then some touch-up paint, a little compound
and wax, and my famous buffing technique did the
job."

"You're good, man."

"Had to replace a headlight, too."

"Looks good as new."

"Thank God the chrome frame was okay. That
would've cost *mucho dinero* to replace."

"Keep forgettin' this car's fifty years old."

"Fifty-six..." Jake picked up a wrench and hung it
in its designated spot on the wall. Everything had a
place. He tossed the empty headlight box onto the
overflowing trash bin. It slid to the edge and stopped.
"Guess I need to dump that thing one of these days."

"Man, you were lucky. Could have been a lot
worse, if you believe Walter's text." Teddy gently
prodded and waited for Jake to say something, but
Jake wasn't biting.

"I can't believe you're lettin' Walter off the hook on this."

Jake nudged him off the car and leaned over the fender with a new polishing cloth. "Walter's not like you." He wiped off Teddy's cheek smudge and greasy finger line. "You never tell the truth. Been that way as long as I can remember. Walter tells the truth. I got no reason to doubt him now."

"I don't tell the truth? Bull. And this isn't about me, Jake."

"Fact is Walter doesn't lie." He kept buffing the car as though his father was standing behind him saying, *put more elbow in it, son.*

"I've told my share of lies growin' up, but nothin' like this one."

Jake pushed his oil-smudged, *John Deere* cap up his forehead revealing the tan line. "What're you tryin' to say?"

"If you don't see, there's nothin' I can say that's gonna matter."

"No. Go ahead and say it. I don't want to deal with it for weeks."

"*Fine.* Walter borrowed your old man's precious, classic '57 Chevy for a date night. He brings it back with a broken headlight, dented fender, and some crazy-ass story about running into a ghost that lives in the drainage tunnels under Memphis. That's the most enormous line of bullshit I've ever heard. I'm sayin' Walter's tryin' to get away with somethin'. He messed up your dad's car. The man's dancing and you're not doing anything about it."

Jake shook his head as he squatted next to a front tire. "Walter's not like that."

"Right. I heard. He never lies. Tunnel ghosts are real. Everybody knows that, Jake."

"We grew up together. You know Walter." He unscrewed the stem cap and checked the air pressure. "He just doesn't make things up."

"You believe in tunnel ghosts...the departed, angry, souls that prey on Memphians?"

"I believe Walter. He's always been straight with me."

"Then you're both nuts..."

"Walter's always been the quiet one. When he speaks, he's a voice of reason. Never blows stuff up. Never misleads. Never lies." Jake moved to the next tire.

"I'll give you that, but I'm not buyin' the story about a tunnel ghost. That kind of stuff only happens in the movies. Normal people know ghosts don't exist. And if they did exist, Walter should have been able to drive right through the damn thing." Teddy laughed. "Everybody knows that."

"For someone who doesn't believe in ghosts, how can you be sure about that? Maybe there are some ghosts out there you can't drive through."

"I'll tell you what happened. Walter ran into somethin' that was alive and real. He was showin' off or doin' somethin' stupid, not payin' attention. Walter doesn't want to look like a dope. That's normal. And he sure as hell doesn't want to pay a ton to fix this classic. Teddy wants you to sympathize and go easy on him. That's why he came up with that lame story. You gotta understand people and motives."

Jake got up, staring into space. Wiping his air gauge with his dirty rag, he said, "When Walter was talking to me last night, somethin' was different about him."

"Different how...?"

"It was like he went through somethin' really bad, just happened. He was tryin' to figure it out. He was relivin' it, not making up somethin'. Walter was scared."

"You've never been good at reading people, Jake."

"I don't need to read people. I keep it simple. There are people who tell the truth and people who don't."

The morning sun peeked through the lowest windows of the garage doors. "You're gonna rub the chrome off that air gauge," Teddy mused. "Walter had a good reason to lie. He wanted to get out of payin' for the repairs."

"He gave me two-hundred bucks before he said anything about the accident. Offered three. I told him two was probably more than enough. This has nothing to do with money."

"He gave you two-hundred bucks?"

"Kind of shoots a big hole in your theory," Jake chuckled.

"Then he had some other reason to make up this crazy story."

"You remember that old, deserted house on Harvester we went inside to smoke pot? You found that dead body in the closet."

Teddy moved to a shadow by the workbench. The station didn't open for a few more hours. "I wish you guys would stop bringing up Harvester. That was years ago. We were teenagers. It's not relevant...has nothing to do with this ghost thing."

"It is relevant. You were the first to run out, to abandon your best friends. When faced with danger, your true colors came out—yellow."

"I told you guys a hundred times I thought you were behind me."

"You didn't look back for two blocks. If you had, you'd 'a seen we were not there. All you cared about was saving your own hide. And this illustrates another thing. To this day you won't deal with the

Harvester incident. You still lie to yourself. You have a problem and we're still your friends."

"I'm not lying about Harvester, damn it."

"You were scared and ran. If you had not opened that closet, never would have known there was a dead body there. You thought the guy was a zombie."

"He was standing there lookin' at me for God's sake."

"No. He was hanging from the clothes bar. The guy hung himself a year before we found him. He was mummified—like beef jerky—except for what the rats ate."

"We didn't know much until the story made the news."

"Walter looked in the closet after you flew the coop. He told me what he saw. Thought it was a zombie too. His description sounded crazy, but I knew he wouldn't make up stuff or play tricks on me. Walter was telling me what he saw in that closet."

Teddy rubbed his eyes. "I still see that dead man in my nightmares."

"Last night Walter had the same look on his face. You couldn't see that in a text message."

"He did? Then cut me a little slack."

"You're the one dissin' Walter."

"Come on, a Memphis tunnel ghost, really. That's just like talking about a zombie."

"I've never believed in ghosts before."

"People who claim to see those things are missing brain cells and usually some teeth."

Jake moved to the back of the Chevy and knelt by the tire. "You're not just a pathological liar. You're a judgmental prick, too. Walter saw something. He believes it was a Memphis tunnel ghost. Walter's not missing brain cells or teeth." Jake stood up and slid his air gauge into his pocket. "I wasn't gonna show you. Follow me."

Jake went to the storage room on the other side of the next bay. Teddy hesitated. Although he acted tough, he was the biggest chicken of the three.

"Come on, Teddy."

He navigated the stacks of tires and teetering cases of motor oil to the dark, cold back room he never liked. Behind the painted cinderblock wall was a pitiful lamp burning on a metal bench in the dark recesses of the dank, cluttered room. Jake stood next to the bench and an old refrigerator. He waved Teddy closer. As he approached, Jake opened the freezer door, and took out a box lid covered with a faded red shop cloth over a lump. He set it on the bench under the lamp.

"I'm gonna show you somethin' that might help you with all of this talk..."

"Unless you caught a baby ghost, there's nothin' you can show me that would change my opinion on all this tunnel ghost crap."

"Don't freak out and run away halfcocked. I gotta show this to someone, and it can't be Walter. Not now. Not until he calms down." Jake stared at the lump. "This is not from our world."

"Quit trying to scare me, Jake. I don't need to see this."

"You're right. I'll put it back—never mind. Forget I said anything."

"No. I'm here now. Show me what's got your undies in a wad."

Jake put on work gloves and pinched two corners of the cloth, and lifted. Teddy's eyes widened as his mouth tightened into a small circle. Jake turned to him and watched the blood drain from his face. "You gonna be okay, Teddy? You're not gonna faint are you?"

"What in the hell is that...?"

Jake turned back. "I don't know. I think it is part of something."

"Holy shit...!"

"I know. Weird huh...?" Jake stared at it under the lamp. "For some reason I feel like it could explode or something. That's why I keep it in the freezer."

"Holy shit...!"

"You said that, Teddy." Jake pulled up a stool and sat. "This was stuck inside the headlight. Walter didn't see it or he would have said something. Most was poking out the back of the light, hanging in the wheel-well."

"Looks like some kind of appendage. If it's a finger, the thing it belongs to is big. If it's an arm or leg, the thing is smaller than us."

"It's gray on one side and bright white on the other—like a shark. Measures eight inches. It's skinny at one end with this talon and muscular at the fat end where I think it was attached."

"No hair." Teddy pointed. "And this cluster of white noodles hanging out of it may be blood vessels. See that honey-like stuff oozing? Not frozen...odd."

"It's syrupy and the color of blood serum," Jake said in a trance. "This cardboard box lid was bone dry a few hours ago."

"Creepy. Still dripping," Teddy muttered.

Jake leaned back, and Teddy looked up over at him. "There's another reason I believe Walter's story. He described the tunnel ghost he hit."

"Oh he did. This is gonna be good. What did Walter say?"

"It was over six feet tall. The grayish blackish color duplicated the night darkness. He said before he hit the tunnel ghost the headlights made the thing glow. He described its head as round with a bunch of eyes, maybe twenty."

"How many...?"

"Too many to count. A few big eyes and a lot of small ones."

"Only eyes on the round head?"

"There was a mouth, an unusually large smile with pointy teeth. And it spoke to Walter."

"He got out the car and talked to the thing?"

"No. It talked to him in his head. It said it was from the tunnel, and it's time."

"I'm not surprised."

Jake leaned against the refrigerator staring at the find. "Walter said it got up and jumped into the culvert."

"Where...?"

"Somewhere on North Second outside the city."

"That's sufficiently vague."

"He did get out of the car to investigate."

"Was he alone...no date?"

"Yes. Dropped her off and was coming here."

"Figures..."

"It was gone. A hundred feet away was an entrance into the city drainage tunnels."

"Sorry. I just don't believe in ghosts, Jake. They do not exist."

"Then how do you explain this?"

"Simple. Walter ran into an animal, a big one with a disease like mange or rabies. It lost a lot of hair and looks spooky and acts weird. When headlights found the sick animal, it reared up on its hind legs, looked way bigger than it was."

"Not a lot of animals in west Tennessee can look six foot, even rearing up and all. Don't think there are bears around Memphis."

"It happened in a flash. It was late. Walter was tired. He imagined things, even the stuff he thinks he heard in his head. That sick animal ran off somewhere to die, simple as that."

Jake dropped the rag over the appendage. "Ghosts would already be dead."

"The ghosts in the movies are shadows or white foggy things that pass through walls. That thing on that cardboard is a piece of a diseased animal, Jake."

"You're probably right."

"The stories about evil demons in drainage tunnels under Memphis are folklore. Someone started that crap fifty years ago because the tunnels are spooky, dark and dangerous. City doesn't want us traipsing around miles of big-ass pipes under Memphis. Lost people would tie up the damn fire department. Best way to stop it from happening is to encourage the junk about the tunnel ghosts, our own underworld taking Memphians in the night."

"I'm not saying I disagree, but I read four thousand people are reported missing in Memphis every year. Half are runaways, but that leaves two thousand nobody knows about. What if these tunnel ghosts are real? What if Walter did hit one?"

"They're not real. It's all bullshit."

Jake straightened the shop cloth on the box lid, and pulled off his gloves. "Walter said he went in the tunnel, Teddy."

"He didn't text me that, although I don't blame him. I was pretty brutal after the first text. So tell me, did he meet his wounded tunnel ghost?" Teddy chuckled as his confidence returned.

"I asked, but he cut me off. Said we'd talk later..."

"What're you guys doing?"

The words came from the doorway behind them. They turned. Walter stood with legs apart and hands hanging at his sides like a gunfighter. Teddy started toward him as Jake moved in front of his find.

"Where the hell have you been, man? You're not responding to texts or answering your phone. We've been waiting to hear from you." Teddy looked back at Jake and winked.

Walter ignored the question and leaned to see. "What are you doing, Jake? You never come back here."

"Nothin' much. I just finished compounding and waxing the fender I worked on all night. Had stuff all over me. Came back here to get it off."

"What's going on with you, Walter?" asked Teddy.

"We started talkin' about your accident." Jake turned pushed the box lid into the dark. "You see my repairs? Fender's good as new." He pushed by both, and snaked through the stacks of tires and boxes. Teddy followed Jake. Walter looked into the room and then joined them at the Chevy.

"Here, take this." Jake stuffed a hundred dollar bill in Walter's hand. "It wasn't that bad after all." *I forgot to turn off the light.*

Walter looked at the bill and then the overflowing trash bin. He saw the box teetering on the edge. "You replaced a headlight?"

"Yeah. It was no big deal. Had one in stock— standard stuff."

"You find anything unusual?"

"Not really." He would not tell him about the appendage until it felt right.

"You gonna to tell us what really happened last night?" asked Teddy. Jake kept busy moving tools from bench to the wall.

"No."

Teddy got in his face. "Why not, Walter...?"

"I'll show you."

"When?"

"Now..."

"Ha-ha, like I'm going with you to meet a *tunnel ghost!* That is not gonna happen, my friend. I'm not gettin' bit by some wild, diseased animal you think is a stupid ghost."

Jake stepped between them. "What do you want to show us, Walter?"

"He probably found its nest in those pipes." Teddy laughed alone.

"It's not something I can explain," said Walter. "It'll take thirty minutes. You'll be back in time to open your garage."

Walter went out the back door and waved them to follow. "I found a way to get there from here." He climbed the hill behind the station pushing through the tall weeds, and stopped on the crest before the woods. The trail had been traveled recently. Tall grass lay flat.

The ten minute trek ended in a small ravine. They followed Walter up a dry creek bed to a thick cluster of bushes. He lifted a limb revealing the opening to a massive drainage pipe.

"Never knew this was here," said Teddy. "Must be seven-foot diameter." They had been in those woods a hundred times growing up, but the trail, ravine, dry creek bed, and drainage pipe were all new.

"Follow me." Walter opened the hanging lone vine and climbed into the pipe.

"I'm not goin' in there," Teddy declared.

Walter turned holding three flashlights. He tossed one to Jake and the other to Teddy. "Come on. This is really cool. Don't be a sissy, Teddy. There're no zombies."

Jake climbed in, turned on his light and went deeper. Teddy caught up. Walter was focused. He stayed far enough ahead to keep the pace moving while avoiding talk. After another ten minutes Walter stopped. When they caught up they discovered they were in a larger tunnel. It was bricked with a thirty-foot ceiling. There were portals in the walls, smaller pipes connecting to the main drainage pipe. Their lights were lost in the cavernous abyss under Memphis.

"We are here," Walter declared as he sat down.

"What the hell does that mean, we are here? Where the hell is here?" Teddy moved his light up and down the tunnel. It was eerie and empty in both directions. Jake sat next to Walter.

"Teddy, point your light down," whispered Walter. They were sitting at the center of a twenty-foot circle of thick, green moss.

"Holy shit...! What's this—moss? Impossible. There's no sunlight down here. Moss needs the damn sun." Teddy slid his foot on the spongy surface. "I don't get it. Vegetation must have sun for photosynthesis. Ten feet into the tunnel the growth stopped. Thirty feet in, there was no sign of animal life. Stuff can't live in darkness like this...except a rat or cockroach."

"This is where it brought me. I hit him on Second. I don't know how it got me to this place so fast. Must be a mile away." Walter got up. "Stay here." He walked into the darkness without his light. Teddy soon lost him. He and Jake waited in silence. Walter yelled from the darkness. "I was supposed to bring you here."

"Supposed to bring us here...?" Teddy whispered. "What the hell does that mean?"

"The *Trintorns* are here," Walter's words echoed.

"What's a *Trintorn*?" Teddy yelled. Jake swallowed hard, got to his feet, and backed away. Then Walter walked into Teddy's searching beam.

"It's one name we use for them—tunnel ghosts." Walter arched his back and looked up. His flashlight was still burning on the thick carpet of moss. He covered his ears and froze in place.

"Now that's just frightening," Teddy said. "Is it me, or is it getting colder down here? And does Walter look grayish to you...?"

"Do I look *what*?" asked Walter. Teddy turned back to glaring eyes inches away.

"I said grayish. I said you look grayish to me, Walter. Back off or I'll pound you."

Walter did not move.

"You brought us through a big-ass pipe we've never seen in our life, and we've been tromping in these woods forever. Did I let that stop me? Hell no...!" He passed the beam over the moss. "And this shit in the middle of nowhere is beyond strange."

"Calm down, Teddy," Jake said, trying to keep under control.

"No. None of this makes sense. Moss needs sun goddamn it! Walter's acting like a weirdo, holding his damn ears, looking at the damn roof of this damn tunnel, and climbing into my face. What's going on with you, Walter? Tell us why we are here."

Walter's face softened as he backed away. "They took me. They did things to me."

"Who took you?" asked Jake. "What did they do?"

"The *Trintorns*...after I hit one in your car. They wanted my *chymalta*. They said after that they'd leave me alone."

"What the hell is *chymalta*?" demanded Teddy.

"DNA. Said they've been taking it from people for a very long time."

"What's a very long time?"

"Said I wouldn't understand. Their time is different."

"Well that's just great. Tunnel ghosts took some of your DNA. That's gotta be the best line of bullshit I've ever heard, coupled with this big tunnel and all this friggin moss. Man, you must be smoking some really good weed to set this one up."

Walter's empty face didn't change. He held his hands out. Both palms were bright white, luminescent. The rest of his arms were dark gray, blending with the surrounding darkness. "What the hell's going on with you, Walter?"

"*Chymalta* is their *tresupta*," he mumbled and dropped his chin to his chest.

"DNA is *tresupta* too? What the hell is *tresupta*?" asked Teddy as he backed to the center of the thick moss circle, and Jake backed to the brick wall.

Standing at the edge of Teddy's beam Walter unbuttoned his shirt. "*Tresupta* means connection." He dropped his shirt and lifted his head, his mouth, an odd and hideous smile. When he spoke, his lips did not move. "*Biovens* have been here four-hundred-thousand years. *Trintorns* are forever...been here from the beginning. This is their world, not ours."

"*Biovens*...that's us, mankind, the human race," Jake mumbled. He leaned back on the brick wall and blinked. His eyes burned.

Walter nodded. "Life has been here four million years. *Trintorns* came before life. They allow *Biovens* to be here."

"So these tunnel ghosts allow us to live on our planet earth? Now I know you're smoking grade-A dope. If that was true, and we knew they were taking our DNA, we'd flood these tunnels in a heartbeat. If that didn't work, we'd blow the place up. They'd be history, Walter."

"*Trintorns* manage the human race. They require a steady supply of DNA. It's like oxygen to them. Our health and procreation are vital. *Trintorns* would never jeopardize our existence. They are everywhere. And they are in the tunnels under Memphis."

"They suck DNA out of us like a hideous parasite, and sneak around the planet managing the human race. We're their personal herd of cattle. Hell, if this bullshit is true, we're nothing more than a next meal for these *Trintorns*."

"Walter's pointed teeth flashed. Jake slid down the wall in shock. Oblivious, Teddy aimed his light in search of an exit. Walter flipped his hair back revealing four eyes on his forehead. They blinked in unison. "It's time for you to go..."

"You got that right." Teddy turned his light back on Walter. "Holy shit...!"

"They want you, Teddy. The *Trintorns* want you."

"God...! What happened to your face, Walter? Are those friggin' eyes? And what are you talkin' about, they want me?"

Teddy tried to back away. He looked down. He was stuck in the moss. It covered his shoes. "What's going on? I can't move my feet." He frantically pulled handfuls of moss from his shoes. It was replaced with more. It climbed over his ankles and up his legs to his waist.

"My God, what's happening? Walter...Jake...help me! My legs, it's squeezing hard. My skin's burning and freezing at the same time. I can't move. I'm getting numb."

Jake watched in horror, frozen against the wall. "Walter," he yelled. "I don't know what's happened to you but we've gotta help Teddy. We've gotta stop this. He's our friend?"

"The *Trintorns* want Teddy," Walter mumbled as the shiny, green moss climbed over Teddy's shoulders, and pulled his arms to his body in a tightening cocoon.

"We've got to do something. He's going to suffocate when that stuff gets to his face." Jake left the wall and stepped onto the mossy carpet ten feet from his struggling friend. But it could have been ten miles. His foot would not move any further.

"They know you're frightened, Jake. They know it's for Teddy, not for you."

"I can't move." Jake looked down. "But my shoes aren't covered with that moss."

"They want you to stay where you are. For now...they want Teddy."

Jake watched in helpless desperation as the moss climbed Teddy's neck and folded over his head leaving only his eyes, nose, and mouth uncovered. Then it seemed to stop.

"We gotta help him now. It's stopped." Jake tried to break free but could not move.

"Look at his face," Walter whispered.

Jake's eyes met Teddy's. Jake would never forget the look the night Teddy thought he saw a zombie, or when Teddy's brother died in the car accident. And he knew the look in Teddy's eyes when he got the red racer for Christmas, and when he fell in love with Emily. Now Jake saw that look. Teddy's eyes were happy, celebrating, filled with wonder.

"He's happy," said Walter. "They said he would be happy."

Teddy smiled and he spoke to Jake. "I'm good. I want this. Let me go." Then Teddy closed his eyes and the moss streamed over his face.

"They won't hurt him, Jake. They never hurt anything." The tunnel started to glow. It got brighter and brighter. They were everywhere. They were standing around Teddy and Jake and Walter. The soft white light emanated from the countless masses of *Trintorns* that filled the tunnel in both directions as far as they could see.

You are as Walter said, Jake thought as he took in the impossible. *You're all alike: six feet tall, multiple eyes and that awful mouth with those hideous teeth, and you have gray and white skin. Your long arms and claws fit the torn appendage I found. And I hear you talking in my head. I don't know the words except for chymalta and tresupta and bioven. You need our DNA to live. "Tresupta" is more than just a "connection". I see now. It's a "hook". It's how you capture us. It's how you take control. How have you taken for so long and not been detected...stopped?*

Teddy was a motionless, moss covered lump surrounded by glowing *Trintorns*. Jake's feet were released. He returned to the wall. Walter's forehead eyes were gone, and his mouth was normal, and skin color back. He was dressed as before. The green, undulating moss that covered Teddy's body turned white in a flash. It fell from him like leaves from a tree.

"Wait. Where is Teddy?" whispered Jake. "That's not him." When all the white flakes settled, a new *Trintorn* stood where Teddy once was.

"He's been converted. One-hundred percent of his DNA is now *Trintorn*. He is happy."

Jake rubbed his eyes. "Teddy turned into one of them?"

"He will need nothing for 1,000 of our years."

"Teddy will need nothing?" The glow in the tunnel grew.

"He will live forever, experience other worlds and other dimensions. Teddy has evolved, Jake. This is evolution. This is where we all go…like angels."

"A person can't just disappear like that, Walter. People will be looking for Teddy," Jake whispered as the *Trintorns* surrounded their new entity.

"There will be an investigation, a lot of questions. If we get out of here alive, we'll be the first they grill. I won't hold up, Walter. They'll find out what happened here. Police will find this place, find the evidence. This is gonna get out. These *Trintorns* will not be a secret anymore."

"Teddy chose to go with the *Trintorns*. Before the moss closed over his face, he saw his future…his options. He could have chosen to stay here as Teddy or become a *Trintorn*. The process would have stopped. Teddy chose, Jake."

"You're not hearing me. There will be a search for Teddy, a major investigation in these tunnels. This whole *Trintorn* thing is going to be exposed."

Walter grabbed Jake's shoulders. "No there won't be an investigation in this tunnel. Teddy is in your garage."

Jake broke free from Walter's grip. "Teddy's alive? Teddy's in my garage?"

"The airlift failed. Your dad's '57 Chevy crushed Teddy. He died instantly. It was a tragic accident. Teddy died."

"I don't understand. There's no airlift accident. Teddy's not in my garage. He's here somewhere in this tunnel under Memphis. They need to get him back."

"The *Trintorns* are good at this stuff. They've been doing it a long time," Walter mused. "They don't disrupt populations. Their 'human conversion process' is what we view as death: accidents, suicides, homicides and natural deaths. And it feeds the missing-persons statistics."

"This makes no sense."

"Once they accept someone into the *Trintorn* realm, they display a copy in a death state. If it's a complicated subject, they'll not leave a copy—a missing person. If there's a mass conversion, it could be a plane crash or war or something big."

Jake turned back to where Teddy once stood. To his amazement the tunnel was empty. Teddy was gone. The thick moss covered circle was gone. The glow was gone. The ghosts that filled the tunnel were gone. Fresh air was replaced with warm, stale, putrid air.

"Where did it all go?"

"They could still be here. We can't see them anymore. They're where they want to be."

"Invisible...?"

"They're rarely detected because they can blend perfectly with their surroundings. It's kind of like a *super-chameleon*. Tunnel ghosts are the highest order, most powerful. They prefer night and dark and underground habitats. The sun makes work for them—too many color adjustments to stay stealthy. The ones you saw here, they are the area *Trintorns* responsible for pursuit and acquisition of *chymalta*."

"*Trintorns* are all over the world?" Jake mumbled. "So when they're encountered, that's when people think they've seen a ghost—it's unexplainable and unprovable." Jake looked at his feet shaking his head. "Now what happens?"

"We forget all of this. We'll be in your garage when it happens, when Teddy has his fatal accident. Won't know it's gonna happen. Can't stop it."

"This is not right, Walter. Teddy was killed! They took him. He was begging for help. You saw what I saw."

"Teddy had a choice."

"The *Trintorns* took control of all of us. They took Teddy." Jake grabbed Walter's arms and shook him. He spit the words in his face. "Teddy did not choose to die today. He did not choose to leave everything and everyone he knows..."

"He chose his future. They all do."

Jake pushed Walter hard against the brick wall. He was always the strongest of the three. "This is wrong. This is murder. We can't let it happen. Teddy's our friend. The *Trintorns* are the monsters. They don't care about you, Walter. They have you under some mind control thing. They'll get around to me next. These tunnel ghosts must be stopped..."

*****

The crowd buzzed as the county medical examiner walked out of *Jake's Gas Station* with head down followed by assistants pushing a long, lumpy, black body bag on a stretcher. In silence they loaded the crash bag into the ambulance and slammed the doors. When it pulled out, the once spinning lights were off and blaring sirens silent.

As crowds thinned as the fire truck finished rolling the hose and were the next to leave. A Memphis police squad car was parked outside the open bay door crossed with yellow tape. An officer sat in the front seat talking into a microphone. Still in shock, Walter and Jake sat on the curb under the rusted canopy with the locked gas pumps. They had watched their best friend die a horrible death beneath the '57 Chevy. The airlift gave way. He was pinned to the floor. 3,232 pounds of metal and 257 pounds of lift dropped six feet in one second—a freak accident.

"We've got everything we need, fellas." The investigating officer flipped a few pages on his clipboard. "Walter Bradley, I need you to sign first. You were the eyewitness to the accident. Jake Mathews was not in the bay at the time. This report has everything you told us."

Jake jumped to his feet and ran around the side of the garage to puke. The officer took a deep breath and waited for him to return. "I know this was awful for you boys."

"Yes, sir." Walter took the pen and scribbled his name. Jake's face was white as snow.

"Mr. Mathews, I need you to sign as the owner and operator of this service station." He passed the clipboard and pen to Jake. His answers to all the questions had been short. He scribbled his name in silence.

Squinting at the setting sun, the officer flipped pages. "Okay. Mr. William Boyle, of *Airlock Lifts Incorporated,* completed his onsite inspection and certifies this was equipment related, a mechanical failure. There was a spontaneous pressure release during lockdown. The safety mechanism was engaged. He couldn't get the release lever out of the lockdown mode. Jake, that's good for you."

"What's that mean...good for me?" He looked up for the first time.

"I'm sorry. Don't mean to be insensitive. You lost a friend today. I'm speakin' from a liability standpoint. This was a mechanical failure. It was out of your control. Not an operator error. This is what we call an 'indisputable event.'"

"Indisputable event...?" Jake had heard that term before.

"Means the insurance company picks up the tab and you're not charged or fined. There are no suspicious circumstances about this accident. You and Mr. Mathews are not liable."

"You mean we could have gone to jail because Teddy died in my garage?"

"Yup. If you fellas were found guilty of negligence or foul play, you coulda lost this garage, and both of ya coulda been sent to jail for a long time." He closed his clipboard. "Your friend was over twenty-one. His decision to get under that Chevy on that rack was his to make. You're not responsible for his decision. You got it posted all over, nobody's allowed in the bays. And you weren't in the area at the time of the accident tah boot."

"This is an indisputable event," *like when our house burned to the ground two years ago killing my parents...*

"Yes...an indisputable event...nothin else tah do 'bout it."

"What about me? I was there. I was standing right next to Teddy before the lift came down. If I had not gone for a wrench, I would have been..."

"The mechanical failure clears you, no tampering with the lift lock, Mr. Bradley. Mr. Boyle said it was a fluke accident. They've seen it a few times. This is the third with this model of airlifts. He said this tragic event will put these lifts on a recall. His company will kill the product. Not worth the time or money to figure out what's going wrong with it."

"What do we do now?" asked Jake. His eyes were red and nose running.

The officer squatted next to them. "You two must learn to accept what happened here today, understand there was nothing you could have done to save your friend's life. It was an accident. This stuff happens." Jake dropped his head. Walter stared, his face empty.

"Let me give you fellas some advice. Mourn your loss. Go to the funeral and say goodbye to your friend. Then, remember the good times. Then get on with your life. He's in a better place."

Jake looked at his shoes until the last policeman pulled off the lot. They sat in silence until the sun was almost down. It kept playing over and over in his head; *this place is all I have left after losing my family in that house fire—my first 'indisputable event'. It grounded me; I didn't feel so alone. But now it's all different. Now it's the place where Teddy died.*

"He died awful, but it was fast," Walter mumbled as he pushed his stick in the dirt.

Jake was jerked from inner turmoil. "Ah...where are your parents?"

Walter seemed alert, less touched by the tragedy. "They left when police took us aside."

I don't want you here. "Call them to get you. You should go home tonight." Jake picked up a handful of pebbles. Aiming at an old rusty oil drum, he skipped one across the lot and missed.

"I called. They're on their way."

Jake hit the light switch. The outside floods popped on. He saw Walter moving his stick in the dirt between his shoes, the accumulation from the last rains where the concrete slab sank deepest. It was always there. Jake skipped another stone. "You ever wonder why people die like that..."

"The way Teddy died?" asked Walter.

"Yeah, like Teddy."

"Not really..."

"The floodlights flickered and one popped out. There were two left. "You believe in God, Walter...?"

He skipped another stone just missing the oil drum on the edge of the lot.

"I think so."

"You think God takes people at certain times for a reason?" asked Jake.

"I do."

"Maybe, but I don't think God decides how someone's gonna die. He didn't hurt Teddy." Jake skipped another and it found the drum. He smiled until the next car slowed on Thomas in front of his garage. "People are already *rubber-necking* this place."

"It'll be in the news tonight. Probably forgotten by most in a day or two."

Jake dropped his stones and went to the pumps. He jiggled the locks on the handles and watched Walter push his stick like he was drawing something. "Wonder why it was Teddy's time to go, not mine or yours."

Walter dropped his stick and got up. He slapped dirt from his pants. "Don't take this the wrong way, but Teddy lied all the time." Walter spit. "Just sayin'..."

"You think God took Teddy because he lies?"

"Don't know. Maybe God's trying to get certain things done at certain times—that's all."

"That's a terrible thought, Walter. No way I believe God's like that."

"Just a thought passed through my head." Walter spit again. He stood there like it was any other day. He could have been waiting for a bus or in line to a football game.

"When I was a kid my mom told me God cares about each of us. He's got a plan."

"I've heard that before. Don't know."

"One time I was in my car with my cousin. He's only five. I put the key in the ignition and started the car. My little cousin said my key was magic."

"Funny. He thought your key was magic..." Walter looked bored, eager to leave. It had been a whole day and they were both tired.

"My cousin had no clue what was goin' on under the hood of my car. He sees a key and then three thousand pounds of metal moves down the road. I was like God because I knew more. I knew there was an engine under that hood, how it works, when it's broke, and when to haul it to the junkyard. God's like that with everything."

Headlights turned onto the lot. "My parents...Better go," Walter said. "They won't come over here, will keep a respectable distance. They don't handle tragedies well." He turned back to Jake. "You wanna spend the night? Probably not good for you to be alone."

The second floodlight popped out. Jake looked up. "Only got one more..." He shook his head. "No thanks. I'm good." Walter crossed the crumbling cement, got in the backseat, and the old station wagon crawled onto Thomas and went north. Jake looked back at his last floodlight. It started to flicker.

Is that how God works? What decides the time we leave this place and go somewhere else? If my parents lived, would I be here now, this place? Would Teddy die in my garage?

On his way back to lock up for the night, Jake stopped at the curb where they had sat all afternoon talking to police. He looked down as he thought about Teddy and the horrific pain he must have experienced under all that steel. *Did you feel anything? Did you have time to be scared? Maybe God takes that away.*

Jake noticed lines in the dirt where Walter had been poking around. There was a line from a square to a circle. There was a large stone in the center of the circle with dozens of white pebbles around it that tailed off in two directions. And there were two black stones outside the circle. *This is weird. But why does it feel familiar...and frightening?*

Jake pushed his hat back, wiped his face, and forced a look into the bay. *I gotta go in there sooner or later to shut things down.* He squeezed closed his eyes until they were wet. Then he blinked them dry and went inside.

Standing in the bay where Teddy died, Jake eyed the yellow crime tape around the lift, the police forgot to take. Although the fire department hosed away the blood, they missed some. Jake could see it on the inner side of the lift. That red splash and the sweet smell were nauseating. He had the dry heaves. There was nothing more to give. Then he saw the '57 Chevy. It sat outside the bay doors. *I'll stay closed tomorrow, clean it up and air it out.*

He hit off the lights and went outside to his car. He stared at the big fins and polished chrome headlights, and thought about the minutes before Teddy died. *I was under there with you. We were gonna unscrew the oil plug. It was tight. I needed a wrench. Then the outside bell rang. I left you and Walter for not even a minute. Was just gonna tell the people I was still closed. But when I stepped off that curb the place was empty; no car at the pumps, no cars on Thompson. Then it happened, that loud crash, the yelling, and then the silence...*

Jake found his favorite buffing cloth on the hood. *What's this doing out here? And it looks like there's been work on the fender.* He picked up the cloth. *It's how I fold, left to right three times. Why don't I* remember? He opened the cloth—*dried compound*— and unfolded it the rest of the way—*moist.* Then he saw the light in the back storage room. *Missed that. Guess the police pokin' around and left it on. Sure wasn't me. That place gives me the creeps, always has.*

The lamp was burning. There was a glossy sheen on the surface of the metal workbench. *This is strange...*

He turned off the lamp and heard something. Jake looked back at the door. "Walter? Is that you? Did you come back for somethin'...?" Jake rubbed his eyes. The doorway was empty. *I'm losing it. Imagining things now.* He took a step forward and tripped. He found it in the dark. A lid to a cardboard box left lying around. And it was sticky. He carried it to the bay and tossed it on top of the trash bin. Jake didn't see the empty headlight box drop to the floor.

Why bring up that Teddy lies? Sure came out of nowhere. Although it's true, it's a lousy thing to say hours after our friend got killed.

Jake went outside, locked the door, and glanced down at the lines and pebbles in the dirt. *Why did you take Teddy, not me or Walter? And why did you take my parents and let me live? They found me unconscious under a tree. No one knows how I got there. My parents were dead. They said the fire that killed them was electrical, an indisputable event...*

He started walking toward the '57 Chevy, and then stopped in the dark parking lot. *I remember. I replaced the headlight.* Jake ran to the car and rubbed his hand over the cold chrome. It too was sticky. The last floodlight popped out. He stood alone in the dark. The road was empty. *I remember! Walter hit a...*

The woods behind the garage started to glow.

*****

Underground Memphis

Every city has its underground waterways and sewer system. Memphis is no exception. The Gayoso Ditch, so foul that it probably bred the mosquitoes that caused the great Memphis Yellow Fever Epidemic, was only covered over in the 1880s. When the new ball field was built for the St. Louis farm team, it was unearthed, and had to be recovered. Even though the system carries only wastewater these days, it is still the dark home to snakes, rats, bats, and who knows what—or who—else?

A Haunting in Midtown
Kristi Bradley

The wood door swung open with a screech. Hailey flipped the switch on the wall. The lights flickered, caught, and burned steady. A noise stopped her in the doorway. "Did you hear that?"

"Hear what?" Lynn asked, pushed past her friend to set the box she carried on a nearby end table with a thump.

"I swear I heard a scream."

Lynn laughed. "Probably the wind. In an old house like this, I imagine you're gonna hear weird stuff all the time. Hey, can I borrow your navy cocktail dress?"

Hailey followed her in with two more boxes. "Of course. I appreciate you helping me move the last of my things. If I hadn't inherited this house, I'd have to move back home."

Lynn flinched at the thought of having to move in with her parents, said, "Now you have no excuse not to fix this place up. It's what your aunt wanted." She glanced around the room. "I just love this craftsman style. This place will be great once you freshen it up a bit. The screened-in front porch is my favorite."

Hailey's aunt had passed away a few months earlier. She'd fallen in the tub, hit her head and drowned. Having no children of her own, she'd left her only niece the property on McNeil Street built in 1920, located in the Evergreen Historic District, not far from the zoo. Hailey had always loved the house, especially the stained glass in the windows on each side of the wood-burning fireplace. "I can't believe it's really mine."

"And Tyler wanted you to sell it."

"I don't want to think about him right now." She turned, led Lynn to the bedroom she'd claimed until she finished the upstairs master, and plucked the dress from the closet.

"I'm sorry if I hit a nerve, but I think it's is a good thing he's out of the picture. Thanks for letting me borrow this."

"It's the least I can do after you helped me move. Have a good time."

"I plan on it. I'll get the dress cleaned and bring it back in a few days." Lynn bounded out the door.

Hailey followed, said, "No rush. See you later." She watched Lynn drive away, then locked herself inside. She sighed heavily, pushed her hair behind her ears, and unpacked the last of her belongings she'd moved from her ex-boyfriend's place.

After cleaning out the room that would be her office, storing the unused furniture in the garage out back, Hailey wandered onto the front porch. Nightfall stirred the streetlights to life. A couple walked past. They held hands, flirted with each other.

Her breath hitched. Tyler and she had been exclusive for three years. His indifference over her aunt's death had infuriated her. Things had gone downhill from there. Hailey stood, strode inside to click on the TV in hopes of a distraction. The love story she found sickened her. She changed the channel. Another love story.

"Ugh!" She flicked the remote again.

Luckily, she had this house and the inheritance from her aunt to soften the blow of losing her boyfriend and her job in the same week. Now she had years of neglect in the house to contend with. Revitalizing the place would be a full-time job for a while. Due to her layoff, she was thankful for the money and the distraction.

Hailey worked late into the night again. After arranging the furniture in the office, she moved to the living room. She filled holes, repaired cracks, and prepped the walls for paint. She was on the ladder cutting in the ceiling, when she heard someone scream. She gasped, turned to see who was there, lost her balance. Her brush stroked the ceiling as her arms flailed, leaving a streak of color against white.

She fell hard. "Ouch!" She struggled to her feet, rubbed her rump. "Who's there?"

Nothing.

Okay, as Lynn said, it was an old house. Just raw nerves causing her to hear things. She climbed back up, finished cutting-in. Tomorrow all she had to do was to roll the walls to finish another room. Worn out, she dragged herself into the kitchen, filled the sink to soak the brushes, yawned.

Her hair pulled. But when she turned around, there was no one there. "Must have gotten caught in my necklace."

In the bathroom, she filled the claw-foot tub, stripped, sank into the hot water with a sigh. Her eyes drifted closed. Immediately, she thought of her ex.

She distracted herself from thoughts of him by making a mental list of the jobs she had to do around the house. Every room needed cracks repaired, a coat of paint, and new curtains. Her aunt had already had the hardwood floors redone. She could update without losing too much of the 1920's charm.

A blood-curdling scream shot her straight up. Water slopped over the side of the tub.

"Who's there?" Her voice shook as her body trembled. Nothing more. After a few moments she relaxed again. Her eyes closed. Suddenly something pushed her head under the water. Held her down. She saw nothing above her. She fought, flailed, but couldn't break free. Her vision narrowed. Her lungs burned for air. Her mind pleaded for help.

As suddenly as she'd been pinned, she was released. Her body burst from the water. She gasped for air, sputtered, coughed, climbed over the tub to fall onto the mat. Shivering, she wrapped herself in her terry robe. Once she'd recovered enough to manage to walk, she staggered to her phone to call the police. Her hands shook so violently, she had trouble turning the thing on. Finally, she succeeded in placing the call.

"9-1-1, what's your emergency?"

The question flabbergasted Hailey. "I...I think someone is in my house. They held me under water while I was taking a bath. I thought I was dying, but then they stopped. M-my name is Hailey Stewart. I live at 555 McNeil." She heard the tapping of a keyboard over the line.

"Someone is in the house with you now?"

"I'm not sure, but I think so."

"A patrol car is in the area. Should be there momentarily. Stay on the line with me. Do you need an ambulance?"

A scream caused Hailey to start, drop the cell phone. She scrambled for the device.

"Ms. Stewart? Are you there?"

"Sorry. I dropped the phone when I heard...something."

"Do you need an ambulance?"

"No. I don't think so."

"And you live alone?"

"Yes."

"The officer should be pulling up now. Do you see the patrol car?"

Hailey peeked out the curtain. "I see it. He's walking up the drive."

"Good. His name is Officer Ryan. Please let him in. I'll sign off now."

"Thank you." She ended the call as the officer approached. She unlocked the iron door, pushed it open for him.

"I'm Officer Ryan. You believe you have an intruder?"

"I live alone, but just now someone tried to drown me in the tub."

He entered the home, scratched notes on a small notebook before he replaced in his shirt pocket. "Stay put. Let me have a look around."

"I'm not sure how they got in. I'm sure I locked all the doors."

"Stay here. I'll be right back."

She fidgeted as he made his way from room to room. Finally, he reappeared. "I can't find anyone else in the home. The back door is locked and doesn't appear to have been tampered with. All the windows are closed and locked as well."

"I'm sorry I wasted your time."

"I'll check with the neighbors on each side. See if they saw anyone lurking around. I'll be right back."

She waited on the front porch as he spoke with neighbors. He ambled to her a short time later.

"No one saw or heard anything."

Hailey's breath whooshed from her lungs. "I swear someone held me under the water." She worried at her bottom lip.

"All I can assure is that no one is in the house at this time. I can't explain what you think happened."

"What I think happened...?" she murmured. He thought she was crazy. Maybe she was. Maybe her aunt's death, the breakup with Tyler, and losing her job had taken its toll on her sanity. "Well, I'm sorry to have wasted your time," she spat, regretting her biting tone.

"Look, it's okay. Better safe than sorry with the problems we've had around here lately. Here's my card if you have any more difficulties. Be safe. Have a good evening."

Hailey closed the door, leaned against it. "What is going on?" she asked the empty room, but it gave no reply. With a sigh, she laughed at herself for letting her mind play tricks, because that's all it could be, her mind playing tricks. She got ready for bed, closed the curtains to keep out the morning sun so she could sleep late, one extremely good benefit to no longer having a job. Slumber took its sweet time to find her.

As she drifted off, a scream rent the quiet house.

Hailey woke with a start, not sure what disturbed her. The room was frigid, so cold, her breath fogged the air. Her eyes focused on the clock. One a.m. The red numerals glowed eerily in dark room.

"Why is it so cold in here?" She wrapped herself in her robe, scrambled to the thermostat. It read seventy-two degrees. "No way it's seventy-two in here." A shiver rocked her body. "This thing must be broken." A thump against the plastic cover changed nothing. "I just can't catch a break. Typical." With a flick of her finger, she turned the unit off. Once she'd returned to bed, she pulled the covers over her head, finally drifted off.

*****

The warm temperature woke Hailey. She kicked the covers off. "Stupid air conditioner." With a flick of her finger, she turned the unit on. Cold air slowly circulated. She searched for her aunt's phone book, flipped through the pages to find the heating and air company she'd always used.

While waiting for the repairman to arrive, she finished painting the living room. She listened to the news as she scraped paint from the windows. The report revealed another unexplained disappearance not far from where she lived. A shudder ran the length of her spine.

She raced to answer when the phone rang. "Hello?"

"Can we talk?" Tyler said in greeting.

"We have nothing to talk about. We don't want the same things, remember? And you wanted to date other people. Leave me alone." She thumbed the off button, allowed the mobile to thunk to the floor. Thinking they were headed for marriage, she'd been floored when he broke up with her over...she shook the memory from her mind, but the truth that he wanted to date other people refused to abate. His ability to turn his back on her after three years still stung.

Now curiosity spurred her. Why did he want to talk now? He'd had no problem avoiding her since the breakup. She'd seen him out with other women, driving his point home. He could suffer her silence now as she had his over the past few weeks. She picked up her phone, then noticed the van in her drive with the heating and air logo.

She opened the door, met the man on the porch. After showing him the location of the compressor outside, she waited for the verdict by touching up the ceiling she'd streaked with paint the night before.

"Ma'am?" the man's voice called.

"Yes."

He entered the room. "I can't find anything wrong with the unit. It's only been two months since we tuned it up, and the Freon levels are fine. Would you like me to check the thermostat?"

"Yes, in fact, since you're here, how about installing a digital one for me? Maybe that will solve the problem."

She chatted with the technician as he installed the new thermostat. He explained how it worked, and after writing him a check, she showed him out. The old thermostat must have been defective. With a new digital one, she figured her problems were over. Heart lighter, she finished painting the living room, and cleaned the space now ready to receive furniture.

Suddenly exhausted, she headed to bed without taking a bath. In fact, she might just stick to showers from now on. As she fell asleep, an orb of light appeared. Her eyes widened, followed its path. It floated about, came at her, caused her to dive under the covers for protection. She peeked over the blanket.

"What do you want?"

It bobbed in the entrance of the room. Her hand snuck from under the covers, reached for the bat she kept at bedside, flung it. The apparition disappeared. The bat clunked to the floor.

Tears flowed. "Why is this happening?"

Unable to sleep, she got up early, exhausted herself by doing more repairs. That afternoon, she crawled into bed for a nap. Sometime later, she woke to loud banging. The clock read eight p.m. Someone knocked on her front door.

It was Lynn.

"Oh, gee. Were you asleep already? I wanted to return the dress."

Hailey motioned her inside. "My nap went too long. Why didn't you just use the hidden key?"

Lynn scooted past. "I couldn't remember where you said you put it. I meant to get by here sooner, but I haven't had time. Kevin has been keeping me pretty busy."

Hailey smiled. "You must really like this guy."

"I do. In fact, we're going out again tonight." Lynn glanced around. "Wow. You've been busy. It looks great. I'm glad you went with this color. I love it."

"Me, too." Hailey frowned.

"You look tired. Wearing yourself out working on the house or worrying over Tyler? Both," Lynn guessed.

"You're right. And those disappearances are disturbing."

"Tell me about it. Has me looking over my shoulder constantly. You know another person disappeared right around the corner. Just last night."

Hailey plopped into a chair. "I haven't seen the news today. Lynn, something strange happened."

"What is it? You're white as a sheet."

"Well, I've been hearing someone scream inside the house. It's not just the wind. Then night before last when I took a bath, someone, or something, held me under water."

Lynn's eyes widened. "Ohmigod. Are you okay?"

"Yes. I called the police, but the officer who responded couldn't find any forced entry or any sign anyone was in the house. What worries me most is the woman screaming."

"A ghost maybe? Your aunt did die here. Do you think she was murdered?" Lynn bounced on her toes. "Murder can result in a soul that can't rest."

Hailey sighed. "Quit being so excited about it. You're not the one living here alone and having to deal with it. And she hit her head, drowned. She wasn't murdered."

"Are you sure? Maybe she was trying to show you her last moments. Maybe someone held her under the water until she drowned."

"Ohmigod. Who would want to kill her?"

"I don't know, but her spirit may still be here trying to communicate with you." Lynn leaned forward, eyes wide. "What else has happened?"

"Well, the house gets really cold during the night. I had a new thermostat put in, then last night an orb of light was in my bedroom." Hailey motioned toward the ceiling with her hands. "I was in bed when it flowed into the room. I grabbed my Louisville Slugger and swung it. It disappeared after that."

"Both your aunt and uncle died here, right?"

"Yes, Uncle Bruce fell down the stairs, broke his neck. Think he was murdered, too?"

"I don't know, but since it's a woman screaming, I'd say maybe there's more to your aunt's death than originally thought."

Uneasy, Hailey rubbed her damp palms on her leggings.

"Ghosts are usually caused by a sudden or brutal killing." Lynn propped her elbows on her knees. "Your aunt never mentioned the house being haunted by your uncle?"

"No."

"And you never experienced anything when you stayed here as a child?"

Hailey bit her bottom lip. "No."

"I really think your aunt is trying to tell you something."

"I don't care. I want it to stop."

"I can do a cleansing in the house."

"A what?"

"A cleansing to rid the place of spirits. You know...burn sage throughout the house. It clears bad influences."

"And that really works?"

"Oh, yeah. Sometimes it takes more than once, but it's usually effective."

"How soon can you do it?"

Lynn smiled. "I'll need to get some supplies. How 'bout tomorrow night?"

"The sooner the better."

Two hours later, Hailey showed Lynn out. Exhausted both physically and mentally, Hailey fell into bed, pulled a pillow over her head. If the haunting didn't stop soon, she might have to stay awake all night and sleep during the day, just so she could get some shuteye.

Even under the covers, she felt the temperature drop. "Please stop," she whispered. "Leave me alone!"

Please help me!

She tossed the blanket from her face. "I don't know how to help you! Why me?"

No response.

"Go away," she whispered.

She lay in bed for a time worrying, but heard no more voices. The temperature rose. Finally she slept.

The rising sun shone through a crack in the curtain, waking her. She groaned, stumbled to the bathroom where she started the shower. After breakfast, she rolled paint the color of the ocean onto the walls of what would soon be her master bedroom. She stretched her tight muscles when the phone rang, realized the time.

"How'd last night go?" Lynn asked.

Hailey could hear the radio in the background, figured Lynn to be on her way. "Started out scary. The voice asked for help, but I don't know how. I asked it to go away, then things settled down. I managed to sleep through until morning."

"You might have chased it off, if you ordered it out."

"I don't want to take any chances, Lynn. Will you still do the cleansing?"

"Don't worry. I'm on my way. Might as well be sure."

"Works for me. I cooked dinner. Lasagna."

"That sounds great. I'll be there in a few."

"I'll be waiting."

*****

Hailey stepped back, surveyed the arrangement of the living room furniture as she waited for Lynn to arrive, quite pleased with the way the house came together. If only she could get rid of the ghost permanently. A knock sounded just before Lynn opened the door with a satin bag in hand, and a big smile on her face.

"Ready to cleanse this place?"

"Definitely. But let's eat before it gets cold." Hailey led the way to the kitchen.

After a dinner of lasagna, salad, and garlic bread, Lynn removed supplies from the bag. She didn't waste any time, lit a bundle of sage, held it over a gray stone bowl. It made a huge flame before she blew it out. She encircled her head with the smoking bundle, down her body. "I'm first cleansing myself," Lynn explained.

Starting at the front door, moving clockwise, she held the bundle high, circling every corner and window as she chanted, "Anything not here for the good of those who live here, be gone! You are not welcome. You are not wanted. I rid this house of all negative energy. As I will it, so mote it be!"

After every nook and cranny of every room had been cleansed, they stood before the front door. Lynn moved her hands in a sweeping motion, walked outside.

Hailey followed.

Lynn circled the door and frame, then gently tamped out the fire in the bowl she carried. "It's done!"

Head thrown back, Hailey laughed, took her friend into a hug. "Thank you, Lynn. I feel the difference already. How about a celebratory glass of wine?"

"Sounds good to me."

*****

Hailey stood with arms akimbo glancing around her freshly painted master bedroom, pleased with her color choice.

Help me!

She stepped from the ladder. "Not again. Aunt Faye? Is that you? Why can't you just rest?"

Help me or you will die here, too!

A tremor shimmied down her spine. "Why? Why would I die by staying here? You left me this house! Why would you leave it to me only to force me out?"

No response.

"Tell me what you want?"

Nothing.

The next morning, after a sleepless night due to dropping temperatures and an insistent ghost calling for help, Hailey dialed Lynn's cell number. "It didn't work!"

"What?"

"You heard me."

"It's okay. I told you sometimes it takes more than once for the cleansing to take effect. I'll be by tonight."

"Humph," Hailey grunted. "I'll be here." She dressed, and waited for the furniture for her master bedroom to be delivered.

*****

Finally, Lynn arrived. "We're going to try something else tonight. First, we use the sage again. Second, we purify with cedar. Third, we use sweet grass to bring good influences."

"Whatever works," Hailey drawled.

Once again, Lynn purged herself of negative energy. She then went through the whole house from top to bottom, in every nook, cranny and closet. Next, she performed the same steps with cedar. Finally, she burned braided sweet grass while she chanted.

From her pocket she pulled a small, satin bag. "I've put herbs inside this that should keep negativity from entering. Hang it above the front door. If this doesn't work, I don't know what will." Lynn placed the cache in Hailey's hand, closed her fist around it. "I'm sorry you have to go through this." She sighed. "If this doesn't work, you have no choice but to open yourself up to what the ghost wants."

Hailey stomped her foot. "I've asked! It won't respond."

"You're angry, closed off. You want it to go away, but it wants you to listen. You've got to let go of the negativity and give it permission to reveal its intent."

"I don't want to do this." Hailey sighed.

"Well, hopefully this worked, and it won't matter." Lynn gathered her things. "I've got to go. See you later."

After a shower, Hailey tied her robe around her, heard a knock at the door. She opened it to find her ex on the other side.

"Tyler," she said surprised. Her hand fluttered to the neck of her robe, pulled it closed. "What are you doing here?"

"You wouldn't take my calls. I need to talk to you. May I come in?" The street lights cast him in a glow, made him appear as a blonde, wingless angel standing on the porch. Hailey's brow furrowed, but she stepped aside, let him enter.

He looked around the living room, hands shoved into his front pockets. "Place looks great."

"Thanks. Um, what did you want to talk to me about?"

When he turned to her, worry etched his face, wrinkled between his eyes. His disheveled hair and stubble-covered cheeks revealed his discontent. He'd always kept himself clean shaven and tidy.

"What's wrong?" she asked, sitting on the sofa, her legs no longer able to hold her.

"Hailey, I miss you so much. I can't stop thinking about you." He knelt before her. "I'm sorry I pressed you to sell this house. I thought we could find our own home with the money from this one. Start out brand new. I didn't think about what this place meant to you. Please give me another chance. I've been going crazy without you."

Tears filled her eyes. "I don't know, Tyler...that was a really crappy thing to do. You basically kicked me out. And what about the other women you wanted to date?"

He lifted her chin with his finger. "That was my ego talking. When you didn't want the same thing as I did, I lashed out. I tried to go out with other women, but my heart wasn't in it. I promise I'll never hurt you again, Hailey. Please give me another chance."

"It's too late."

"Is there someone else?" he asked, voice shaking.

"No!"

"Then it's not too late." He placed his hand at the back of her head, pulled her close, kissed her deeply. They ended up in her new bed, skin to skin. They lay entwined, her head on his chest. He stroked her dark hair.

"You really want to get back together?" she asked softly.

"If you'll have me."

"I already have." They laughed. Hailey propped herself on an elbow. "And you'll move in here?"

"Hailey, this house gives me the creeps. Why can't we just sell it, and find something new?"

She couldn't argue the creep factor, but she couldn't let it go. Her aunt remained in the house, and she owed it to her to help her out of her purgatory. "I can't give up this house, Tyler. I just can't. You came here telling me you understood why I need this house so much, and after getting me in bed, you tell me to sell?"

He wrenched from her embrace, shoved his legs into his pants. "Why can't you do this for me? I thought you loved me."

"That's not fair. I do love you, but this house is special to me. It's mine, and I want to raise a family here. Leave it to our kids one day."

"Why can't we leave our kids something else? Why this house, Hailey?"

"Because my aunt is still here and I need to help her."

"Well, I hope the house will keep you warm at night, because I can't stay here." He stalked from the room. She heard the door slam with his exit.

She blinked away tears. If he couldn't understand, then maybe she was better off without him. She could swear she heard her aunt sigh.

*****

Hailey woke the next morning, forced herself to smile. She'd decided not to fret over that jerk Tyler. No matter her good intentions, depression rode her all day, growing in intensity as she went to bed alone.

Then the orb entered. It stretched, grew until a frothy form appeared. She stiffened. It motioned for her to follow. Tears stung her eyes, but she bolted from the bed, crying and laughing at the same time. She had to finish this somehow. She'd had a reprieve when Tyler had been with her, but now? Now, it was back.

She followed the form to the downstairs bathroom, watched the death scene replay over and over. In trying to better understand, she climbed into the tub. "Please Aunt Faye. Show me who killed you. Please."

The faucet turned. Water filled the tub. Hailey started. Hands on the rim, she almost catapulted herself out, but forced herself to remain even as the tub filled within inches of the top. Her heart thundered in her chest, but she remained still even as the water drenched her clothes.

Nothing happened, so she reclined in the tub as her aunt had done in the vision. Closing her eyes, she waited. The feeling of no longer being alone rose. Her eyes blinked open to see someone standing above her. A blood-curdling scream forced its way from her throat. A hand clamped over her mouth.

"Shhhh," the smooth voice cooed. "I just want to talk."

"You scared me. How did you get in?"

"You have a faulty lock on the back bedroom window. When you didn't answer, I let myself in to check on you."

Her eyes narrowed. "How did you know about the lock?"

"I scoped out the place when I came for dinner once. Easy access."

"And you didn't say anything about it?"

"Of course not. I've been in this house several times. You have quite a few things of interest. Or did, I should say."

Her mind raced. "W-what do you want?"

"I'm in trouble. I need money."

"I have about five hundred in my purse. Take it." Her voice shook. She hated to show fear.

Laughter. "That's a start, but I need way more than that puny amount."

"I don't have access to anything more."

Laughter rumbled again. "You are worth plenty."

Realization hit her between the eyes. "My death won't bring you any money. There's nothing..."

"That's where you're wrong. I influence the one who is listed in your will." Pushed under water, held down with one hand to her head, one to her chest, she fought uselessly. Couldn't win against the attacker. She was held under without a problem. Her lungs burned, forced her to take a breath, sucking water deep into her lungs.

*****

She came to little by little, her voice hoarse from screaming. Lynn hovered over her, shaking her shoulders. Hailey sprang into a sitting position, scrambled away.

"What are you doing here?"

"You didn't answer your phone. So I came by to check on you. When I got here, I heard you screaming. I let myself in with the hidden key. Have mercy, you scared the crap out of me."

"What happened?"

Lynn sighed. "I have no idea. You were flailing about in the empty tub. It was all I could do to get you out of there and on the floor before you knocked yourself out."

Hailey scrambled to the tub, peeked over the rim, stuck one arm inside. "No water? I...I could swear I was drowning." Her hands smoothed her dry shirt. "What's happening to me, Lynn?"

"I don't know, Hailey. I'm beginning to think you need to leave this house. This is bigger than I understand. I need to consult with my mentor."

"I can't leave." The identity of the killer niggled at the edge of her consciousness, but she couldn't grasp hold. "I have to find out what happened to Faye. Leaving won't accomplish that."

"And your sanity is on the line if you stay here. I'm really worried about you, Hailey. Maybe you should call the police."

"Her death was classified an accident. You think if I walk in the precinct that they will believe me based on what? Ghosts? The police can't help with this and you know it. Let me figure this out."

"Boy, you've sure changed your tune. At first you can't stand the idea of finding out what happened and now you're like a woman possessed."

"I am not." Hailey stood, stomped from the room. "You wanted me to do this from the start and now that I'm on my way to finding out, you want me to stop. You are the one that doesn't make sense. I think it's time you leave."

"Hailey, I..."

"No. Go. I've got this." She raked a hand through her tangled hair. "I was dreaming of drowning. Of Faye's drowning. I need to remember the rest." When Lynn didn't move, Hailey pointed toward the front door. "If you can't handle it, go!"

Lynn stalked out the door, slamming it on her way out.

*****

The next day as Hailey unloaded groceries, she heard a knock on the door. She opened it to a detective with the Memphis police, which gave her quite a start.

"Ms. Stewart?"

"Yes."

"I'm Detective Walters with Memphis Police Department. We've got a missing person's report for Tyler Morrison. Have you heard from him?"

Brow furrowed, Hailey stepped aside to let him enter. "Not since Wednesday."

"According to his mother, he's been missing since then."

"Well, he was here that night. We'd broken up a few weeks ago, and he came by to reunite, but he left mad instead. He wanted to sell this house, and I didn't."

He asked more questions that Hailey answered to the best of her ability. She swallowed hard, shuddered. "Do you think he's become a victim himself?"

The detective didn't answer her question, posed one of his own as he made a note in his book. "Did he drive here?"

"Yes. He left in his truck." She clenched her fingers in her lap. "Did he go to work?"

"He never made it to work Thursday. Can anyone verify when he left?"

Her heart kicked. "No. But maybe the neighbors saw his truck parked here, or saw him leave."

He nodded. "We're doing everything we can to find him."

"It makes me nervous to know I was the last one to see him."

His eyebrows rose. "That's a good reason to be anxious." His skeptical gaze served to unnerve her further.

When the detective finally left, Hailey leaned against the closed door, slid down, held her legs tight as she cried. She didn't know what to think, or what to do.

That night, Hailey woke to the bed shaking violently. The vibrations stopped once her eyes popped open.

"What is it?" she whispered to the form she now knew to be her ghostly aunt.

He's here.

"Who?"

Hide!

Then she heard what sounded like a window scraping open downstairs. Her heart pounded. She scrambled for her phone, dialed the police. When the call connected, she whispered, "There's an intruder in my house. 555 McNeil. Please hurry."

"I'll dispatch an officer."

Hailey ended the call. She couldn't stay on the line, and hold the baseball bat. She dropped her phone to the bed, flung the bat onto her shoulder. Down the stairs she crept, tip-toed through the kitchen, past the butler's pantry, and into the hall. After carefully checking the other rooms, she glanced into the back bedroom to see a window wide. A shudder ran through her. She backed from the room.

Watch out! her aunt's ghostly voice screamed.

A thud sounded. Pain radiated from the top of her head to her toes.

*****

Hailey groaned. She flinched as she touched the knot on her head as her eyes popped open. Tyler sat on a chair across from her, gun in his hand, pointed directly at her.

"What are you doing?" she asked, surprised her voice remained calm. She rose to a sitting position slowly.

"I tried to be reasonable, Hailey, but I'm in a bind and you're the only one who can help me."

"Of c-course," she stuttered. "W-what do you n-need?"

He stood, extended a stack of papers and a pen. "I need you to list me as your beneficiary in your will."

Her heart thudded. "Excuse me?"

"You refuse to sell the house and I need the cash."

"Y-you're crazy," she whispered, pushing herself against the cushions.

Tyler flashed an eerie smile. "That's what your aunt said, too."

"Y-you killed her?"

He sighed. "I had no choice, Hailey. This place is worth a lot and I needed access to it."

Her head shook. "How did killing her give you access to...oh." She realized his plan. "Even if you get away with killing me, this house might not sell for months. There's no guarantee…"

"I've already got someone interested, so don't worry your pretty little head about that." He stood, strode to her. "Just sign here and it'll all be over soon."

"I thought you loved me," she accused.

"I do, but I need money more than I need you."

"What have you gotten yourself into? Maybe I can help figure out another way?"

He clucked his tongue. "There is no other way, Hailey. Now sign!" He jiggled the papers below her nose.

When she didn't reach for them, he slapped her. She gasped.

"Sign the freaking papers. NOW!"

"So you can kill me? I don't think so." She darted from the couch, ran for the back of the house. He tackled her in the dining room. Held face down beneath him, she fought for freedom, but he outweighed her by a hundred pounds. He straddled her body, knocked her head into the hard floor until she no longer resisted. Her wrist in his tight grip, he forced her to scrawl her signature on the page.

A sob wrenched from her throat as he jerked her up by the hair, shoved her toward the bathroom.

"You'll never get away with this," she cried as he forced her into the tub.

"Oh, I think I will."

"Two deaths the same way? It'll raise suspicions."

His brows furrowed with thought.

*****

Officer Ryan shook his head as he slipped from the cruiser, back again for another fruitless search of the old house. He sighed, wishing he'd taken the night off. He'd had enough crazy for one day.

The disappearances had everyone in uproar, the chief, the population, and the press that continued to sensationalize the vanishings of several people in the area. They hadn't found one clue to find the missing people, not even bodies. He hoped that meant they were still alive, had just decided to disappear on their own.

Quietly, he made his way to the porch, tried the front door knob. Locked. He heard a scream and a loud thump. He drew his gun, made his way around the house. He peeked into a window to see a man roughing up Ms. Stewart. And the man doing it resembled the APB he'd seen on one of the missing people.

"Holy hell," he muttered. Into his shoulder mike, he called for backup, then rounded the house, looking for an entrance. The back door was also locked, but he found an open window, shimmied through. Gun pointed at the ceiling, he quietly moved outside the bathroom door, listened.

*****

"So, I'll just shoot your ass," the intruder said.

Ryan stiffened, peeked around the doorframe. Hailey met his eyes for an instant, then returned to the assailant, but her shoulders visibly relaxed.

"Why? Why do you need to kill me?"

He sighed. "I told you. I need money. I have a buyer for this house and since you left it to me in your will, it's mine as soon as you're gone."

"Why do you need money so badly, Tyler?"

"I've got to get out of this town before they figure out what I've done. I've already got a buyer lined up for a quick sale. Now I just need the property to be mine."

"W-what have you done?"

"They'll find the bodies soon, Hailey. I can't seem to stop. I like it too much."

"Stop what?" She hated how her voice shook, but hated the sinking feeling in her heart worse.

Tyler paced the small bathroom. "The killing, Hailey. I like it and now I can't stop. It's the ultimate high, kidnapping someone, holding them hostage. I like to hear them scream when I torture them, like the way their eyes go dim once they're dead. It's such a rush!"

Hailey sputtered. "H-how many people have you k-killed?"

He stopped the pacing, stood with his back to the doorway. "Six. The first was an old lover of mine. I saw her out one night and we hooked up. Then she tried to kick me out of her bed when I mentioned you. We fought. I strangled her. God, what a rush it was."

Hailey shivered as she faced the monster before her.

"Remember those nights I didn't come home?"

"Ohmigod."

"Yeah," he laughed. "Victims are so easy to find. And you didn't have a clue. Didn't even realize I'd killed your own aunt. Then I met someone, said they'd get me cash for this old house if I could get my hands on it. I knew your aunt left it to you, and I thought you'd sell it to make me happy. You weren't even living in it, so what did it matter. Then I could disappear before they found me out."

"They haven't found any bodies. You apparently hid them well."

His smile turned fiendish. "That took some work, but you know the old Sears Crosstown building?"

"Yes. I can see it from the porch."

"Well, it's not just a skeleton of a building now, but has a few bodies to add to the creepiness."

"They are about to start renovations there! They'll be found."

"That's why I need cash to disappear. I've got a contact in Mexico, said he'd help me if I can get down there. Any more questions, sweetheart?"

Her nose scrunched at the endearment. Her brain worked to think of more to ask, but he extended the gun. Her mind went blank.

"Say goodnight, sweetheart." His finger tightened on the trigger.

Goodnight, sweetheart.

Tyler jerked around to see Aunt Faye in the hallway. His eyes bulged. "I killed you," he screamed, fired his weapon, but the apparition disappeared. He jerked when a bullet hit him in the shoulder, rammed into the wall behind him. He slid to the floor, clutching his wound.

Officer Ryan stepped forward, kicked the gun out of his reach as sirens and tires screeched out front.

Hailey threw herself into Officer Ryan's arms.

"You were great, Ms. Stewart. I can't believe you held it together and kept him talking. He won't be getting out of prison any time soon."

She stepped out of his embrace. "I can't thank you enough. I was worried no one would come after to the false alarm last week." She glanced at Tyler's slumped body. "I can't believe he killed my aunt and all those missing people. I can't believe I didn't know I was dating a serial killer."

"They're sociopaths. They can blend in with normal society. That's what makes them so dangerous."

Paramedics took Tyler away with a police escort while a barrage of cops stormed through her house. Her voice turned hoarse from repeating her story.

Finally, Hailey closed and locked her front door. She leaned against it with a sigh. Movement in the hallway caught her eye.

Her Aunt Faye stood smiling outside the bathroom door where her life had ended. "I'm sorry for what he did to you Aunt Faye. I'm so sorry. I should have known."

Not your fault, child. He was truly insane. I'm just so happy he's out of your life.

"I hope you can at least rest in peace now."

Her body faded. *Oh, I will. And you will find happiness and have a large family to fill this house.*

Hailey smiled as her aunt waved goodbye.

*****

The Evergreen District

The Evergreen area was split in half and many homes were destroyed to make way for the expansion of Interstate 40. The neighborhood fought, going all the way to the U.S. Supreme Court, which finally ruled in their favor. The land cleared to make way for the interstate stood bare for many years after this fight ended.

In the early 1990s, builders began construction that filled in that area once again. It now has an eclectic mix of new and old homes. Today, the Evergreen Historical District is listed on the National

Kristi Bradley

Register of Historical Places, and is home to Overton Park and the Memphis Zoo.

The Misadventures of Mama Lou: Victorian Mayhem

Angelyn Sherrod

"I won't do it, you hear me?" Mama Lou rapped her cane against the polished wood floor for emphasis. "That woman is ornery enough to make a Baptist preacher cuss. Besides, I want to get home in time to watch Maury."

Ethel Mae expelled a long-suffering sigh, drawing from the well of patience she'd needed when teaching the Pythagorean theorem to a bunch of hormonally-charged teenagers years ago. She and Louisa Metcalf, *aka Mama Lou*, had been friends for over fifty years and Ethel Mae was well familiar with the tilt of her friend's sharp chin. Mama Lou was gearing up for a fight. Ethel Mae had known the discussion wouldn't be easy but she knew her friend's heart. That woman would give her last, if she thought it would help somebody else. Mama Lou Metcalf, for all her spit and vinegar would, eventually, come to see things her—*ahem*—the Lord's way.

"Louisa," Ethel Mae pasted on a patient smile. "Agnes Bradshaw asked for you specifically. She needs our help."

"She did no such thing, Ethel Mae," said Mama Lou, glaring in challenge. "That over-sexed cow hates me. The truth of the matter is that, if she asked for anybody, it was you and that's only because she

209

wants to keep you close to make sure you don't try to steal away any of her men."

"Louisa," Ethel Mae chided.

"Well, it's true. Remember that time at the annual church picnic? Who was it that nearly started a riot because you offered her husband a slice of sweet potato pie?"

"Okay, that's true, but she's in real trouble. She may lose the house."

Willie C Bradshaw, Agnes's late husband and his family, had been founding members of the Friendship Community Church established in 1897. The Bradshaw family was one of the few black families in Memphis with money. Old money. Willie C's great-great-grandmother was a former slave born on the Tiddle estate. When the last of the Tiddles died out in the early 1900's, the family home—as well as a healthy trust to maintain it—was deeded to the Rosetta Bradshaw and her descendants. There'd been a Bradshaw living at the Tiddle place in Victorian Village ever since. Agnes married into the family, but to hear her tell it, she was to the manor born, even though everybody knew she came from a family of sharecroppers in Sugar Ditch, Mississippi.

"I told you that woman didn't have enough sense to fill a thimble. What's she done now?"

"Louisa, show some compassion. Times have changed, the trust isn't enough to maintain that house the way it used to. And now with Willie C gone..." Ethel Mae allowed her voice to trail off, allowing the silence to do what her words could not.

"What does she expect us to do?" Mama Lou said, with just a hint of belligerence that told Ethel Mae that her friend was thawing. "She should probably just sell it and live off the proceeds in some swanky retirement home."

"She's got an idea of how she may be able to maintain things, but there is a problem, which is where we fit in." Ethel Mae raised a palm and shushed. "And before you ask, I'm going to let Agnes explain herself."

*****

"I just can't see how we can help you, Agnes."

Agnes Bradshaw was a tall, bird-like woman with a hawkish nose and light-caramel complexion. She was eighty if she was a day but still wore five inch heels and hemlines above her bony knees. Her religiously-attended, monthly visits to the hair salon resulted in jet black hair that drew attention to the network of creases next to her mouth and eyes.

"Louisa, you're such a pessimist." Agnes gritted out through clenched teeth, her mouth twisted in a rictus. Mama Lou reacted the way she always did when Agnes pasted on that fake, frozen smile: with snark. Ethel Mae could hardly blame her; Agnes was a challenge at the best of times, but when she pasted that vacuous smile and spoke in that high-pitched, child-like tone, she could test the patience of a saint. "You're one of the busiest bodies I know. I'm sure if you put your mind to it..."

Mama Lou narrowed her eyes to squints. Ethel Mae closed her eyes and silently prayed that the good Lord would forestall her friend's tongue.

"Still," Mama Lou drawled out. "This is a beautiful home." She glanced pointedly at Agnes. "Even if it is starting to show its age."

"*Well!*"

Mama Lou smiled her satisfaction that the barb had found its way home. "You should be able to find a buyer easily enough."

211

Agnes sniffed but otherwise ignored the dig. "Willie C doesn't want me to sell."

"Your husband, Willie C?" Mama Lou kept her expression deadpan.

"Of course, my husband. Who else?" said Agnes, oblivious to Mama Lou's sarcasm. "He wants the property to remain in the family. He's been quite insistent about it."

"Your *dead* husband?" Mama Lou inquired again.

"Yes, my dead husband. You spoke at the funeral, remember? I swear sometimes, Louisa..."

Ethel Mae, who'd learned long ago to stay out of her friend's squabbles, decided it was time for her to speak up. "I think we may be missing something, Agnes. Perhaps if we sit down, you could tell us all about it?"

As they processed into the parlor, Mama Lou caught Ethel Mae's eye then with a side-eye towards Agnes, rolled her finger in a circle next to her head. Ethel Mae slapped her hands down as Agnes turned back towards them. She gestured for them to take a seat. Mama Lou opted to remain standing near the door.

"I've wanted to sell since right after my dear Willie C's funeral. I've even had a couple appraisals done and received some really good offers. But each time, Willie C refused. He's been quite vocal about it too."

Ethel Mae glanced back at Mama Lou who shook her head. Ethel Mae sighed and asked, "He's vocal?"

"Well, I mean, he hasn't come right out and said anything in English, you understand – that would be crazy; but when he locks the doors and refuses to let strangers inside, what else am I supposed to think? He almost knocked me down the stairs once. If I hadn't caught the rail at the last minute, well, we wouldn't be sitting here together now."

Mama Lou mumbled something under her breath that sounded suspiciously like, *we'd all like to knock you down a flight of stairs.*

"And all that caterwauling," Agnes continued. "All night long—I haven't had a decent night's sleep in ages. He's breaking dishes—fortunately I keep the good china locked away but he's costing me a small fortune in dinnerware. And the smell? *Whew!*" Agnes pinched her nose and fanned a hand in front of her face. "I think Jesus must be feeding him cabbage."

"Are you saying that the ghost of Willie C. Bradshaw is *haunting* you?"

"But of course, haven't you been paying attention? Do sit down, Louisa. Perhaps you need a rest."

Ethel Mae leaned back against the sofa. She had no idea how to respond. She kept a steady eye on Agnes, trying to determine if perhaps she should get in touch with the woman's daughter. She glanced over her shoulder at Mama Lou, who had re-adjusted her purse on her arm and mouthed, "I'm out of here." Ethel Mae vigorously shook her head, then turned back to Agnes.

"Um," she cleared her throat. "How long has this— Willie C—been...um, visiting you?"

"Since I started trying to sell the house. That's how I know that Willie C is angry and wants me to keep it, though I really can't afford to do that now, can I? But I've come up with a reasonable compromise." Agnes raised her hands like a maestro in an orchestra pit. She watched them beneath her lashes and when she felt she had their attention, she said. "I'm going to turn the house into a bed and breakfast. We've got twelve bedrooms. I can keep the third floor for the family and the rest," she twittered. "I can fix up and charge an extravagant rate for guests."

Ethel Mae and Mama Lou remained silent. Agnes continued, "It'll give me a whole new lease on life. You know how much I love entertaining, and the income could be used to make this place fabulous again. That's why I wanted you to come."

"I don't understand?"

"To talk to Willie C, of course. He was always kind of sweet on you." Agnes sucked her teeth and then rolled her eyes at Ethel Mae. "- and so I know he'll take the news better from you. He always said I was too flighty, with no head for business, so make certain you convince him this was all your idea."

"Agnes Bradshaw," Mama Lou proclaimed. "You are three gallons of crazy in a two gallon bucket." Mama Lou's expression was incredulous. "But to show you what good Christians we are, we're going to give you a lift to the looney-bin. C'mon, let's go."

"Louisa!" Ethel Mae shot her a quelling glance. "Agnes, what Louisa meant..."

"I meant exactly what I said."

"What she intended to say was..."

The air shifted, and the ambient temperature in the room dropped to freezing. Ethel Mae was startled by the sight of her frosty breath on the air in front of her. She rubbed her hands up and down arms suddenly pimpled with goose flesh. The hairs on the back of her neck lifted and she fought the primal instinct to run. Before she could activate her muscles, Ethel Mae felt a presence behind her as two heavy hands settled on her shoulders. Expecting to see Mama Lou behind her, she turned to look over her shoulders but the space behind her was empty.

"Willie C Bradshaw! Take your hands off that woman this second," Agnes demanded, staring at the empty space over Ethel Mae's shoulder. "I don't care if you are dead; I will not have you disrespect me in my own home."

Ethel Mae lowered her head to her shoulder again and glimpsed the hazy outline of a man's hand. She recognized the pinkie signet ring Willie C had worn since she'd known him. Ethel Mae lost her breath and fainted.

When she came to, Mama Lou was bent over her, trying to force a delicate china cup to her lips. Her friend's mouth was moving but Ethel Mae had no idea what was said. She felt a sharp sting against her cheek and realized that Mama Lou had slapped her. Ethel Mae raised her own hand to return the favor.

"Whoa," said Mama Lou. "I was just trying to make sure you were okay."

"What happened?"

"You fainted. Why'd you do that? I've never known you to have the vapors in all my years knowing you. Maybe we'll stop to have your blood pressure checked after we drop this mad housewife off at the asylum."

"Willie C," said Ethel Mae. "I think I saw him."

"Now you sound as dingy as Agnes, I'm calling the doctor as soon as I get you home. I sent Agnes out to the kitchen to stop her hysterical babbling about her dead husband cheating on her. Don't you start."

Ethel Mae swallowed and considered her next words. She wasn't certain what she'd seen but there had been something. It wouldn't do any good to try and explain to Louisa. That woman could be as stubborn as the day was long. But if the house was indeed haunted, what could they possibly do about it?

Agnes returned bearing a tray loaded with a carafe, cups and pastries. She lowered her burden to the table then looked sharply at Ethel Mae. She then glanced around the room, presumably for her dead husband's ghost. "I want your help but I want your word right now that there won't be any funny business between you and my husband while you're here."

Ethel Mae was nonplussed. None of the thoughts racing through her head would come out in a kind, Christian way, so she mutely nodded her head.

"Good," said Agnes, taking a seat across from them. "Sit down, Louisa. You're giving me a crick in my neck. Okay, here's my plan: I've invited the children over this afternoon to discuss the B&B idea. This is their inheritance too, so I thought their input would be good. But y'all know as well as I that, if Willie C keeps throwing tantrums whenever people come into the house, we won't get any boarders. So, while I'm talking to the kids, you and Louisa can bargain with Willie C, get him to understand that the place will still belong to the family and that it is a sound business proposition. Well, I won't tell you what to say, but I'm depending on you."

*****

Mama Lou complained the entire twenty-minute drive back to her home in Central Gardens. Ethel Mae was quiet, trying to make sense of her *paranormal?* experience in Agnes's home. Had she really seen a ghost? Felt the presence of a spirit? Flights of fancy were Mama Lou's purview; Ethel Mae had always been the sensible one. Still, she couldn't shake her belief that something profound had happened to her.

"I did see Willie C's ghost." There. She'd blurted it out. Maybe saying the words would help bring a lie to the whole experience.

Mama Lou's prattle and complaints ceased. She didn't speak another word until they pulled into her driveway. Not an easy feat for her old friend. She turned off the engine and faced Ethel Mae. "You are one of the most level-headed people that I have ever known. So, if you're telling me you saw or felt something strange in that house, I believe you. Tell me about it."

"I didn't see anything at first. The air around me got really cold, cold enough to see my breath. Then I felt hands on my shoulder. I saw his hand, Louisa. It had that dang pinkie ring you and I both hated. He touched me." The memory of that phantom touch brought shivers, even in the middle of the hottest day of the year. The creepiness ceased, however, when Mama Lou took Ethel Mae's hand into her own.

"All I saw was your shocked expression and then you fainted. And of course, that dag-blamed Agnes Bradshaw yelling at you to stop flirting with her man." Mama Lou chuckled then drew in a deep breath. "I don't like to see you scared." Mama Lou patted her gently on the back of her hand. "We'll go back. And we'll find out what's really going on in that Victorian madhouse."

*****

Mama Lou and Ethel Mae returned as promised the next afternoon for dinner. Agnes had gone all out. The formal dining room had been aired out, the red-oak floors gleamed and the room was fragrant with both live flowers and potpourri.

Agnes's daughter, India, and her husband, Napoleon, were already seated when Mama Lou and Ethel Mae arrived. India had her mother's height and build but was softer around the edges. She was sweet natured, kind-hearted and a little overwhelmed by the force of her mother's personality. Her husband, Napoleon, was a big man with the shoulders of a former football hero and the middle girth of a man who now instead of a pigskin, tossed six-packs of beer instead. Louis Bradshaw arrived shortly after. He was Willie C's first cousin on his father's side; he was also the executor of Willie C's will.

The six of them—Agnes at the head of the table, Louis at the end; India and Napoleon seated opposite to Mama Lou and Ethel Mae—consumed the meal with a scattering of small talk. It wasn't until the dessert and coffee were served that Agnes introduced the topic of her new venture.

"I wanted to speak with the family about something. I wonder, Ethel Mae, Louisa, if you could excuse us for just a bit and then we'll all come back together in the parlor." Agnes sent them a sharp, meaningful look then glanced towards the open doorway. Mama Lou and Ethel Mae took the hint and left the room.

"So," Mama Lou said as they stood in the hall. "You got a plan to seduce Agnes's husband into haunting someplace else?"

"Shush," Ethel Mae laughed, just as Mama Lou intended, despite her anxiety about being in the house again. "I didn't do anything before. Maybe if we go somewhere and be still, he'll show?"

Mama Lou rolled her eyes, just a little bit, and led the way to Agnes's home office. The room was the definition of girly female—pink and mauve wallpaper, delicate furniture, and impressionist art on the wall. Mama Lou suppressed an urged to gag as she sat behind the French reproduction writing desk with its elaborate metal scrollwork and curlicue feet.

Ethel Mae chose to perch on a mauve damask-covered chaise lounge with pink stuffed silk pillows. She didn't speak but maintained a watchful eye on the corners of the room.

Mama Lou said, "Oh, this is ridiculous. There are no ghosts, I'm not sure exactly what is happening here, but sitting around waiting for some specter to show is just plain foolish." As she spoke, she picked up or moved various objects across the blotter. Her rant finished, she moved to step around the desk but her purse clipped the small jar filled with metal ball bearings, knocking it over. The jar was used to clean the antique fountain pen tips—*Who used fountain pens anyway these days?* Mama Lou muttered as she struggled to contain the spill before any of the small balls fell to the hardwood floor. *Nobody but a pretentious busy-body like Agnes, that's who.* As Mama Lou scooped up the last of them, she pulled a document from beneath the blotter, a legal document, Ethel Mae surmised from the official-looking letterhead. It had been dislodged during her fight to right the ink jar. Ethel Mae watched as Mama Lou pulled it clear and began to read.

Ethel Mae debated reminding her friend that whatever was in that document was none of her business but gave up the idea before it was fully formed. Instead, she chose to focus on their purpose in the room. She closed her eyes. Ethel Mae wasn't a medium, so it wasn't like she could call the ghost to her, but she thought maybe if she were really still and concentrated?

There was a commotion from the dining room, voices raised in anger, the clammer of stampeding feet. Ethel Mae turned to Mama Lou, who hadn't moved, a quizzical expression on her face as she read. Ethel Mae rushed to the door and as she pulled it open, the cries of Agnes and her daughter India, mixed with the rage of one of the men. Napoleon? Or Louis? Ethel Mae couldn't tell.

India ran to the front door, frantically trying to open it. Agnes stumbled out of the dining room and shoved her daughter out of the way and grabbled for the doorknob. She repeatedly glanced over her shoulder, jerking the knob left, then right but the door would not budge. Napoleon fell out of the room and landed on his butt. It took several tries for his feet to find purchase on the glossy floor. When they did, he joined the women at the door but even in his adrenal-fused strength, he couldn't budge it.

The hallway was freezing, Ethel Mae watched her breath coalesce in front of her again and felt a renewed twinge of fear. A howling wind developed in the entry, causing flower-stuffed vases to twirl around as if caught in a tornado, one by one, picture frames, bric-a-brac from the corner table, joined in the swirling mix; chairs and tables were picked up and dropped. Agnes and her family fell to the floor and covered their heads, waiting for the maelstrom to end.

Louis stumbled from the dining room, his expression shocked but not afraid. He backed down the hall towards Ethel Mae, babbling under his breath, spittle striking his chin as the wind poured around him. At first, the space was empty and then Ethel Mae glimpsed a figure, a shape, the size and form of a man. It was more of a distortion in the air, like a gelatinous blob; Ethel Mae could see right through it. It followed Louis down the hall, and the closer they two figures were to Ethel Mae, the more the figure took shape. Willie C Bradshaw. The expression on his face was one of pure fury.

The focus of all that rage was Louis Bradshaw who, incredibly, appeared to be equally furious. "You're supposed to be dead. I killed you. You're dead." He caught sight of Ethel Mae in the doorway and pulled her in front of him, placing her in a choke hold. "If you don't stop this right now, Willie C and return to the pit of hell, I'll kill her. I swear it."

The ghost of Willie C smiled gently at Ethel Mae and she felt the arm around her throat pull away. She felt the warmth of a hand on her upper arm and she was pulled away. The warmth shifted to her back and she was propelled towards the front of the house.

There was an instant of terrifying silence. The howling wind ceased and the various objects hovered above the floor. There followed an explosion of sound. A gust of energy swept past Ethel Mae and into the body of Louis Bradshaw. The force of it swept him down the length of the hallway and out through the kitchen doors.

For several long moments, no one moved or said a word. The air shifted in front of Ethel Mae and she caught the vague outline of the man. She felt several hairs of her bun rise then fall against her neck, then a pair of warm lips touch her cheek and then...nothing. The temperature returned to normal. Household sounds like the air conditioning unit, refrigerator and grandfather clock were audible again. The only evidence of any supernatural energy was the cyclone level mess in the foyer and hall.

Ethel Mae heard the click-clack of Mama Lou's heels as she reached the office doorway. She waved the same documents she had been reading at the desk. "Ethel Mae," she began but then catching sight of Agnes, directed her attention to her. "Agnes, you couldn't sell this place even if you wanted to and you certainly can't transform it into a business. You don't even own—what in the world...?"

Agnes, India and Napoleon were still huddled on the floor, clutching each other, for dear life. Mama Lou counted heads before turning back to Ethel Mae. "Where's Louis? He's got some explaining to do. Agnes, how could you just sign you rights away like this?"

Agnes stood up, glaring harshly at Ethel Mae. At Mama Lou's words, her head swiveled on her neck. "Oh, you found the papers. Well, I was trying to find a way to save money and I was watching Alex Trebek on TV and he suggested I look into a reverse mortgage. Louis thought it was a wonderful idea and he drew up the papers for me."

"You nitwit," said Mama Lou. "This isn't a reverse mortgage. You signed everything over to Louis, the house, the land, the trust, all of it. Some development company has made an offer on this place, Louis stands to make millions. Where is he, by the way?"

"Look around you, Louisa. Don't you want to know what happened here?"

"Nope, because you're going to try to sell me some story about a dead guy wreaking vengeance and I don't want to hear it. You've got all the drama you need right here in these documents. Given all of this undercover shadiness, you might want to check in with the cops to find out whether poor Willie C was murdered."

"But Louisa..."

"Nope, I told you, getting involved in this mess was nothing but trouble. Now, it's time to get me out of this Victorian mayhem. God willing and the creek don't rise, I can still get back to the house in time to catch the last thirty minutes of Maury."

*****

Victorian Village
In the mid-19th century Memphis, if you took a walk down Adams Street, near the edge of what was then downtown Memphis, chances are that your journey lead you past Victorian Village. Known also as 'millionaire's row', everyone who was anyone in Memphis lived there, from cotton magnates to riverboat tycoons and everyone else—with the right level of coin—in between.

The Tiddle House featured in *Victorian Mayhem* is fictional, however visitors to Memphis can still access these homes, including the Woodruff-Fontaine house, the Mallory-Neely House, and the James Lee house. The Magevney House is the oldest of the remaining residences. Several of these grand Victorian-style homes have been repurposed into museums, a bed and breakfast, and one of the city's hottest night spots. These beautiful homes, which range in style from Neo-classical through Late Gothic Revival, are sure to please.

The Adventures of Sonny Etherly: Special Powers

James C. Paavola

BOOM!

Lightning struck and struck again.

I jerked awake. The hairs on my arms stood out like porcupine quills. The house shook and the windows rattled as if some giant pounded his fist on the roof. I threw my covers back and reached for my glasses. Lightning lit up the room. I stood as thunder vibrated the floor. I eased to the window and looked out. Complete darkness. No moon, no street lights. A lightning flash illuminated my bike, now on its side— tires smoking and the safety flag on fire at the end of the antenna, even in the rain.

BOOM!

Was that two seconds apart, or three?

Another lightning bolt! Two people across the street, running. *Teenage boys, I think.* The flickering lightning caused a strobe effect. The boys' movements appeared jerky like in a silent movie. And after the darkness between strikes, they reappeared in different places, different positions.

The second boy carried something in his hand, sticking out in front of him. *Is that a gun?*

Darkness. Another clap of thunder exploded.

In the next lightning flash, I saw the first boy stretched out on the sidewalk, face down. The second boy was gone. My breath fogged the window. I pulled the sleeve of my pajamas down in my fist and wiped it clear. Nothing but darkness and the sound of pounding rain. The street flickered to life. No one. *Not even the boy on the sidewalk? Did he get up and run away?*

Boom! The window rattled.

I took my glasses off and rubbed my eyes. I put them back on. *Still no boy. Did I imagine this? Was this a dream? But it felt so real. Only one way to be sure—gotta go outside.* I turned toward where my desk should be. My hands searched the darkness. My pinky finger made contact. I stepped forward and waved my hand side to side until I found the lamp. I pushed the switch—no light. I found the side drawer, pulled it open and stuck my hand inside. I felt around until I touched a short, cool, metal cylinder. I lifted out my flashlight, switched it on, and walked to my grandmother's bedroom. I knocked. No answer. I opened the door slowly.

"Grams," I said softly. Then a little louder. "Grams."

"What is it, child? Get that flashlight out of my face!" Grams snapped.

I moved closer to the bed. "Grams," I said. "The power's off, and I think I just saw a murder."

"Benjamin Sonny Etherly," Grams pronounced, raising herself up on her elbow. "You've just been dreaming. Your mom and dad will be back next week. You can tell them all about it then. Now, go back to bed."

Lightning lit up the bedroom. Two seconds later—Boom!

"I have to go outside and look. I'm sure something happened."

"You can't go out in this weather," she said and rolled back on her side. "That lightning will fry you like a piece of burnt toast."

"But—"

"But nothing," she interrupted. "Go back to bed. You can check all you want in the morning."

I returned to my room, got dressed, shoes and all, and lay on top of my covers. I must have dozed off, because the next thing I knew, light was streaming through the window. I hurried to look. No rain. My scorched bike was in the driveway. The sidewalk glistened from across the street. I swung into my coat, grabbed my iPhone, hurried downstairs and pushed through the door.

Leaves and pieces of tree branches covered the yard. Trashcans lay in the street—lids open, junk falling out. The cool air surprised me. I zipped up my coat and ran across the street to the place I saw the boy fall. A red circle the size of one of Grams's pancakes stained the sidewalk. I took pictures, then walked up and down the sidewalk looking for another red stain. Nothing. I ran home to tell Grams.

*****

Grams stood over the stove, holding a spatula. "Wash your hands, child," she said and added, "and set the table."

"But, Grams. I found blood. I took pictures with my iPhone."

"You wash up and set. Then, after we eat, I'll drive you up to *Walgreen's* so you can get the pictures developed."

"No, we don't need—"

"You going to argue with me, boy?" Grams interrupted.

"No, Ma'am."

*****

I couldn't see my plate because Gram's huge pancake covered it up, no room for the bacon. I just piled it on top. When Grams had her mouth full I stuck out my iPhone with a picture of the blood. She began choking. I ran to bring her a glass of water, and hit her on the back like I'd seen in the movies.

"Lands, Boy," she said coughing. "Stop pounding on me. You trying to kill your grandmother?"

I plopped in my chair but didn't take my eyes off her.

Grams finally stopped coughing and looked at me. "You think that's really blood?"

"Yes. I saw one boy shoot another boy. I found the blood where he fell."

"Okay. Just in case something did happen we need to call the police."

*****

I couldn't believe how long it took for the police to come. It must have been an hour before a cruiser pulled up in front of our house.

"Now, don't let them police officers scare you 'cause you're only twelve," Grams said. "Or 'cause you wear glasses or 'cause you're black."

"No, Ma'am. Will you stay with me?"

"I won't leave your side, child."

*****

"Okay, Sonny," the female officer said, putting her hand on my shoulder. "Tell us what you saw."

"I saw one boy chasing another boy," I said. "Then the one boy pointed a gun and shot the other boy."

"You sure?" she said. "The storm knocked out power in this area. It had to be pitch-black last night. Did you have your glasses on?"

"Yes, Ma'am. And I saw them real clear when the lightning flashed."

"And you saw the gun clearly?"

"Well, not really."

"And you heard a shot?"

"No, the thunder drowned it out."

"What did these boys look like?"

"I couldn't tell. But they looked like teenagers."

"Like teenagers?"

"Yeah—"

"Ahem!" Grams interrupted.

"I mean, *yes, Ma'am*," I said. They had long legs and they ran real fast."

"I'm sorry Mrs. Etherly," the male officer said, looking at his watch. "We have no report of any shooting in the area, or of any missing person. And, Sonny doesn't seem to be clear on what he saw or heard."

"Wait," I said. "What about the blood?"

"What blood?" he said.

"Here," I said, handing him my iPhone.

The two officers looked at each other.

"Show us where you found this," the female officer said.

*****

Grams let me stay home from school to watch the Crime Scene Investigators. It was so cool, just like on television. They took tons of pictures and rubbed the red stain with long Q-tips so they could test for blood.

After that, they walked up and down the sidewalk looking for more red stains, just like I did.

*****

The next day my brain felt like mush. I know it sounds crazy, but I don't remember a single thing about that morning. I must have walked to school and sat through my morning classes because, the next thing I remember, I was sitting at my usual table in the cafeteria—the one in the back corner where nobody else sits—my lunch bucket open, an unwrapped sandwich in my hands, and my mouth full. I remember because I almost choked to death when I saw a girl sitting across from me. After I finally stopped coughing and caught my breath, my brain shifted into popcorn mode. *Who is she? Why is she sitting at my table? Is this a trick, so the other kids can laugh at me? Wait. They were already laughing at me, because I'd been gagging and coughing like an idiot.*

The girl didn't move. At least I never saw her move, not even her little finger. She just sat there kind of bent forward, looking into her fruit cup. She seemed tall, skinny with long arms. Her straight brown hair hung in front of her face and covered most of her red rimmed glasses. *Braces? Did I see braces? Maybe.* She took a spoonful of fruit. *Yes, braces.* She flicked a glance upward. *Green eyes.*

"*Who* are you?" I said.

She mumbled into her fruit cup.

"I couldn't hear you."

"Breanne," she said, barely above a whisper.

"You're new here, aren't you?"

"I've been here the whole school year."

"All year?"

Breanne nodded.

"I'm Sonny."

"I know," she said from behind her hair.

"You know? How do you know?"

"I'm in most of your classes."

"Huh? You're in my classes and I don't even remember seeing you before?"

"You don't pay attention to anything but what's on your desk, and sometimes you let a teacher interrupt you."

"That doesn't sound so good when you say it like that. I suppose I stay to myself because the other kids are always picking on me. I just keep my head down and my pencil high."

"You weren't yourself this morning," she said. "Like your mind was somewhere else. You didn't answer when the teachers called on you, and the kids laughed when you didn't know the questions."

"Not a good day, huh?"

Her hair shimmered like a Hawaiian grass skirt when she shook her head.

"But, you still sat with me?"

"I didn't mean to bother you," she said.

"No. No bother. Sorry for almost throwing up on you."

"At least you didn't laugh at me."

"You, too? Kids laugh at you, too?"

"All the time."

"I won't."

"You won't what?"

"I won't laugh at you."

Breanne seemed to relax. "You're smart, aren't you?" she said.

"Smart enough, I guess."

Breanne looked at me like she was thinking about whether or not to say something. "And there's something else about you," she said. "I've sensed it all year, and it's been getting stronger."

"Something else?" I said. "You *sensed* it? Stronger? What does that mean?"

"Yeah. It's quite strong today. You have special powers."

"What? What powers? What're you talking about?"

"I'm not sure. Probably because *you* don't even know yet."

The bell rang.

Breanne gathered her things and left.

I still had my mouth open. I know because kids were pointing and laughing as they filed out.

Sure enough, Breanne was in my last two classes. In fact, in math she sat in the next row, just behind me. I tried to sneak a look but I couldn't see her face, only her long hair hanging like a curtain as she hunched over her desk taking notes.

*****

When I got home Grams told me a man had called, a Mr. Thurman. Used to be a policeman. She said he'd be coming over to talk to me about the two boys I saw in the storm. No sooner than I'd dropped my book bag, the doorbell rang. I heard Grams open the door. She called me.

I walked around the corner and was surprised to see Breanne standing in front of an older white man.

"You must be Sonny," the man said to me. "I'm Junior Thurman, Breanne's grandfather." He turned to Grams with his hand on Breanne's shoulder. "These two kids are in the same classes at school."

"Well don't just stand there like a lump, Boy," Grams said. "Close your mouth and mind your manners." Then she whispered, "You can sit at the dining room table."

"This way," I said, and led them to the table. "Would you like some water?"

"Sonny," Grams hissed.

"I mean would you like something to drink?"

"No thank you, young man," Thurman said. "But it's kind of you to ask."

Breanne didn't say a word

Mr. Thurman took Daddy's chair, the one at the head of the table. I slid into the end seat to his right, and Breanne sat across from me, just like in the cafeteria. Grams sat beside me, her hand on my shoulder.

Thurman looked at Grams. "Like I said on the phone, Ma'am, I'm a retired Memphis police officer. I worked homicide. My former partner is now a Major in the department. Yesterday the Major showed up at my house, pretty upset about a murder case we investigated over thirty years ago but never solved. He'd just read a police report that made him think the old case deserved another look with a fresh pair of eyes. He gave me a copy and asked if I'd check into it." He looked out a window and pointed. "Happened right across the street." He turned to me. "Same place you saw whatever you saw this past weekend, Son."

"Wow," I said slowly. *What are the odds of two murders happening in the same place, and so many years apart?*

Breanne looked up, her green eyes sparkled. "You really don't understand, do you?" she said, flashes of her multi-colored braces showing.

Did she just read my mind?

"You're thinking about the wrong things, Sonny," Breanne said. "You should be trying to find the odds of a twelve-year-old having ESP."

233

"Did she just say you had a disease?" Grams whispered to me.

"I think she believes I can see things that other people can't see," I whispered.

Grams turned to Breanne. "Are you saying my grandson is crazy?" she said loudly.

"No, Ma'am," Breanne said, ducking behind her hair.

Thurman opened his hands just above the table top, palms out. "Far from it, Mrs. Etherly," he said. "The police report my old partner gave me was the one written by the officers who came to your house. It said Sonny went to Snowden Middle School, the same school as Breanne. I called her last night and asked if she knew him and could she tell me something about him. She told me they are in many of the same classes, and that Sonny is a quiet boy who keeps to himself. Then she told me Sonny has special talents which go outside the bounds of science."

"Come again," Grams said.

Breanne's face reappeared and she looked at me. "You remember how you were able to guess every symbol on the ESP cards Ms. Phelps held up in math class last week?"

I nodded.

"You were the only one who got them all right. Well, the only one besides me. What were the odds of that?" She paused. "It wasn't just luck, Sonny. And how about the other day when Alexander tried to snatch the pencil off your desk and slug you? You grabbed your pencil and leaned down pretending to get something from under your desk just as he made his move. He got nothing but air with his right hand and missed you with his left fist. How'd you know he was coming?"

"I saw him."

Breanne shook her head. "He came up from behind you," she said.

"I must've seen his reflection or a shadow."

"Even so, neither would've told you what he was trying to do. I think you sensed him coming, and you read his mind."

Read his mind? I felt Gram's eyes on me.

Thurman looked at Grams. "In nineteen eighty-two, a boy named Darrell Swift was shot in the back and killed across the street," he said, jabbing a finger in the direction of the window. "A pool of his blood was left on the sidewalk." He placed an eight by ten color picture on the table.

Grams winced, and pulled back.

"The blood stain was visible for months. Neighbors requested the city break up the sidewalk and pour fresh concrete. They did. But within a few days the blood stain returned." He laid a second picture down. "Lab boys even liquefied a sample and found it matched Swift's blood. People really freaked out. Some moved away." Thurman laid down a handful of photos and spread them out like playing cards.

Grams's eyes widened.

"Since then, that one section of concrete has been replaced no fewer than seven times. And the blood stain always returned, except for these last five years. That is, not until Sonny discovered it this past weekend. That's why my ex-partner was so worked up. Darrell's blood spot is back."

"We've only lived here three or four years," Grams said. She looked nervous. "No one ever said anything about this. I don't think my son would have moved here if he'd have heard about the bloody sidewalk."

Thurman smiled, closed lipped.

Breanne flicked her hair away from her face. "The murderer was never found," she said. "It's as if the spirit of Darrell Swift has been crying out for justice all these years."

"What does this have to do with the boys I saw?" I asked.

"Sonny," Thurman said. "There was no murder last Sunday."

"Are you saying I never really saw two teenagers?"

"Oh no, Sonny," Breanne said. "You saw them all right. They just weren't alive."

Grams rose up off her chair. "God in heaven. You *are* saying Sonny is crazy."

Thurman shook his head. "Not crazy. Just gifted. Your grandson has powers very few people do."

Grams settled back in her chair, looking from Breanne to Thurman and back again.

Breanne turned to her grandfather. "As far as I can tell, this is all brand new to him. He doesn't know he has the power."

I looked at Mr. Thurman, then at Breanne. "What about you, Breanne," I said. "Do you have powers?"

Breanne lowered her eyes.

Thurman patted his granddaughter's hand. "The spirits talk to Breanne," he said, keeping his eyes on her. "They trust her and ask her to do things for them. Things they can no longer do."

Grams narrowed her eyes. "What kind of things?" she asked.

"They usually want her to correct some mistake they made when they were alive or send a message. Right Bre?" Thurman said.

Breanne nodded.

"Do you hear spirits talking right now?" Grams challenged.

"I've learned to turn them off," Breanne said softly. "Otherwise I'd go crazy. There are so many spirits who wish they'd done something different when they were alive or are desperate to protect a loved one."

I traced the pattern in the tablecloth. "I'm pretty sure what I saw was real," I said quietly. Thurman leaned forward with his forearms on the table. "Okay, Sonny," he said. "Let's go with that for now. Can you describe the shooter?"

"I never saw him clearly. The lightning was like a big strobe light. I could only see when it flickered. It was pitch-dark between lightning strikes."

"I need you to concentrate, Son," Thurman said. "Close your eyes and focus on what you saw that night."

I closed my eyes. I could feel Grams looking at me.

"Tell me about the boy with the gun," Thurman said. "What's he wearing?"

"A hat," I said. "A baseball hat. T-shirt and jeans. And he held the gun out in front of him."

"Good," Thurman said. "How about his build, maybe even his height?"

"Skinny. He was skinny," I said. "I don't think either boy was tall, but they were about the same size." I opened my eyes.

"Sonny," Breanne said as she reached across the table and touched my hand. "Close your eyes again."

"Huh?" I said, jerking my hand back.

"Please," Breanne said.

I looked at Grams, took a breath, and stuck my hand back out.

"Good," Breanne said, and laid her hand on mine. "Close your eyes and find the second boy. You can see him better, right?"

"Whoa," I said. "How'd that happen?"

"What do you see?"

"I see him real clear. His baseball hat is red and so are his running shoes."

"How about his hand?" Breanne said. "The one holding the gun."

"The left one. There's something on the back of it, a tattoo I think. Not sure what it is." I squinted to get a better look. "It's like a sideways fat V that's coming off a large circle."

"Keep looking," Breanne said. "I can see it too. Go back to when they were running and his hand swung down so we can see the tattoo right side up."

"Wait," I said. "That can't be. It looks like the head of a rabbit."

"I agree," Breanne said. "A rabbit looking to the left."

"Yes," I said.

Thurman's eyes flashed. "The *playboy bunny*," he muttered to himself. "Great work, kids." Thurman shifted his eyes to Grams. "This is so much more than our investigation uncovered," he said. "The first youth gangs in Memphis began showing up in the eighties, many being sent by Chicago judges who ordered them out of town to live with relatives. One gang in particular called the Vice Lords seemed to have a large number of relatives in the mid-south—Arkansas, Mississippi, Tennessee. Each gang has its own colors and symbols. Red is the Vice Lords' color and the *playboy bunny* is one of its symbols. Juvenile court processed quite a few of these kids back then. I need to have a look at those old files."

I couldn't take my eyes off Breanne. "Did you really see the two boys?" I said. "Just by touching my hand?"

Breanne nodded. "Your psychic vision is clear, Sonny. And you'll learn how to use it."

*****

The next day in school Breanne seemed different—she stood tall and held her head up.

"Hey, Breanne," I said. "Look, I've been thinking about last night. I have to say—"

"It scared you?" Breanne interrupted. "You think you're going crazy?"

"Yeah...how'd you know?"

"Because that's exactly the way I felt when it began happening to me."

"But this couldn't have happened. It's not logical."

"How'd you feel yesterday when I touched your hand?"

"Calm. And it was like you were standing beside me looking at that kid."

"I was."

"But how?"

"Look, Sonny. I can't answer how or why, or even better, why me?"

"Yeah. Those are my next questions."

Breanne took a breath. "All I know is that, thanks to you and your special powers, my grandfather found him."

"Found who?"

"He found a picture of a skinny kid with a *playboy bunny* tattoo on the back of his left hand. His name is Thomas Bradley. Grandpa says Bradley is now fifty-two-years-old, still goes by the name of *Lil' T,* and he's left handed. And get this, he was just released from jail after serving a five-year sentence for attempted murder. That explains why the blood stain didn't reappear on the sidewalk until last weekend."

I'm sure my mouth was wide open. I didn't know what to say.

"I'll walk home with you after school," Breanne said. "I want to check out the sidewalk. If everything went the way I think it did, Darrell Swift's spirit will have been released now that his murderer has been found."

*****

After school, Breanne and I walked to my house and crossed the street. I couldn't believe my eyes. The blood spot was gone.

*****

Vollintine-Evergreen Historic District

The Vollintine-Evergreen neighborhood is located in the northwest section of midtown Memphis, historically anchored by the religious community - notably Baron Hirsh Synagogue surrounded by its orthodox members living within walking distance, Saint Therese Little Flower Catholic Church/School, community outreach programs of churches like Evergreen Presbyterian and Trinity United Methodist, and acclaimed Snowden Middle School and Rhodes College. VECA, the neighborhood association, successfully countered the real estate "block busting" strategies of the 1960's-70's, and contributed to the stability of the neighborhood during its racial integration.

War is Hell
Geoffrey Meece

I thought this weekend would never arrive. I had been preparing for months. My first Civil War reenactment. Finally it was time. I left work early that day and was on the road by three thirty. Destination, Shiloh. No rush. I had oceans of time. This is where the saying, *the best laid plans of mice and men*, bit me on the ass.

"Damn, damn it to hell," I cursed as the red warning light flashed on my dash-board followed by a burning smell. Smoke seeped from the hood of my car. I heard my phone buzzing from the console. As my car slowly coasted to a stop on the edge of the road, I took the call.

"Hello, Mary."

"How's it going, baby? Are you there yet?"

"No, and it isn't going very well. I'm stuck on Highway Twenty-Two with an overheated radiator."

"Oh, Virgil, I'm sorry. I know how much you've been looking forward to this."

"That's okay, I'll make it. Worst case scenario, I might be a little late. I passed a farmhouse about a half-mile back. If I'm lucky, I'll be back on the road soon. I hope they don't think I'm a ghost in my uniform and have a heart attack."

"That would be bad." She laughed.

"I was so busy checking out my gear for this weekend that I forgot about everything else, like the car and charging my phone. It hasn't beeped yet, but if you lose me, you'll know why."

"In that case I'll let you go, but call if you need me to come get you."

"I will. If you talk to Randy, explain why I'm late."

"Be careful. Bye."

"Bye."

I felt better now. The sound of Mary's voice always blew away the dark clouds of self-pity.

The farmer didn't seem shocked by my uniform and was kind enough to fill several jugs of water and drive me back to my car. He stayed until my radiator was filled and the engine was running.

As he was getting in his pickup he hollered, "Give 'em hell boy and tell old Bedford I said hello."

"I'll do that, sir, and thanks again."

I called Mary to give her an update.

"Well that wasn't too bad. I'm driving again."

"Glad to hear it. I was worried about you. I called your cousin, Randy, but his phone is off."

"He leaves it in his car when he does reenactments. I think I'm close, so I'll, aw hell." *THUMP, THUMP, THUMP.* "You've got to be kidding me."

"What's wrong, Virgil?"

"Other than a flat tire everything is rosy."

"This is turning into quite an ordeal for you, isn't it?

"Well what can I say, war is hell. On a bright note, I have a good spare. I guess I'd better hang up and take care of this. Call you back shortly."

As I closed my phone, the low battery signal beeped. I might be able to make one more call, but that was a big maybe. Changing the tire went smoothly. I should have been smart enough to keep my mouth shut. As I tightened the last lug nut I asked the dumbest question a person can come up with.

"Hell, what else can happen?"

The roar of thunder followed by a downpour answered my question. I didn't say another word. Why tempt fate?

I put my wet carcass behind the steering wheel and drove into the outer skirts of the park. The rain and heat from the road created a misty fog. I definitely drove defensively. Visibility was a bitch.

If it hadn't been for that dog I might have made it. Funny how a slight turn of the wheel to avoid hitting a stray can put you in a ditch, but that's where I landed.

I grabbed my phone. It was as dead as my hopes of making it to the battlefield. Men aren't supposed to cry, but hey, I was close to breaking that code when I heard music, a harmonica with singing in the background. It came from over the rise beside the road. I grabbed my gear, locked the car, popped the magnetic key box under the fender and headed toward the sounds. At the crest I spotted a campfire in the distance. As I approached the music stopped.

"Halt. Who goes thar?"

"Virgil Jackson."

"Show yourself and be quick about it."

"I'm a showin', hold your fire." I was proud of my realistic response. Now I was starting to have fun.

A man behind him said, "Lower your piece, Zeke. That boy is one of ours."

"I see that now, Josh. Come on in, Virgil. Boy, you look like something a bobcat played with."

When the laughter died down, I said, "Thanks."

The man called Joshua invited me to sit by the fire and relax. He poured me a cup of coffee.

"Here, son. Sip on this. It'll warm you."

"Thanks, sir." Maybe it was due to the fact I was damp and chilled to the bone, but that was the best cup of coffee I ever had.

"How'd you get so wet?"

"Believe it or not it was raining just below that rise, a real downpour."

"That's strange. Seems like we would've seen it from here or heard the thunder? Oh well, April weather is funny like that. Who you with?"

"The Thirteenth-Tennessee. If you can point me in the right direction, I'll try to find them."

"That's not a good idea. It's almost dark. You'd be better off stickin' with us. We're the Twenty-second. Besides, we can always use the help."

"I guess that'd be all right."

"It's settled then. Hey, boys, Virgil, here, is joinin' us."

Nods of approval from the men around the camp reassured me.

"Virgil, you already met Zeke thar. That mean looking one next to him is Lem, then we got Abner, Clyde, Andrew, and I'm Joshua, but the boys just call me Josh."

With slight hand gestures they gave their approval and acceptance, I responded with a slight wave. "You can call me Virg."

"Store your gear over yonder and you're welcome to bed down in my tent. Thars room enough for both of us."

"Thanks, Josh, I'm obliged."

"You know there's something about you that seems familiar. Kinda like we've met before."

"I know what you mean. I was thinking the same thing."

"Where you from?"

"Memphis. And you?"

"Franklin."

"I heard that's a nice town, but I've never been."

"Well now, I have been to Memphis, but I was just a boy. Pap took me in to see the big city. I don't remember much about it other than the fact it was a busy place and the river was bigger than I thought it'd be. It was nice enough but too many people for my taste."

"Maybe we were brothers in a past life," I said with a smile.

"Brothers in a past life. I like that. Virgil, you're a hoot. That's what you are, boy, a genuine hoot."

He laughed, and I had to laugh with him. Usually, I'm slow when it comes to making friends and feeling relaxed around strangers, but this was uncanny. I felt an instant bond with Josh. Hell, maybe we were kin in a past life.

"Well whatever the case we know each other now. We'll have to get together after this is over, have y'all over for dinner. My Mary is one hell of a cook."

"Sounds nice, I'm sure my Esther would take right to you like I have, but I guess for now we should just concentrate on tomorrow and take it a day at a time."

I enjoyed sitting by the fire. My clothes were now dry, and the everyday pressures of work and bills seemed a million miles away. I was a little surprised how exhausted I was. I guess the long day and obstacles to get here were catching up with me.

"I hate to end such a pleasant conversation, but I'm ready to call it a night."

"That's all right, Virg. I'm about ready myself. Go on in. I'll join you shortly."

I was at the point of dozing off when Josh entered the tent with a lantern. He bedded down and blew out the flame. I was amazed how quiet and peaceful it was. I sat up and looked out enjoying the serenity of my surroundings. I could see the soft glow of the campfire's hot embers. Several of the other men remained around the fire. Every so often, someone threw a log on the fire, reviving the flames.

"Son of a..."

I didn't finish, afraid I'd wake Josh, who snored lightly. I rubbed my eyes. The men had moved to the side. I'll admit I was exhausted, and a tired mind can play tricks, but I swear I could see the flames of that fire through several mist like forms. They turned and stared in my direction. For a split second I was looking through them and then it was Lem and Zeke, solid as rocks again. The scene I witnessed left me breathless, but what else could it have been other than an illusion created from an over active imagination and a fatigued mind?

"I thought I heard you stirrin'."

"Sorry if I woke you."

"You havin' trouble sleepin'?"

"It's just that when I looked out at the fire I thought I saw..."

Josh turned his head and stared out.

"What fire?"

I stared out at a black quilt of night with a million stars forming its patchwork pattern.

"I don't get it. I saw, or I, ah..."

"That's fairly common out here. Why me and the boys have seen a number of things that can't be true, but a good night's rest always makes things better with the sunrise."

"Sounds like good advice. Sorry, I woke you."

"Nothin' to be sorry about."

I vaguely remember saying goodnight for a second time and rolling over. I dozed off in seconds, dead to the world. Suddenly, I had the sensation of being shaken. It seemed as if I had only been asleep a few minutes, but I opened my eyes to sunshine. I heard gunfire, and the roar of cannon in the distance. Josh was leaning over me. He had an odd grin, and his eyes sparkled with excitement.

"Get up, Virg. Yankees are hittin' us with all they got! Grab your gun! All hell is bustin' loose!"

I came out of the tent to a surreal scene. These guys could have won an academy award. The chaos and panic were awesome to behold. Now this was neat. With Hollywood quality, I played my part in the reenactment to the hilt.

"Let's get 'em," Zeke screamed as our small band ran like a pack of starving wolves on a blood trail towards the enemy.

"Keep your head down, son. Make yourself a smaller target."

While running in the middle of the group, I was on the verge of doing my well rehearsed rebel yell when Andrew to my left let out a scream that made the hairs on the back of my neck stand up. Several others chimed in. They sounded like a choir from hell.

"Thar they be in that thicket yonder."

We turned and ran full speed towards them. A soft breeze caressed my face. Smoke from gunpowder floated like a mist around us. The indescribable sounds of screams, guns, groans, and curses echoed through my brain. The spectators who came to view this battle were getting their money's worth. I turned to Josh and smiled, then reality slapped me hard. There weren't any people, only us.

"Josh," I screamed, "Where are the people?"

"Virg, I don't know. I imagine folks are in church praying for a victory. Wherever they are, they're in a safer place than we are. Just shoot straight and try to keep your head down, son."

Josh turned, charging a wall of blue emerging from the thicket.

My breathing grew rapid, and my heart pounded like a bass drum in my chest. The smell of gunpowder and blood nauseated me. Sweat burned my eyes as it dripped from my forehead. Bile rose in my throat. I fought the urge to vomit.

This isn't real, it can't be, but if it's not, what the hell is it?

A Yankee private lunged at me driving his bayonet into my chest.

Panic and terror consumed me.

I stopped and waited for the pain I knew was forthcoming but nothing. From behind me, an agonizing scream of pain erupted.

I turned.

Lem stared in disbelief as the Yank passed through me and drove him to the ground with the point of the bayonet imbedded in his throat. Looking up at me in disbelief, Lem spit blood and gurgled, whispering, "Virg, how did you do that?"

Tears filled my eyes as I watched him die.

Abner, to my left and a few paces ahead of me somehow lifted upward. As his body shuddered, he spun quickly. In horror and disbelief I realized half his face was blown off. A scene that should only exist in nightmares.

"Oh my, God!" I screamed as the butt of Abner's musket spun full force with him towards the side of my skull. Instinctively, I ducked, but in the process I lost my balance and fell backwards. I hit the ground hard. I lay there dazed, unable to rise, and to be honest, not really sure I wanted to. I turned my head to the side and witnessed the battle still raging in the meadow around that thicket. The sounds of war softly faded away, and the men slowly vanished from view until none were left.

That's when I blacked out.

*****

"Quick bring some water! I found him. Virgil, snap out of it. Virgil."

"Ohhhh, where am I?"

"Take a sip of this. What happened to you, cousin? We've been looking all over for you."

"Randy?"

"Yeah, it's me. Here, take another drink. Slow, easy does it. Splash a little on your face."

The cold water on my face made me more alert. "How did you find me?"

"When you didn't show up, I figured something happened, so I called your house this morning. Mary said you left early yesterday. I knew you had to be in trouble. We found your car in the ditch. It took a little while to find you in this tall grass."

"Tall grass? What are you talking about?" I tried to sit up, "Ow, damn that hurts."

"Take your time. You got a pretty good goose egg there, Virg."

I rubbed the knot and grimaced. The bright sunlight painfully blinded me. Gradually, my vision cleared, and I took in my surroundings. "How did this tree get here?"

Randy grinned. "I'm no expert, but I'd be willing to bet it grew right there from an acorn."

"Help me up."

"You sure that's a good idea?"

"I'm sure. Help me up." I stood on wobbly legs for a few minutes before I was able to walk. "I'll be right back. Give me a couple of minutes. Call Mary, I know she's freaking out."

I slowly walked the short distance to camp, or at least to where it had been. All signs of a campfire and tents—gone. I found my gear and bedroll neatly laid out beside a blackberry thicket. I returned to Randy.

He stood holding my rifle. He knelt beside the tree and showed me a limb, with signs of a fresh break. "I have no idea how you ended up here, but I think I found what got you. This must've fallen on you and knocked you out."

"No that's not what happened. I was..."

I stopped and considered what I was about to say, and the undoubted aftermath.

"You were what?"

"Wait. Give me a second to get my bearings."

"It's okay. Take your time."

"It's starting to come back to me. I went off the road dodging a dog. My phone was dead. I thought this was a shortcut to the reenactment camp. I stopped here to listen for voices or spot any fires when that branch must have clobbered me just like you said."

It was a slow process, but with a little help, I managed to gather my gear and make it back to their camp. Despite the pleasant conversation with Randy, I wanted to leave. I needed to be alone and mull over my thoughts.

My car was towed from the ditch, no damage, and Randy insisted on following me home as a precaution. As I pulled into our driveway, Mary ran to meet me.

"Virgil, are you all right? I was worried sick."

"I'm fine."

"You don't look it. To be honest you look like hell."

"Don't hold back on my account. Tell me how you really feel."

"I'm sorry, but when they told me you didn't show up, my imagination took over. Well, you know how I get, but I'm really sorry your trip was ruined."

The thought of confiding in her crossed my mind, but I instantly dismissed the notion. A selfish part of me wanted to protect those memories. They were mine, and I didn't want anyone to rationalize or explain them away.

I did promise on the next reenactment, I would ride with Randy. That seemed to make everything okay. She could live with that.

Almost any experience in life can be rationalized with the passing of enough time. I was close to that point until my birthday, July twenty-eighth.

"Wake up, birthday boy. We've got things to do and places to go."

"Can't I just sleep in? You can join me in bed, and make this day really special."

"Maybe later. Right now the car is packed and ready to go. Get up."

No use arguing. When her mind was made up, it was a lose, lose situation. Thirty minutes later we were on the road.

"Now, Mary, since it's my special day, will you tell me where we're going?"

"Shiloh," she said, with a huge smile.

"Shiloh, but you're not into history. Isn't there something else you would rather do?" I asked.

Actually, the thought of returning scared me. I don't know why, but I was on the verge of a panic attack.

Breathe deep breaths. Slow. This day had to come. It didn't happen. It wasn't real.

"Vigil, are you all right? I thought you would love spending the day there. I read online they have a new exhibit opening today in the museum."

I felt like an ass. She had gone to a lot of trouble packing a picnic lunch and planning this getaway.

"I'm fine. This is going to be great birthday. Thanks, Mary." I squeezed her hand.

We made the rounds. I told her about the bloody pond, Hornets' nest, General Johnston's death. Now I was starting to relax and have fun. We stopped at the mass Confederate grave for a moment, before heading to the museum. It was Mary's turn to guide me. She led me to the new exhibit.

The sign read, *Skirmish of the Bloody Thicket.*

My heart leapt to my throat. I moaned as my knees buckled. I caught the edge of a display table with my hands to keep from falling.

"Virgil, what's wrong?" Mary screamed, "I'll get help."

"No, I'm okay, don't."

"Are you sure? You don't look okay."

The section I viewed honored a small band of brave Southerners from Franklin, Tennessee. Faces on tintype stared at me, familiar features of friends.

"Mary," I said, as I pointed to the men, "The handsome fellow on the end is Joshua, next is Andrew, then there's Lem, Zeke, Abner, and Clyde."

Mary flashed me an amused look.

"Virgil, you nut, you really had me going there for a minute."

"Excuse me folks. This won't take but a second. We almost overlooked this"

We stepped aside for the museum director to open the glass display. He smiled as he placed a brass plate under the photograph.

Mary paled as she read the names off the latest addition to the display.

"Virgil, how did you know?"

"Let's find a nice shady spot for that picnic lunch you made. As a matter of fact, I know the perfect place in a meadow by a big oak tree. I have a story I want to share with you. A story I now know to be true."

*****

Shiloh Battlefield Park

A historic site in southwestern Tennessee, near Pittsburg Landing on the Tennessee River, Shiloh was the site of one of the first major battles of the Civil War and took place in April, 1862. The numbers of dead and wounded were horrendous on both sides. The park is frequently used as a venue for Civil War reenactments.

Kolopin
Seth Wood

"Son," Dad said. "Don't beat the water with your paddle. Dip it into the water. Turn it. Push it out. The canoe ain't going to paddle itself."

Dad said the same sentence at least five times a day. Sitting in the front of the fiberglass canoe, Andrew did not steer the canoe, but he did provide the forward thrust and steady movement.

"Really dig in there," Dad said. "But don't splash me. The river is cold this time of year."

Andrew dug his cheap, wooden paddle into the muddy Mississippi River water and pushed. The cold, wintery water swirled around the wide, flat end of the paddle.

"I hate this," Andrew mumbled from the front seat of the canoe.

Andrew shifted in his winter coat as a freezing breeze ripped across the front of the canoe.

"What was that, boy?" Dad asked.

A partially submerged tree limb drifted alongside the canoe. Andrew wondered if there was a whole tree just below the surface. What if the canoe was floating above a gigantic, fallen tree that travelled the entire length of the river just until the moment when Andrew looked at it?

"What was that, Andy?" Dad asked again.

He always did that. It was not a pet name. It was an insult. He called him by what he assumed was the weaker name. Andrew thought that perhaps Dad had named him just so that he could put him down. Andrew hated being called Andy.

"You think there is a whole tree under there?" Andrew asked, and pointed at the limb.

Dad took his aluminum paddle and pushed on the floating limb. It rolled over in the water to reveal a short splintered carcass. Bits of rotted wood broke free, but there was no large tree rolling beneath the canoe. It was just a broken branch that fell off of a tree somewhere upriver.

"Nope," Dad said. "Keep paddling. If you want your Mom to pick us up by tomorrow morning, we have to call from Cates Landing by tonight. We've got a couple more miles to go."

"Why couldn't we bring a cell phone?" Andrew asked.

Dad did not answer.

During his 'float trips' as he called them, Dad was a bit of a Luddite. Sure, if he was out alone on the River, he would take a cell phone, but it would stay OFF until he was ready to be picked up. Since he and Andrew were both on this trip, he declined to take a cell phone. At twelve, Andrew hated every minute of being on the river without video games or television.

"Do you really think any place in that town has a payphone?" Andrew asked over his shoulder.

Dad steered the canoe by pushing his paddle into the water and allowing it to drag a bit before digging in to guide the canoe towards shore. While they were still several miles from the small town, traveling from the middle of the nearly mile wide river to the shore took some time.

"Someone is bound to have a phone that we can use. Now help me get us to the shore. We are close enough to Cates Landing." When the boy didn't move, Dad said, "Get out and pull the canoe ashore."

Andrew sighed. Whoever sat at the rear of the canoe steered. Whoever sat at the front was responsible for landings. Dad did not trust Andrew with steering, or he could not give up that particular control. Either way meant Andrew had to get out of the canoe and into the freezing, dirty water, and haul the heavy, metal canoe ashore.

Andrew slid the paddle into the belly of the canoe and gripped both sides of its metal frame.

"Don't flip us," Dad said.

Andrew leaned his chest to one side of the canoe, lifted his legs over the side, and into the frigid water. He kept his weight in the canoe by pushing down on the sides to keep the boat steady. Andrew stood up in cold water that came midway up his calf. The wind pants and water shoes did nothing to keep the freezing water out. The cold seeped up his pant legs.

"Thanks for not tipping us," Dad said.

Andrew grabbed the wet rope that hung from a mooring hole bored through the front tip of the canoe, and pulled the canoe towards the shore.

"Come on, boy," Dad said. "Don't use the rope. Grab the side of the canoe. I have told you how to do this."

Andrew dropped the rope back into the water, grabbed both sides of the canoe, and pushed it forward onto the shore.

"There you go," Dad said. "If you just use the rope, you could tip me, and I don't want to get wet."

Andrew looked down at his wet pants.

"I told you to wear shorts," Dad said.

"Why would I wear shorts?" Andrew asked. "It's winter. It's cold. We are in an open canoe."

"Are you talking back?" Dad asked.

Andrew did not answer. Out on the River and alongside it, Dad seemed less restrained. He seemed to lose a bit of himself to the wildness that he was trying to recapture with the canoe trip. Andrew considered pressing the issue but thought better of it. Dad would never call Mom to pick them up, if Andrew had a black eye.

Instead, Andrew hauled the canoe as far as he could onto the riverbank. Dad got out and slid his paddle into the canoe before pushing the heavy canoe the rest of the way onto the bank.

"Why'd we have to stop here and not closer to town?" Andrew asked.

They were about half a mile north of the small town, and Dad had steered them onto a part of the bank that was thicker with brush and undergrowth.

"This ain't a car, Andy," Dad said. "There aren't any locks or anything."

"So, we are hiding it?" Andrew asked.

"Bingo," Dad said.

Dad and Andrew pushed and pulled the canoe further ashore, and out of sight of the river.

"That should do it," Dad said.

Dad bent over the canoe and beneath his seat. He threw Andrew a towel and his hiking boots. Dad then pulled a small revolver from beneath the seat and slid it into his belt. He covered the handgun with his coat.

"What's that for?" Andrew asked while drying off his pants with the towel.

"Just a little assurance."

"Assurance for what?"

"You never know," Dad said. "Let's go."

"Let me change shoes really quick," Andrew said.

"Well, hurry up."

Andrew quickly changed shoes. They picked their way over rocks around bushes along the riverbank towards town. Of course, Dad led the way as he always did. Andrew tried to keep pace.

"Keep up," Dad said.

It did not matter at what pace Andrew followed his Dad, it was never the right one. Andrew either heard "Keep up" or "Stay back." He was not allowed to walk alongside his father. Andrew had to walk behind him at whatever arbitrary distance Dad chose for that particular journey.

Keeping pace with Dad proved difficult. The large rocks were cold and slippery, and where Dad skillfully moved around them as someone with his experience on riverbanks should, Andrew fumbled along awkwardly. Abruptly, Dad turned from the river, and moved up the bank towards a field away from the river.

"Where are we going?" Andrew asked.

"We don't want to let people know which way we came from," Dad said.

"Would anyone care?" Andrew asked.

Andrew slipped on a particularly wet rock and wedged his knee into the ground between two stones. He grunted in pain.

"Come on," Dad said–ignoring the question and Andrew's pain.

Andrew pulled himself up and brushed off his pants. They were still damp, and stuck to his legs at the ankle, causing the wind pants to parachute unfashionably.

"Stop," Dad said. "Look back at the canoe."

"I don't see it. We hid it. Remember?"

"Son, don't look at the trees. Look through them."

Andrew did the trick that his Dad taught him. When most people saw a forest, they saw exactly that: a large mass of trees, underbrush, and wood debris. They see a natural fence that is tens of feet high with green at the top. But, Dad had shown Andrew another way of looking. A forest was also a

large group of individual trunks and leaves and
branches. Once he understood that, Andrew could
see past the initial line of tree trunks, and then the
second line. And then, the third. The sensation of
looking beyond the trees and into the forest was like
looking at one of the once popular 3D artworks that
required the viewer to place his or her nose on the
two dimensional paper, and pull back until the image
leapt off of the page. It was eye-opening.

"I can't see it," Andrew said.

"Good. Let's go, Andy."

Andrew grumbled, and followed his father into the
field and toward the town of Cates Landing,
Tennessee.

*****

A low, swirling fog rolled across the town's empty
main street. Along either side of the single main
street sat rows of squat brick buildings with glass
fronts edged by sloping, aged sidewalks. Even from a
distance, Andrew could see that the buildings
encompassed a small store, a barbershop, and what
looked to be a cleverly named, but vacant religious
coffee shop, 'He Brews.' The rest was lost in the fog
that seemed too thick with the sun shining so
brightly overhead. No one and no thing moved along
the street or sidewalks. The town exuded an almost
tangible silence as if the fog muffled everything that
should be making noise.

"Dad, I don't want to be here," Andrew said.

He felt uneasy. With the fog, uncertain malaise
drifted along the ground in tendrils that licked at
Andrew's feet. He did not want to go into Cates
Landing.

"I know, Andy. That's why we are calling your Mom."

"No. Not the canoe trip. This town," Andrew said. "Can't you feel it? It feels off."

Dad looked at the town. Andrew guessed that Dad also felt some unease. And for one of the first times in Andrew's life, Dad agreed with him.

"Yeah," Dad said. "It does feel a little off."

"Where do you think everyone is?" Andrew asked.

"School's out," Dad said. "Everyone left town. Can't say that I blame them. This place looks miserable."

The town looked as if it had aged poorly. Potholes and pitfalls peppered the road with loose asphalt and black grit.

"I don't think that's it," Andrew said. "Let's go back to the canoe and go farther down river. We can find another town."

"You wanted to quit, Andy. We *are* quitting. Besides," Dad said, and patted the gun beneath his coat. "I have this."

Maybe Dad had felt something after all. Maybe it was the reason he had brought the gun in the first place.

"That doesn't make me feel any better," Andrew said.

"It should. I'm a good shot," Dad said.

And he was. Dad was good with a pistol but poor with decisions. Andy considered him dangerous.

"Go on," Dad said.

Andrew stepped forward out of the field and onto the town's main street. A single low-slung stoplight swayed lazily in the breeze. "Come on, Dad," Andrew pleaded one last time.

Dad threw Andrew an angry look, pushed past him, and walked briskly into town. Once Andrew followed Dad deeper into town, the fog thinned and seemed to burn away.

"The barbershop is closed." Andrew pointed to the sign hanging inside the door.

"You want a haircut?" Dad asked.

Andrew ignored the question. Dad was clearly in one of his moods. His moods swung about like a sailboat trying to catch the wind. But, Dad would never see that. From behind, Andrew could see his dad's shoulders squared off as if he was ready to fight the next person he came across. Andrew kept behind him at a pace that either Dad found acceptable or showed how little he thought of Andrew at the moment.

Dad's feet beat the sidewalk as if it owed him money. The sound of his feet smacking the concrete reverberated against the brick buildings.

Otherwise, the town was silent.

"Hey, Dad," Andrew said. "We could try the store."

"Where do you think we are going, Andy?" Dad huffed.

Whatever unease lay over the town was getting to Dad. Andrew could see his mood worsening with each heavy footfall. Andrew felt an itching slightly at the edge his mind: the feeling that something was off. Perhaps, it was the lack of cars on the town's main thoroughfare. Perhaps, it was that the only lights on in any of the buildings were in the store that they were walking towards and some other rundown building across the street.

The store had a large glass front with a black and orange 'OPEN' sign hung from a plastic hook stuck crookedly onto the window with adhesive. Dad pushed the glass door open.

Andrew jumped as the store's doorbell banged against the glass once, and then a second time as he waved Andrew inside.

"Well, go on," Dad said.

Andrew grimaced. The store smelled as if they were the first customers in a long while. An old man smell permeated the entire establishment. Behind a long counter reminiscent of a soda shop, sat the old man that the smell most likely came from.

"Morning," the old man said.

"Good morning," Dad said.

"You two look a little worse for wear there," the old man said. "Car trouble?"

"Something like that," Dad said. "Andrew, go get us a couple of cokes, ok?"

Andrew nodded and walked between the sparsely stocked shelves towards the coolers in the rear of the shop. The shelves were mostly bare. The store looked to be a lifeless snapshot of the brands and marketing lingo from at least fifteen years ago. A squat, blue bottle of menthol chest rub sat alone on a shelf with 'Medicine' stenciled into the shelf's leading edge. The faded label was nearly illegible, but bore a label that Andrew had never seen, though he recognized the brand.

"You all walk into town?" the old man asked.

"Yes," Dad said.

"Did you see any of them wild kids out there?" the old man asked.

"Wild kids?" Dad asked.

"Yeah. All of the kids in the town went crazy a couple of weeks back. Started spray painting all kinds of satanic symbols on the buildings here in town. Didn't show up for school. Then they all just left and never came back," the old man said.

Andrew plucked two barely cold cans of coke from the whirring cooler, and let the door close behind him.

Dad was humoring the man. "No we didn't see any wild kids on our way in to town."

"Well, they are all over those woods out there. You had best be careful."

"Hey mister," Andrew said. "How many kids were there anyway?"

"About eight," the old man grumbled. "It about wiped the high school out."

"How much do I owe you for the drinks?" Dad asked.

Andrew set the two cans down on the counter next to the cash register.

"Ah, don't worry about it. Looks like you could use them."

"Thanks," Dad said.

"I can't really blame those kids for leaving," Andrew said.

"Andy!" Dad snapped.

"Oh, it's quite alright," the old man laughed. "Your boy is right. There isn't much to do here. And, that is what kids here do. They grow up and leave, but this was different."

"Was it because they all left at once?" Andrew asked as he cracked open the drink.

"Yep. And the satanic symbols of course," the old man said.

"Satanic?" Dad asked. "You didn't say anything about there being satanic symbols."

He had, of course. Dad hadn't been listening.

"Oh, yes. That is what they spray painted all over the buildings," the man said. "Horrible things."

"We didn't see any," Dad said.

Kolopin

Dad was right. The buildings were not spray-painted. Actually, they barely looked occupied much less vandalized.

"Oh, we cleaned it all off." The man added, "Bunch of hooligans if you ask me."

Dad changed the subject, "Can I use your phone to call my wife?"

"Sure. I'll just chat with your son while you make your phone call."

"You don't want to talk to him. This one here is a quitter," Dad said.

He gestured to Andrew. He looked away from the old man behind the counter to out beyond the storefront, and into Main Street.

"Say," the old man asked him. "You ever hear of Kolopin?"

"Kolopin?" Andrew asked.

"Yeah. The old Indian?" the man asked.

Andrew looked over at Dad, who was speaking angrily into the phone. Andrew was being blamed for ending the river trip. It was a trip that he never wanted to go on in the first place. Of course he did not want to keep going. Who wanted to waste a week of winter vacation floating from St. Louis to Memphis in a canoe?

"I haven't heard..."

"You should get your father to take you to the museum across the street." The old man pointed out of the large front window. "It's all about Reelfoot Lake and Kolopin. And, tonight is a special night!"

"What's so special about tonight?" Andrew asked.

The old man smiled, and said, "Well you'll just have to learn about that at the museum."

Dad slammed the phone down on the counter.

"Do you have any hotels or motels anywhere here?" Dad asked.

265

"We had a bed and breakfast, but that closed up shop," the old man said.

"Well that doesn't help me and the boy, here, now does it?" Dad said.

Andrew looked at the old shopkeeper apologetically.

The old man grinned, and said, "Well, we have a Hotel Seven out on the old highway. I could drive you and your son up there after I close up shop later this afternoon."

Andrew knew the answer before Dad even said it. He guessed the shopkeeper knew the answer as well.

"We won't be needing that," Dad said.

"Well then, have a nice day," the old man said.

"Yeah." Dad added, "You too."

Dad pushed Andrew towards the store's front door. Main Street looked empty. An old sign atop a ragged awning on the front face of the brick building across the street read 'Museum.' As Dad pushed the store's front door open, Andrew threw the old man another apologetic look.

"Hey, be careful out there. Like I said," the old man called, "the kids around here have gone crazy."

"Thanks," Dad said.

"And, you watch out for old Kolopin," the old man said to Andrew.

He nodded, and then he pushed out onto the sidewalk in front of the street.

"Your Mom will be here tomorrow morning to pick us up," Dad said. "What was all that 'watch out for chloroform' stuff about?"

"Ko-lo-pin," Andrew enunciated. "He was some Indian from around here I think. There is a museum over there about him and some lake."

Dad looked up and down the empty main street.

"This is a weird place for sure," Dad said. "This whole place looks abandoned."

"Can we go?" Andrew asked.

"Go where?" Dad asked.

"The museum. It's just right over there."

"Museum? You want to go to a museum? I wanted to finish this float trip and you want to go to some Indian museum."

Andrew sighed.

"Fine, Andy," Dad heaved. "We can go to your museum. We need to kill some time, and it doesn't look like anything is really open anyway. Let's hope your museum is."

The Reelfoot Lake Museum and Gift Shop crammed itself into one long room. The 'exhibits' blended into the gift shop in such a way that Andrew was not sure that anything in the museum was not for sale. The front half of the room consisted mostly of shelves with bits of colored quartz, plastic Native American figurines, and rain sticks.

"Don't touch anything, Andy," Dad said.

"Oh, he can touch anything in here if he wants to," a woman's voice called from the back of the museum. "None of the dioramas in here bite. I assure you."

Dad looked at Andrew, and repeated, "Don't touch anything."

"Sure, Dad."

"Well, good afternoon to you all!" A short, late middle-aged woman appeared between two shelves.

"Is it afternoon already?" Dad asked.

"Well, it's just after noon," the woman said. "Glen said you guys might pop in over here."

"Glen?" Dad asked.

"Why yes. Glen owns the shop across the street," the woman said. "Oh, I am being so rude. My name is Martha."

"I'm Andrew!"

"All right, boy. Calm down," Dad said.

"Well, Andrew," Martha said. "It is nice to meet you. Are you fine gentlemen here for the anniversary?"

"Anniversary of what?" Dad said.

"Why the New Madrid earthquake of 1812!" Martha said, "It happened two hundred years ago today."

"I've heard of that," Dad said.

"Was it a big one?" Andrew asked.

"It was so powerful it rerouted part of the Mississippi River causing the river to flow backwards," Martha said. "The church bells rang in Philadelphia. You'll have to learn the rest of the story yourself. Check out those dioramas. And, read the placards for more information."

"Thanks," Dad said. "Do you have a restroom that I can use?"

"Sure," Martha said. "In the back."

Dad turned to Andrew. "Remember, don't touch anything."

"Yes, sir," Andrew said.

Dad strode through the maze of dioramas to the back of the small building. Andrew wandered into the maze of cheap glass counters containing plastic painted figurines.

Martha retreated to the front of the store.

Andrew looked over the first few exhibits. The first glass case had a map of the central United States with what must have been the New Madrid fault line running along the Mississippi River from Missouri, through Arkansas, Kentucky, and Tennessee before ending in north Mississippi. The map showed in yellows, oranges, and reds where the fault line and its inherent danger lay.

The second exhibit showed a 'hypothetical' pre-earthquake path that the Mississippi River could have taken, and it explained how Reelfoot Lake was formed from the remnants of that pre-earthquake path.

"Mrs. Martha?" Andrew called.

"Yes?"

"When do I get to Kolopin?" Andrew asked.

Martha said, "Oh, you see Reelfoot Lake there? It is named after him."

"But, I thought his name was Kolopin," Andrew asked.

"Reelfoot is what the settlers in the area called him," Martha said. "It was a nickname because of a birth defect."

"What kind of birth defect?" Andrew asked.

"He was born with a misshapen foot that caused him to look to like he was rolling his foot every time he took a step," Martha said. "Reelfoot."

"Is he bothering you?" Dad said from the back of the museum as he wiped his hands dry on his pants.

"Not at all!" Martha said. "It is always great to have visitors. We don't see many good kids around here these days."

"Hey, Dad!" Andrew said. "Come look at this."

"What is it, Andy?"

Andrew ignored the patronizing tone. "It says here that this whole area was washed away by the Mississippi River during a big earthquake in 1812. See that Indian village on the map? It was washed away by the river!" Andrew pointed to the map.

"That was Kolopin's village," Martha said.

"Really?" Andrew asked, "Was he killed?"

"Of course," Martha said. "But, that isn't the right question to ask."

"What is the right question?" Andrew asked.

"Andy," Dad said.

"Oh, I promise your son is fine," Martha said. "The right question to ask is: why?"

"Why?" Andrew asked.

"Well, you have to go through the exhibits to find out!" Martha said.

Andrew smiled, and turned back to the story of the Great Earthquake of 1812 laid out along the maze of poorly lit exhibits. Dad came up alongside him.

"You really like this stuff?" Dad asked.

"Yeah. This is the stuff that I like," Andrew said. "It is a mystery, you know? Like the missing kids."

"We will stay out of that mystery," Dad said. "We don't want you to go missing."

Andrew eyed his dad, while he moved farther into the exhibits.

As he moved through the maze, Andrew learned the story of the 'why.'

Kolopin, or Reelfoot, had desired a wife from a neighboring village to produce a viable heir. He attempted to negotiate a trade for the daughter of the neighboring chieftain but was rebuffed. So, Kolopin decided to steal the chieftain's daughter. Upon returning to his own village, Kolopin was warned by the village elders that nothing good would become of stealing a potential wife.

Kolopin did not listen.

The ground shook once. The elders told Kolopin that it was the earth telling him to return his wife to her village, but he so wanted an heir that Kolopin refused.

The ground shook twice. The elders told Kolopin that the third time would mark the doom of the village and his people, but he so wanted an heir that Kolopin again refused.

Kolopin

The ground shook for a third time. And, it did not stop. The earth shook and shook. Still Kolopin refused to return his stolen bride. The earth shook so hard that the River writhed across the land like a great serpent. It washed away Kolopin and his village. It drowned any chance of Kolopin's line continuing.

"The real legend of Kolopin starts here," Martha said while leaning over Andrew's shoulder.

"Oh, yeah?" Andrew asked.

He looked over to see Dad perusing the gift shop to kill time.

"Yes," Martha said. "What you don't see among the exhibits here is that Kolopin is still looking for someone to take his place."

"You mean like an heir?" Andrew asked.

"Exactly like an heir," Martha said while flourishing her hands wildly. "Since his chances of one by birth were destroyed two hundred years ago, he has been hunting for a worthy replacement ever since! And if you aren't worthy, he throws you into the Great River!"

"Is that where all of the kids have gone?" Andrew asked.

Martha abruptly shut her mouth. Andrew felt a heavy hand clap him on the shoulder.

"With that," Dad said. "I think we will be leaving."

"But Dad," Andrew said.

"We are leaving, Andy." Dad pushed Andrew towards the gift shop, and the front door. He looked back apologetically at Martha, but she turned away, and moved towards the back of the museum.

As he was pushed through the front door, Andrew asked, "What, Dad?"

"You don't know when to not pick," Dad said.

"What?" Andrew asked.

"I know you, Andy," Dad said. "I know where you were going with that question."

"About the kids?" Andrew asked.

Dad walked down the sidewalk away from the museum. Andrew followed.

"Yes, about the kids," Dad said. "You couldn't tell that it upset her?"

"I know it shocked her," Andrew said.

"Don't always ask what is on your mind," Dad said. "It can hurt people's feelings."

"But, I thought it was a good question!" Andrew said.

"Come on. Let's cross the road and head back towards the canoe," Dad said. "It was a good question. Probably not about an Indian. And probably not the right person to ask. She looked to have been old enough to have one of the kids that the shopkeeper said went crazy and disappeared."

"Is that why she got all flustered?" Andrew said.

"That would be my guess," Dad said.

A bell clanged.

Andrew turned around to see the old shopkeeper standing outside his door looking at Andrew and Dad. Andrew turned back towards the museum to see Martha watching them from the museum's wide front window.

"Dad, they are watching us," Andrew said.

"Andy, they have been watching us since we got here."

"Who?"

"The whole town," Dad said. "There are more people here than just the old man in his store and the museum lady."

"So, they are hiding from us?" Andrew asked.

"From us?" Dad asked. "I don't think so."

"This place is really strange," Andrew said.

"You're telling me," Dad agreed.

"Is there any way that Mom can get us tonight?" Andrew asked. "I really don't want to stay here."

"No. She still has to work the rest of the day and deal with your sister," Dad said. "She said she'd leave early tomorrow morning and be here by ten or so."

"Where are we going to stay?" Andrew asked.

"We will stay near where we dragged and hid the canoe," Dad said. "There were quite a few trees there, and we can throw our tent up."

"I don't know," Andrew said.

"We are stuck here," Dad said. "But, I do think we should take the long way back to the canoe."

"The long way back?" Andrew asked.

"Yeah. Just in case anyone tries to follow us."

*****

"Did you see that the Mississippi River ran over this whole area during the earthquake?" Andrew said.

He and Dad picked their way through the forest in the general direction of the canoe. Andrew was glad that Dad knew where the canoe was; the winding and twisting path that they were taking to avoid being followed proved difficult for Andrew to keep track of.

At times, Dad's usual high level of paranoia was irritating and frustrating to endure, but in this situation, Andrew was thankful for the paranoia. Andrew felt it too.

He stumbled over a rotting log. There was something in the air of Cates Landing. It was like a subtle buzzing in the back of his brain. It was like the low warble of an airplane at cruising altitude. And, like that low warbling, Andrew was afraid that he could get used to the fear, and that he could get used to the sense that something was 'off' with the town. He could grow comfortable with it.

Dad's paranoia was keeping them safe for once.

"Yes, Andy," Dad huffed. "I saw. I was at the museum, too."

The river was nearby. The air grew colder with each step. Andrew shivered in his jacket.

"How much farther?" Andrew asked.

"We are just about there."

"Do you think anyone followed us?" Andrew asked.

"Not with the route we took," Dad said. "We took a couple hours to walk a couple of miles. If anyone was following us, they'd have been bored and gone by now. I didn't hear anyone following us anyway."

"What was wrong with that place, Dad?" Andrew asked.

"The town?" Dad asked. "I'm not sure. It seems like something bad happened there. Some kind of tragedy. Some people just can't get over that stuff, son. They cling to the hurt forever."

"Huh," Andrew said.

He was surprised. It was rare for Dad to speak so deeply with Andrew.

"What do you think?" Dad asked.

"About the town?"

"Yes. What do you think?" Dad asked again.

"I don't know. On the one hand, I think they are just a small town not used to strangers. I mean there isn't even a bridge crossing the river. They must get no traffic from anywhere," Andrew said.

"Good point," Dad said. "And?"

"And, I think someone killed all of the kids in that town," Andrew said.

Dad stopped, and looked back at Andrew.

It was a large leap of logic to go from a few missing kids to murder.

"Well, there's that," Dad said.

"Do you think it is possible?" Andrew asked.

"I suppose it has to be possible," Dad said. "The kids probably just ran away though. That place is dead, and just doesn't know it yet."

Andrew's stomach growled. "How much farther now?"

"We are here," Dad said. He pointed to the gray canoe concealed in the bushes nearby. "Start grabbing some twigs and sticks to build a fire while I unpack the tent. Get some dry leaves, if you can find them."

"Yes, sir," Andrew said.

"And Andy," Dad said. "Watch out for poison ivy."

"I will, Dad."

"We don't want a repeat of last time."

"I know!" Andrew said.

"I'm just saying that the last time I asked for dried leaves you picked the poison ivy leaves right off of the vine, son."

"Dad!" Andrew said.

He laughed as he pulled the bright yellow tent bag from the canoe.

"Oh, here. Take this." Dad pulled the firewood hatchet from the canoe. "Now, go on."

Andrew walked a short distance away from the canoe and his Dad, and bent down and started gathering sticks from the underbrush. He wondered if Kolopin had done the same thing so many years ago, but surely, a great Indian chief did not pick up his own sticks.

Dad built a small fire so as not to attract unwanted attention. As dusk fell, the woods felt as if the spaces between the trees grew smaller; the forest seemed to grow more crowded. There was no way that the forest could multiply, but he had to admit that he felt a twinge of fear. He was not accustomed to being in the woods at night. Even though he had spent the last several nights outside during the canoe trip, Andrew could not get used to the constant movement of the forest at night. Sounds came from every direction. Wind caused a tree branch to scrape against another branch. A rabbit or other small creature pushed through long dead leaves on its way to somewhere that surely could only be gotten to during the night.

Andrew shivered. Being so close to river at night during the winter made for a very cold experience. The small fire was not much help. He held out his hands to the meager flame.

*****

"Get enough stew?" Dad asked.

Dad stretched out and reclined deeper into his foldaway chair.

"Yeah," Andrew said.

"I can put another can of stew or chili in the coals if you want," Dad said. "We won't need the rest since tonight is our last night."

"I get it, Dad," Andrew said. "We aren't finishing this leg of your trip. You don't have to keep rubbing it in."

"Andy," Dad said. "I'm just disappointed."

"Quit calling me Andy. I hate it," Andrew said. He looked off into the forest–through the forest.

"Well, with that," Dad said. "I think it is time for bed."

"I didn't want to come on this trip," Andrew said.

"I know, Andrew," Dad said, "It's, just...there are things that I wish that I had done with my dad, that I never got the chance to do. They were things that I hated at the time, but looking back now, they weren't so bad."

"I somehow have a feeling that won't be the case for me with this," Andrew said.

"It probably wasn't a good idea to do this during the winter anyway," Dad said. "I just thought it'd be a fun adventure for you to be able to tell your friends once winter break is over."

"I probably won't tell them," Andrew said.

"That's fine," Dad said. "Well, I will see you in the morning. No need to get up early. We will have to float the canoe down to the boat ramp in Cates Landing before your Mom gets here, though."

Dad stood and walked to the tent.

"Kick out that fire before you go to bed, OK?" Dad asked.

"I will," Andrew said.

*****

Andrew shot up from a deep sleep to the sound of a loud thunder crack that seemed to come from everywhere at once.

"It's ok, Andrew," Dad whispered groggily. "A storm is coming in."

Andrew rubbed his eyes. "Won't the tent get flooded?"

"We should be ok," Dad said. "I put the tarp down beneath the tent to keep the water out. It hasn't even started raining yet."

Even in the dark, Andrew could see the different panels of the inside of the tent bulging inward and then outward as the wind beat against the canvas.

"I am going to turn the lantern on. Watch your eyes," Dad said.

A very low light flickered on in the center top of the tent. The light slowly grew brighter. Andrew could make out Dad slowly turning the propane valve on the lantern up for more light. Andrew looked from the brightening lantern to Dad, and screamed.

A large human torso shape bulged against the outside of the tent wall just behind Dad. It pushed inward.

Andrew fell backward against the tent wall–snapping one of the tent's load-bearing support rods.

The tent collapsed into a maelstrom of all-weather canvas and flailing bodies.

"Watch out for the lantern!" Dad yelled.

Andrew writhed among the folds of slippery cloth trying to find a way out. What had collapsed the tent? Were those footsteps coming from outside the tent?

"Dad!" Andrew cried. "Someone is outside the tent!"

"I have a gun!" Dad bellowed to whoever was outside. "Get away from here!"

Andrew felt along the bottom seam of the collapsed tent until he found the zipper. He wiggled through the canvas and mesh towards the zipper pull. As Dad thrashed about, Andrew felt around until he found the tab.

Smoke filled the collapsed tent.

"The lantern fell!" Dad yelled. "Get out. Get out of the tent!"

Andrew pulled the zipper upward and pulled himself forward. Something, hard and cold and metallic dug into his stomach: Dad's gun. Andrew grabbed the pistol and rolled out of the tent into darkness.

"Dad! I'm out," Andrew cried.

"Run towards town!" Dad yelled from inside the collapsed tent.

Flames erupted.

"I've got the gun!" Andrew shouted.

"Take it and go!" Dad yelled.

Andrew turned and ran barefoot into the forest. He ran fifty feet before Dad started screaming.

Blackness. Blackness all around. Trees. Cold air. Andrew ran until he could no longer hear Dad's screams. His bare feet hurt. He rubbed his arms to keep them warm. The sweatshirt and sweat pants did little to combat the cold.

Andrew fell against a tree trunk and gripped its rough, cold bark for support. He tried to catch his breath. The small revolver in his hand scraped the wood. Where had he run to? He moved around the tree to look for the fire that must have completely engulfed the tent by now. Andrew rubbed his eyes. They refused to adjust to the darkness quickly enough.

A twig snapped.

"Who's there?" Andrew called.

No answer.

Andrew raised the gun and pointed it towards where he thought the sound had come from.

"Dad?" Andrew asked.

No answer.

Andrew fumbled around for a better grip on the gun. Completely devoid of any sound beyond Andrew's own breathing, the forest felt completely dead.

He closed his eyes and listened.

Nothing.

Where the woods had previously been alive, there was only silence.

A twig snapped.

Andrew's eyes snapped open and he looked towards the sound through the trees into what lay beyond.

Something coalesced out of the blackness between the tree trunks. A purple silhouette of a broad-shouldered man flickered between the trees and dead underbrush. Instead of walking straight toward Andrew, the figure twitched and lurched towards him. He blinked. The figure burned its way into his retinas in an after image of purples and greens that moved all on their own.

"Get back!" Andrew screamed.

The figure continued to solidify as its gait became more that of a man, but the purple afterimage of the figure still burned when Andrew blinked. The figure kept coming. Andrew raised the gun and pointed. The thing did not walk. It rolled and stumbled its way between the trees.

"Kolopin." Andrew shuddered.

The figure slowly turned its head towards Andrew. The Indian chief's face was difficult to see in the dead of night, but Andrew could make out some sort of dark face paint that covered a shaved forehead. A thick black ponytail stood high on its head.

The figure opened its eyes.

Luminescent white filled the sockets. The soft glow of Kolopin's eyes failed to light the face, but from the open mouth sneered a row of clenched, white teeth. The figure stepped with a slight limp towards Andrew.

Andrew pulled the trigger.

A loud report echoed in the trees, but the figure did not flinch. It continued its slow, rolling gait towards him.

Andrew pulled the trigger again.

A second report interrupted the absolute silence. The figure maintained his path towards Andrew.

He carefully looked down the barrel and through the iron sights towards the approaching Indian. He pulled the trigger. Bark erupted from a tree directly behind Kolopin.

"I am not your heir!" Andrew cried at the figure.

The figure limped closer.

The limp.

Kolopin had a disabled foot. He could be outrun. Well, the *living* Kolopin had been disabled.

Andrew turned and sprinted back towards the tent. The sound of crunching leaves and intermittent footsteps followed. Andrew dared not look over his shoulder. Kolopin had been a native to the area and a child of the forest. Andrew had little hope of outrunning his hunter in the area Kolopin knew so well. He stumbled several times in the cold, dark forest. Through the gaps in the trees, Andrew could make out orange and yellow flickering flames of the burning tent.

"Dad!" Andrew yelled as he ran into the clearing.

The fire was dying out. The tent was a pile of barely burning canvas and sleeping bags.

Dad must have run off in another direction to avoid attracting attention, or perhaps, he wanted to draw attention to himself in some misguided attempt to draw the ghost away from Andrew.

"Dad!" Andrew yelled again.

No answer.

Kolopin still shambled towards him. The chief was hard to see–out of focus. There were no hard edges separating the figure from the surrounding night. He blended into to the darkness, as if he had emerged from it partially formed.

Andrew looked past the tent and the forest beyond. He looked through the trees as his dad had taught him.

The canoe.

It was the only way.

Andrew bolted around the smoldering tent and to the nearby canoe. Still nearly fully loaded, the canoe was too heavy for him to drag by himself. He rocked back and forth until he got the canoe propped up on its side; all of the contents spilled to the ground. He let go, and it rocked back onto its bottom with a resounding clang. Andrew grabbed the front of the canoe, and leaned forward with all of his might. The canoe lurched forward. Its fiberglass bottom scraped loudly against the rocky ground.

Looking over his shoulder, Andrew saw Kolopin reach the smoldering tent. The Indian stepped through the smoking debris unaffected.

"Get back!" Andrew screamed.

He pushed the canoe hard over the crest of the hill to the shore. It slid down on its own momentum. Andrew raced downhill after it.

The canoe lodged itself in the shore mud, but Andrew dug his toes in, and pushed the canoe into the water. He waded in and turned the canoe into the current. Andrew hopped into the back of the canoe just as the river took it.

He looked back at the shore.

Kolopin reached the edge of the water and stood looking at Andrew as he drifted away.

"I am already somebody's heir," Andrew yelled at the ghost.

The ghost faded away from the bank and back into the woods.

Andrew pulled the paddle from the center of the canoe. He dipped his paddle into the water as he had seen his Dad do so many times. He turned it. He pushed it out. The current carried the canoe away from the shore. He let the current carry the canoe, until he could no longer feel the tickling wrongness that was the ghost. Andrew pushed his paddle to the opposite side and dug into the water. The canoe front tipped back towards shore.

Dad was still out there with Kolopin.

Andrew guided the canoe back to the shore and towards the malicious spirit's lands. He paddled hard just as the canoe hit the bank–driving the canoe's front deep into the sticky river mud. Andrew bounded down the length of the canoe and leapt onto the riverbank with Dad's gun still in his hand.

No Kolopin. The normal, chaotic sounds of the forest at night called to each other. They were comforting in their own way.

Andrew knew roughly where the tent lay. He pulled the canoe farther onto the bank and set out back towards the tent, taking the long way.

At the campsite, the tent still burned in the center of the clearing. A figure sat on the ground next to the low flames.

Dad's eyes reflected the white-hot remains of the still smoldering tent.

"Dad!" Andrew said.

"Andrew!" Dad said. "I thought that you'd gotten away. Are you hurt?"

"Nope. I just floated down river a little ways and then came back ashore," Andrew said. "Did you see it? Did you see Kolopin?"

"No," Dad said. "I went looking for you and came back here when I saw you leave with the canoe."

Dad tried to get his feet, but he stumbled forward.

"What happened, Dad?" Andrew asked.

"I fell in the woods. I hurt my foot," Dad said. He rolled forward with a limp as he took a few testing steps.

"So, you didn't see the ghost?" Andrew asked.

"No ghost. Just an overexcited boy," Dad said.

"I saw it. I saw Kolopin. I saw the ghost," Andrew said.

"Let's get our things and get ready to go. Morning will be here soon," Dad said.

Andrew grabbed his bag from its place hanging on a tree branch. Dad did the same.

"This is a trip that I will definitely tell my friends about when I get back," Andrew said.

Dad started walking.

He ruffled Andrew's hair with his heavy, rough hands and said, "Let's go into town. Walk with me, son."

Andrew smiled. He caught up, and walked alongside his Dad.

"I thought we were going to float the canoe down to Cate's Landing," Andrew said.

"No more canoes. No more of that river," Dad said.

"I don't understand," Andrew said. "Just a couple hours ago, you said you were disappointed about finishing early."

"It is too dangerous." Dad smiled. "I can't risk losing my heir."

*****

The New Madrid Fault and Reelfoot Lake
The legend of Kolopin is tied to the creation of Reelfoot Lake and the massive earthquake along the New Madrid fault line that is said to have caused the Mississippi River to flow backwards for a time.

The Nature of Ghosts
Carolyn McSparren

I never believed in the spirits. I am a Capricorn, of the earth earthy. I have always felt that ghostly manifestations are supra-normal, not super-natural. In the sixteenth century, if I had flipped a switch and turned on an electric light (batteries included), I would have found myself tied to a dunking stool or going up in flames. And ghosts? Only leftover energy like the ghost on an old television set after it's turned off.

I do, however, think that there are parts of the human brain that most of us can't reach, but a very few of us can. Mostly those people haven't a clue how to control what they can reach or understand what they can see or do. There are half a dozen methods of bending spoons that have nothing to do with magic, but that doesn't mean the occasional person isn't capable of bending a spoon without tricks.

I have never considered myself one of those people. Being caught up in the supra-normal was not my fault, although it became my problem.

I figure so many hauntings happen in old houses, cemeteries, etc., because the electrical remainders have been concentrated and grow with the layers of time like grime on an undusted chest of drawers. But just as I ignore the dust in my house or on my car, none of it ever penetrated my consciousness.

I no longer believe that.

I am of an age where any oddity is put down as incipient dementia. I cannot tell anyone this story for fear I'll wind up in a small bedroom in assisted living surrounded by the truly demented. So I will write down what happened and hope that someone will find and read it after I'm dead. At that point, my mental state will no longer be germane.

I taught English for forty years. I know how to do research. I decided my only out lay in discovering who my spirits were, why they were here, why they were picking on me, and send them off to wherever they actually should be. They were somebodies. The trick was to make certain they were no longer *my* somebodies.

None of this would have happened if I hadn't decided to add a new kitchen and keeping room to my old farmhouse.

I am not a gourmet cook, although I have prepared many Thanksgiving and Christmas dinners quite well in my old kitchen. It was, however, an abomination. Small, ill-equipped, badly designed, about as far from ergonomically sound as possible. I decided to go whole hog, bump out the back wall twenty feet or so and build myself a kitchen and keeping room with everything top of the line. And fit for me if I were suddenly to wind up in a wheelchair. Not there yet, but it could happen.

Anything to remain here. Let my daughter and my grandchildren deal with forty years of detritus after I'm dead and sell off the treasures that Alan and I collected over the years. Those things are the repository of memory for me, but not for them.

My present house is over a hundred years old, but a Johnny-come-lately among its pre-Civil War neighbors. Although Alan and I added onto and redid during the years we lived in it, we never got around to the kitchen. This was my first major project since my husband of fifty-three years died four years ago.

Now wouldn't you think it I were to develop a 'haint,' it would have been Alan? But I've never heard a peep nor seen a shadow of him.

Instead, the minute my construction type, Billy Reynolds, dug the first trench for the new addition outside my present kitchen, he disturbed something—or someone. It refused to go back to sleep.

"Hey, Mrs. Waldran, you need to come out here and see this," he said, peering down into the newly turned clay soil.

"What'd you find?"

"Lookey here, like as not they're from the foundation of the original house."

"I wasn't aware that there was one."

"Me neither, but then you and me both count as strangers in Fayette County."

He was correct. Alan and I moved out here from Memphis forty years ago to this acreage carved out of my next-door neighbor's pasture. Billy's father grew up in the county, but that's only two generations. It takes at least four to be considered a native.

Billy jumped into the trench, picked up a brick, brushed off the dirt and handed it up to me. An old rose-colored brick, much larger than our present day bricks and solid, without the holes for mortar.

"Handmade. Are there more?" I asked, peering into the trench.

"Yes, ma'am. Looks like could be a bunch more." He took it from me. "See this? Them's scorch marks. Must have been a fire. Probably busted most of 'em up, but could be enough to say, maybe, add you an old timey hearth and fireplace in your new room."

"Can you get them out?"

He rubbed his stubbly gray hair. "Cost you some, have to dig 'em out by hand. I can get me some old boys to come help."

"How far does the old foundation go, do you think?"

"Back under your house at any rate. Looks like your slab was poured partway over the old crawlspace."

"Don't disturb the present slab, but get as many as you can out of the trench," I said and went back to my knitting inside. In early October in West Tennessee it wasn't really cold yet, but the wind was whipping. I don't know what we let loose that day, but we sure as shooting opened up a can of more than worms.

That night I had my first 'visitor.' I have never been afraid on the farm, and not simply because we have the world best wireless alarm system, outside motion sensor lights and a gravel driveway that makes as much racket as a bushel of lady peas rolling in a barrel when someone drives in.

I was finishing my TV dinner on a tray in front of the television in the den when both my cats decanted themselves off the sofa beside me and disappeared with their tails up and as big as bottle brushes.

A moment later he was there standing right in front of me. I yelped, shoved the tray table out of the way, and reached for the Glock I keep beside me at night. I might have shot the television set—a nearly new fifty-four inch flat screen—if he hadn't disappeared just as fast.

I assumed I'd fallen asleep over my Healthy Choice and waked up in the middle of a dream. Took a few minutes for my heart to settle down. I felt really stupid.

I did walk the house with my Glock in hand to find nothing untoward, but the cats refused to come back into the den until the following morning. Nothing else happened for more than a week. The piles of bricks grew, and although many of them were scorched or cracked, an amazing number had survived intact.

One morning Billy came to the back door with brick in hand. "Mrs. Waldran, Mrs. Waldran—I can't come in 'cause of the mud on my boots, but would ya look at this here?"

I walked out onto the patio and took the brick from him.

"See, right there on the side?" He pointed. "Says right there in the brick, 1885. Musta been when this old house got built."

I was as excited as he was. I had been meaning to go into Somerville to the library and the historical society, but hadn't gotten around to it. Now I had a date from which to start looking for my house. Already I was calling it my house.

I bundled up, drove the thirty-odd miles into the county seat, and threw myself onto the good offices of my favorite librarian, Cheryll. Unfortunately, she's in her mid twenties and an incomer like me.

"No, ma'am," she said. "I don't know anything right off the bat, but if there was a fire, we ought to find something in the *Fayette County Gazette*. Could have happened anytime after the house was built and before y'all bought the property."

"More likely not after the war." She looked at me blankly. "The Second World, not the Civil. Surely it would be within the memory of people living here after that."

"Remembering and talking about's two different things, ma'am. Let me set you up with the microfiche from 1885. Sorry, it's the old-fashioned kind where you have to crank the spool by hand."

My cataract surgery helped my eyes, but they still tire easily. By lunchtime I was up to nineteen hundred with no mention of my house, definitely no story about its burning down.

"Where would I find the old land titles and tax rolls?" I asked. She told me. So I moved to the courthouse after a barbecue sandwich for lunch. This time I found the original farm plot so fast I kicked myself for wasting time.

The place had originally comprised over five hundred acres of rolling crop and pasture land that ran back from the road. Taxes were paid by the owner, a Mr. Norton McRae, until his death in 1940. He apparently died intestate and with no heirs. The land went to the state of Tennessee and was sold at auction to the people who eventually sold us our part.

Okay, off to the genealogy sites back home on my own computer on my old roll top desk in the den.

It's amazing how easy it is to trace one's ancestors these days. I called up Norton McRae's taxes in 1886, the year after the house was apparently built, and there was a picture of him.

I looked up from the computer screen at that point and guess what, there he was.

I knocked over my chair and yelped. He continued to glare at me. I gulped past the log in my throat and managed to croak, "Mr. McRae, I presume?"

He started to fade, so I held up a hand. "Please Mr. McRae, I mean you no harm."

The point was, actually, did he mean me any. I couldn't see how.

"Leave him." His lips didn't move, but I heard his voice as clearly as though he'd spoken.

"Leave whom?" But he was gone.

I considered calling my eldest daughter to tell her I might actually be ready for the padded cell. Then I got angry. "Mr. McRae, you are rude. This is my house. You didn't even say please."

That's when I started laughing.

And when the other two showed up.

They were laughing too, and waltzing, whirling around me. They had shadowy faces, but she wore a ball gown that looked as if it might be from the early Edwardian period—I am very good with costumes—while he wore a tweed jacket and breeches tucked into tall riding boots.

Her dark blonde hair was beautifully coiffed. She was neat and clean. He was filthy and unkempt.

I had not liked Mr. McRae, but these two were the very definition of blithe and bonny. I sat at my desk and watched them waltz. "How can you be so cheerful?" I asked. "You're dead."

That sobered them up.

I heard the male's voice. "Bring us together."

"No!" McRae's voice shook the house, although he didn't reappear.

"Now, you listen, Norton," I said. "You leave those two kids alone and get out of my house right this minute!"

"What have *I* done?"

I spun my desk chair around. My daughter Parker stood in the doorway with a strained look on her face.

"Oh, sorry. I was cussing the computer."

"Momma, do you do that often?"

"Every chance I get. Now, what brings you to the country? Haven't seen you in a month of Sundays."

"You have made a terrible mess out back. What on earth possessed you?"

"My homage to the kitchen God. Once before I die I want to cook in a real nice kitchen. It should be ready by Thanksgiving. Christmas at the latest. We'll all be able to eat in the keeping room and I won't be stuck off away from the party."

"Must be costing a fortune. You'll never get your investment back when we sell the house."

"You mean *you* won't. Want a cup of tea?"

"I can't stay. Audrey wants to know can she come after school Wednesday of Thanksgiving and stay through Sunday night?"

"Why on earth would she want to do that?"

Audrey is twelve.

"We are all planning on going to Jim's parents in Birmingham right after Thanksgiving dinner. She doesn't want to go. I'd rather not put up with the sulks for three days. So can she come?"

I nodded. I knew that in a couple of years I'd lose her. Children always have to separate from the person who is most important to their young lives. Alan and I were always Audrey's bastion. Like to have killed her when her grandfather died. Me too, but that's another story. I might as well enjoy her while she wanted my company. "Tell her to give me a call and let me know what she wants to do."

Having accomplished her mission, my daughter was out the door without so much as speaking to Billy, who waved to her.

Then it hit me. What on earth would I do if McRae and the dancers showed up while she was here? Would she see them? Would she flee from them and me in horror? Was I truly losing it?

Leftover energy or not, I had to get rid of them—lay them—before Audrey came to visit. And to do that, I needed more information. So back to the computer.

Which levitated from my desk, spun on its cord and flung itself at my head. I dove under the desk. The computer fell into my heavily padded desk chair. I grabbed it on the bounce, slammed it shut, and held it down.

"Norton, you cut that out! I mean it!"

The house went dead still. Old houses are never still. They creak and snap, the trees blow around outside. I gasped as though I were trying to breathe in a vacuum.

"Mine...forever mine..." The words came out half moan, half snarl.

"This is *my* house and I refuse to have you toss expensive computers around. You darn near brained me. Git, or I swear I'll take the broom to you."

"Mine..." The word whispered as though from a long distance. The moment he was gone, I realized the room was freezing cold. But a nano-second later I felt warm air surround me.

"Not his, never his." It was the first time I'd heard the voice of my female ghost, lovely and very southern, but with an edge of steel in it. A moment later they swirled around me again in their headlong waltz.

"Look, you two, stop that for a minute and tell me what's going on here," I said.

"Together," he whispered. "Bring us together."

"And how do I do that? That old doofus Norton obviously is against whatever it is you want to do, and he considers something..."

"Me!" said the female.

"Or someone," I continued, "his."

"He never owned me," she said clearly.

"Do you two have names? Dates of birth? Something I can get a handle on?"

"Sally," she said. "Sally McRae."

Then they were gone.

So she was some kind of kin to Norton. She was obviously young, so probably his daughter who wanted to marry somebody he didn't like. Niece or cousin maybe. Grandchild? Then there was the other possibility, the one I didn't want to think about. Her voice was very young. Norton's was middle-aged. Could she be his wife? The male ghost her lover?

If he had come to take her away and been caught by Norton, that would explain his attire. He was dressed to ride.

She wasn't. She was dressed in her prettiest ball gown, but maybe that's what she was buried in. Nothing said they died at the same time. As a matter of fact, their emphasis on wanting to be together militated against that.

If old Norton found out about him, whoever he was, he might have killed him. I know that's a big if, but it did make sense. If I were attached in some way to old Norton, I'd glom onto any decent stranger to get me away from him.

And the way they waltzed said love.

She was Sally McCrae. I could trace her, assuming Norton hadn't managed to disable my computer. Who was the *man*? A neighbor? A traveling salesman?

I opened the computer and turned it on. It booted, miracle or miracles, and seemed to be working properly. Good thing it hit my padded chair and not my head. Norton would have a second body to his credit. Or third? Maybe he killed Sally too. I felt certain he'd either killed the man or gotten rid of him somehow.

I found out how the next day.

"Oh, Lord, Mrs. Waldran! Call the sheriff!" Billy staggered into my den completely unmindful of the mud on his boots. He didn't have to tell me. I knew he'd found the man.

While we waited for the sheriff, I fixed Billy a cup of coffee, laced it with lots of sugar and milk, and thrust it into his hands. As he gulped it down, he looked at the mud on my floor. "Oh, Lordy, I'll clean up the mess."

"Don't worry about it. Drink your coffee." I grabbed my quilted vest and went out the door.

"Don't look, Mrs. Waldran!"

But I was already standing beside the trench looking down at the skull. The rest of him was still buried, but I could see a tiny bit of brown tweed where his neck would have been. The skull was brown too, not white the way they are on television. I expected the skull to be crushed by the weight of dirt on his skeleton, but it looked intact. Except for the round hole where his third eye would have been.

Oh, dear. I sat down hard on the edge of the trench. I'd never seen a bullet hole in a skull before, but I was willing to bet I was looking at one now.

The minute the sheriff pulled into my driveway, all hell broke loose. The skeleton in the crawlspace between the foundation walls had to be treated as a fresh death, of course, complete with detectives and crime scene people followed by the medical examiner. I drove to the road and shut the gate before the news people arrived. I don't know who in the sheriff's department is on their payroll, but they hear bad news as soon as it happens.

Sheriff Crawley is a bear of a man with the bulbous nose and raw red cheeks of a man whose fondness for bourbon has allied with his rosacea to make him look boiled. He is, however, a good man and a competent sheriff. He sent Billy out to be interviewed in his squad car by one of his detectives, and talked to me in the den.

"From the preliminary report, the ME guesses it could be close to a hundred years old."

"Can't you carbon date bones?" I asked. I watch the same CSI shows everybody does.

"Takes forever and costs a fortune. I'm already on a tight budget. We'll dig him out, take him to the funeral home in Somerville, clean him up, and put a story in the paper asking if anybody knows who he is. He'll be buried in the unknown and indigent section of county cemetery otherwise."

"He will not!" I didn't even know we had a county cemetery. "You're going to hang on to him for a little while, aren't you? Try to find out who he is, trace any family he may have left?"

Sheriff Crawley ran a hand down his face. "Well, for a few days anyway. Can't afford to keep him too long."

"I'll pay for his keep. I want to know who he is."

About that time a hysterical Parker called me, screaming that all the news stations were saying they'd found a murder victim in my house.

"Nobody says he's a murder victim," I said, although he must have been. "And he's a hundred years old. And he's not in the house. He's where the crawlspace for the old house would have been. Lord knows how they managed to dig the hole to bury him in. Can't have been much clearance between the foundation and the floor above."

"You can't stay in that house another minute! I'll be out to get you in an hour."

"No you won't. If you come it'll be a wasted trip. Not likely a hundred year old skeleton is any danger to me."

"I'll have somebody drive by and check on you every whipstitch tonight, Mrs. Waldran," the sheriff said. "You keep the front gate latched. Anybody climbs over and wants to talk to you, dial nine-one-one."

The whole kit and caboodle left at dark. I stuck the Glock in the back of my jeans and swore I was going to get a dog. A big mean dog. I finally took the landline off the hook and put the security system on. I did watch the six o'clock news. They had pictures of my house from the road, but that's all. They did, however, give my name. Great.

"Now look what you've done, you old coot!" I snapped at the empty room. "I know you killed him. I wish you were still alive so they could hang you."

I felt like an idiot speaking to an empty house. Maybe finding the skeleton had gotten rid of him, but I didn't think so.

I settled down at my computer to trace Norton McRae's female kin. Took some digging—women being of lesser import than man and not owning as much property—but I did eventually find Sally. She was the granddaughter of Norbert's aunt Estella, and as such was his first cousin once removed.

She was thirty years younger than Norbert. And his second wife. Double cousins, then. She died young in childbirth along with her baby. Norton's baby? Or her lover's? Did Norton kill both of them too? And where was she buried? Obviously the lovers wanted to be buried together.

So I needed to find where she was buried, find out who the man was, and bury his remains alongside Sally. If that meant disinterring Norton and moving him as far away as I could, that's what I'd do, even if it meant hiring Billy to do some grave robbing for me.

If Parker heard me talking like that, she'd go for a mental conservatorship in a heartbeat. Still, I had to do it. Norton couldn't be punished at this late date except by getting that poor girl's remains away from him.

I had never believed whatever constituted ghosts could touch the living. Then Norton tossed a computer at my head. He wouldn't like what I was planning.

So, while Billy and his crew dug out the area between the old footings where the skeleton was found without finding so much as an additional mouse bone, I went hunting for Sally's grave.

That meant discovering all the old graveyards in Fayette County, both still in use and long abandoned.

Parker griped because the only way she could get a hold of me was cell phone. I didn't tell her I generally ignored her calls. I don't answer my cell when I'm driving, and I was doing a lot of driving.

The ME certified the skeleton was old, and whoever put the bullet that they found in the skull cavity was no doubt long gone to a higher authority than the State of Tennessee. No identity in the bits and pieces of clothes and the shreds of his boots that remained.

Once the new footings were poured and the concrete pad laid down, I moved everything out of my old kitchen into the guest room, which looked like the sort of food bank you wouldn't want your children to eat out of.

Then the new construction started.

Billy put up heavy plastic drapes to keep the wind out of the old space, but they popped and snapped and still let in the cold air. I bought a small dorm refrigerator so I wouldn't have to live on fast food all the time, and kept the doors closed so the cats couldn't get out—not that they would. The outdoors terrifies them.

No ghosts.

I made reservations to have Thanksgiving dinner for me and my family at a restaurant in Somerville because no way would my kitchen be ready by then. Audrey would be coming home with me for three days. Two weeks left to discover where Sally was buried.

Defeated, I went back to Cheryll at the library with my graveyard problem.

She agreed to help find abandoned churches. We located a couple, but none with lists of the buried, so I had to go hunt the actual yards—mostly overgrown. Too late for snakes, thank God. Pygmy rattlers love overgrown graveyards.

The outside walls went up around the new addition. Cabinets from the old kitchen went to the dump. New cabinets were delivered. The boxes took up most of my den. New wiring, gas lines, windows, walls, new wood floors. It was starting to look like a room. A darn big one, with plenty of space for the keeping room with its fireplace. I planned to turn the old den into a library. Billy could tackle the floor to ceiling book cases in there after the kitchen.

I'd decided the ghosts had departed. The whole town now knew that I was searching for a name for the skeleton and looking—so they thought—for where the rest of his people were buried. The sheriff didn't have missing persons reports before 1930, and his clothes looked more like nineteen hundred. So did Sally's, although I didn't mention that to the sheriff.

"I'm stumped, Mrs. Waldran," Cheryl said over her homemade vegetable soup at the local café, which is the luncheon hangout for most of the town. "We've checked every church and cemetery I can find."

An elderly white-haired lady at the next table leaned across and asked me, "Have you checked the graveyard at your house?"

"I beg your pardon?"

She turned her chair around. She looked like a little dumpling person until I realized that her forearms were more muscular than mine. A farm woman used to hard work, although the size of her diamond solitaire said her husband was probably rich.

"Before the war..." This time I knew she meant the Civil. "People who owned slaves buried them at the home place. After the war, with so many dying of the yellow fever, plenty of farmers buried their families in their own plots too."

I felt my pulse quicken. "But the original house on my land wasn't built until 1885."

"Huh. Wouldn't stop them. Lotta country folks planted their dead close by. Mine certainly did. Doesn't your house have a graveyard? Maybe a mausoleum?"

"I have no idea. How on earth would I find out?"

She grinned at me and turned her chair back around to her own table, where a woman who must have been her daughter listened to us. "Walk your land, honey. If you have one, it'll be close by."

I could hardly wait to get home, but on the way I realized that the task was huge. A hundred year old abandoned graveyard? Even the gravestones would be buried under leaves and dirt.

The next morning dawned blustery and rainy. No way was I stalking around outside and taking the chance on slipping and breaking my hip.

The day after that the sheriff called. "Mrs. Waldran, I know you're paying the undertaker, but he wanted me to call you. You got to make a decision on what to do with your skeleton."

"Give me a week, sheriff."

"Three days."

"Oh, all right. I'll let you know."

Mud or no mud, I had to find that graveyard or satisfy myself that it didn't exist. I felt certain it did. Norton probably forced Sally to marry him. I couldn't see her doing it without duress. She was barely sixteen when she married and only twenty when she and her baby died. Norton's baby? Or the unknown man's? Had she wanted to marry him and been unable to? Judging by his riding gear, I wondered if he'd come to fetch her from Norton, been surprised and killed.

Would Norton tell her he was dead and buried? I didn't think so. She'd watch and hope for a man who was buried underneath her house. Bastard. And I don't mean the baby.

And when she died, he'd want to keep her close to him so he could continue to gloat.

I printed off a plot of my land, set up a grid, and hoped that the lady in the café was right. It would be fairly close to the old house and therefore part of the land we owned. I put on my muckiest clothes, took my heaviest cane, and started.

I consider myself in good shape for a woman my age, but two hours and I was flat worn out. I had me some lunch, then sitting right on my sofa I went to sleep. And here came ole Norton hoofing it into my dream with his little piggy eyes and his mutton-chop whiskers. He held a big old hog-leg pistol pointed straight at me. I knew I was Sally's lover, and I was about to get my head blown off.

"Let her go. She never loved you." A male voice. Me?

"Her body is mine whenever I choose to use it. I will have your child to use as I like as well, and I'll beget my own afterwards. Why would I care about her love?"

Of course the *I* in my dream went for him. Stupid! Played into Norton's vicious hands. I saw the bullet leave the gun and woke up in a sweat.

A pale early November dawn was breaking when I wrapped myself up and went hiking. "Sally McRae, if you want me to bring your man to you, you are going to have to help me. Where the Sam Hill are you?"

Since Alan died and we no longer keep horses, I've kept the pastures bush hogged, but haven't touched most of the underbrush. Between the love vine and those horrible locust trees with their three-inch thorns and the wild privet, plus the saplings and leaf mold, a goodly portion of the land has reverted to jungle. I walked all the pastures with no result. Then I had to start on the copses—where the worst of the vegetation and the snakes lived. I whacked away at the underbrush with the crook on the top of my cane until I wore out.

There had to be some indication of where the graveyard had been. I brought up aerial photos of the land from Google and stared at them for hours. They had been taken originally in the spring when the leaves were new.

At some point that graveyard must have been tended. I went over the pictures with my big magnifying glass looking for some pattern. I didn't find one. What I did find was azaleas. Oh, I knew we had azaleas growing wild, but it had never hit me that they were an unlikely plant to volunteer. At some point someone had planted them. Then I saw scraggy roses. Not wild roses, but real red roses. Again, not a usual volunteer. The next morning I was excited, although the wind was blowing a mile a minute and it was forty degrees.

The new cabinets were going in that morning, so Billy had a full crew working. He barely heard me when I told him I was going for a walk. I had my medic alert around my neck and my phone in my pocket in case I needed help.

The previous night looking at the aerial photos I had thought finding the place from the ground would be simple. Not so in the fall without the colors of the roses and azaleas to guide me through the thick stands of trees. I wasn't altogether certain I could even recognize the foliage without the blossoms.

One would think that after living in a place thirty years and raising horses there for nearly that long I would be completely familiar with the land, but I assure you, that's not true. One copse looks very much like another. I only knew the paths the horses had worn. I'd already walked those.

So I had to get down and dirty—literally—in the underbrush. Using the hook of my cane, I clawed my way into the copse that I was most certain wouldn't toss me down a sinkhole.

Not a sinkhole, but a four-foot stretch of rusted iron fence lying on the ground half covered with leaves. I caught my foot between the posts and twisted my ankle. While I tried to dislodge it, something hit me right between my shoulder blades. Hard. I catapulted over the fence and six feet into the underbrush, dragging the fence section with me.

It fell over, pinning me under it. One of the spikes that topped each pole grazed my cheek. Hurt like hell! Warm blood trickled down my cheek. I would definitely need a tetanus booster.

I spit out a mouthful of dead, wet leaves, grabbed for my cane and used it to haul myself to my knees. And howled.

My ankle was trapped at a dangerous angle. I didn't think I'd broken it yet, but wouldn't take much to fracture the bone. If I didn't get myself out, it very well could turn a sprain into a break.

Wouldn't Parker love that? I had to get back to the house without anyone's noticing I was limping.

That's when it hit me. I'd been pushed. Norton really could *hurt* me.

I started yelling, but I knew no one could hear me up at the house with chain saws and hammering. I reached for my cell phone, but my pocket was empty. It must have fallen out. I'd never find it in the dead leaves.

My medic alert button cheerfully notified me it had no service.

My tears were more frustration than pain, but I have never felt so alone nor scared in my life. I kept waiting for Norton to come at me with one of those spikey fence posts. Billy would find my impaled body once they realized I was still gone and came hunting.

Now, when I get scared, I get mad, and I was very, very scared.

"Norton, you bastard, you leave me the hell alone or you'll spend the rest of eternity wishing you had!" I screeched.

That's when I smelled the roses. Roses don't bloom after frost.

And as I looked down, the old fence section twisted sideways ever so slowly. A moment later, I was free. Then my hand touched my cell phone. And when I picked it up from the leaves, I felt the oblong stone it rested on. I brushed aside the leaves and the dirt.

I could just read it. No 'beloved wife and mother' stuff for old Norton. It said "Sally McRae and issue" plus the dates of her birth and death. He hadn't even bothered to name the child, and he'd buried them together like a mamma cat and a dead kitten. Well, they wouldn't be alone much longer if I had any say in the matter.

I struggled to my feet. The ankle wasn't bad. I could make it to the house if I hobbled slowly and used my cane. I could soak it and wrap it. Nobody would ever know how close I'd come to getting truly hurt.

In the next few days, Billy left one crew to finish my addition while he brought some more men to clean up the graveyard. Once you knew where to look, it was obvious. We found all the sections of the iron fence and the gate that had enclosed the little plot, repaired, painted, and set them back up. Only a few graves. Norton's first wife was there, and his mother and father. And, of course, Sally and her baby.

Norton's was the last headstone we located. He outlived her by many years. Sweating bullets about the man he'd killed, I hoped.

This time the Somerville papers gave me a huge story. We still had no idea who brown suit was, but I made arrangements to have him buried the Friday after Thanksgiving so Parker wouldn't be around, but Audrey would. She thought it was very romantic.

My own rector offered to do the service, even without the deceased's name.

The afternoon before the funeral, I went out to look at our handiwork. As I stood beside Sally's freshly scrubbed headstone, I said, "Norton, I'll make you a deal. You leave Sally and her man alone to sleep through eternity side by side and don't bother us or them again. If you do that, I'll leave *you* alone. If, however, you try a single bit of haunting, I swear I'll dig you up, buy you a plot up in Jackson and plant you a hundred miles from Sally. Do I make myself clear?"

"Gram, who're you talking to?"

I jumped a foot. "Nobody important, Audrey honey. Come on, we got to bake cupcakes in my brand new oven for after the funeral tomorrow."

I wished I had a name for our new guest. No fair he should have 'unknown' on his headstone.

After the funeral a bunch of neighbors, reporters and people I knew from the county came up to the house for refreshments. Among those I'd never met was a very old lady wearing an elegant dress of gray Alaskine that must have been twenty years old. And black kid gloves.

She took me aside and introduced herself. "My name is Teresa Mitchell. I've seen you, but never met you. I came because I think I know who the deceased was."

I left Audrey to hostess and took Mrs. Mitchell into my little sewing room, since the addition was not quite finished and the party was going on in the den.

She sat on the sofa, pulled a large brown envelope from her copious handbag and handed it to me. "I think his name is Earl Vincent and he was my great, great uncle. He disappeared in 1906."

I started to rip open the envelope, but she laid a hand on my wrist. "Let me tell you first. Earl was chief engineer on the Memphis to Charleston railroad—quite a prestigious job for such a young man. He got off the train in Collierville one evening and rented a horse at the local livery stable. Neither was ever seen or heard from again. The family hired private detectives even, but no one found anything.

Do you have any idea how he ended up in the crawlspace of your old house?"

I told her everything I surmised without, of course, telling about the ghosts.

"He could have met Mrs. McRae on a trip to Memphis," she said. "Well-to-do ladies did most of their shopping in town. He was handsome enough to turn any woman's head." She pointed at the envelope. I opened it and pulled out the restored five by seven photo. If you ignored his slicked down hair, he was drop dead gorgeous. The other items were cuttings from the newspapers about his disappearance and a hand-written report from a private detective saying he'd reached a dead end.

"My great-grandmother always said he must have been shot by an irate husband. He frequented all the dances he could get to and danced with any woman who would partner him." She shook her head. "Sad."

"He disappeared on April twentieth," I said. "The back part of the old house burned down on the twenty-third. McRae took Sally, moved to town and never rebuilt the part that had been destroyed. That wasn't done until the forties. Norton must have torched it to cover up what he'd done. She died in childbirth four months later."

We went back to the reception. She left the envelope with me. I had the photo framed. It hangs on the wall of my new kitchen.

Norton has kept his end of the bargain. We've had no more hauntings. We now maintain the little cemetery in pristine condition—the local garden club has made it a priority.

But every once in a while when the spring breeze is light and out of the east, I hear the faint sounds of a waltz.

I wonder what happened to the horse.

Carolyn McSparren

*****

LaGrange, Tennessee

LeGrange is a country town in Fayette County, Tennessee, one county east of Memphis. Spared most of the destruction of the Civil War, the town's farming interests was largely destroyed by the boll weevil during the depression. Thank goodness most of the ante-bellum houses were restored in the second half of the twentieth century. Today LaGrange and the farms that surround it are burgeoning with young families.